hip-hop high school

Also by Alan Lawrence Sitomer

The Hoopster
The Hoopster: A Teacher's Guide
Homeboyz
Hip-Hop Poetry and the Classics

hip-hop high school

by Alan Lawrence Sitomer

Jump at the Sun

HYPERION PAPERBACKS

New York

Copyright © 2006 Alan Lawrence Sitomer
All rights reserved. No part of this book may be reproduced or transmitted
in any form or by any means, electronic or mechanical, including photocopying,
recording, or by any information storage and retrieval system, without written
permission from the publisher. For information address Hyperion Books for
Children, 114 Fifth Avenue, New York, New York 10011-5690.

Printed in the United States of America
First Hyperion Paperbacks edition, 2007
10 9 8 7 6 5 4

This book is set in 14-point Perpetua.
Designed by Ellice M. Lee

Library of Congress Cataloging-in-Publication Data on file.
ISBN-13: 978-1-4231-0644-9
ISBN-10: 1-4231-0644-X

Visit www.un-requiredreading.com
ILS No . V475-2873-0-12209

Dedicated to all my students

Yet none of this is possible without Tracey . . .
I love you!

ﻞ

Special Shout-Outs go to . . .

That-H, my U-turn Momma

Don Roberto, mi hermano, mi corazón

ALS #1—the original (& Grammy D.)

Catnip Girl & BK—Big, Big Props

Ruby2Shoes, 4 much support

G-money (dat's U, chuck!), J. Marx (BIG THX!!)

Turntable Adam & his magic sista' T, my homie Vignone, Larr-Dogg & the Purple Crew, Jr. in SF, Richard C. (w/ da' bombin' Farm ess. app.!), Dontae & J.J., all my Trojan Homies (Fight On, Bay-bee!!), my peeps at the Wood & LMU, Mrs. K., The Goofy B's, Julie Jam, J. Burke, tha' Eng. teecher's teecher, Manda, E.B.S., I.J., & folks who have moved on like G. Sam., Sweet Bev, Gram L., and the inimitable S.J.S.

ﻞ

And how about some luv for the Team . . .

Wendy L.—from da' rooftops . . . AIN'T NONE BETTER!!

Angus K.—Perpetual Magic

Al Z.—where would I be without thee? 4-ever thx!

Jerry the K.—class, tenacity, brains, and patience . . . Wow!

Dana T.—pushin' pedal to da' metal

Kim-from-L.A.—workin' it, feelin' it, & workin' it some more!!

EeeeLeee—wutta cover!! E-Hog w/the Web magic!

Scottie B. & RasShahn—sweatin' behind the scenes, G, A, P, & V @ SCBeee!!

Abbie K., Mark M., Barb F., Jenn L., Jeanne M., Brenda B., Kelli M.—so many doin' so dang good . . . THX!

misspelled *seesaw*, so it read *cee-saw*. That's where she got her name, or at least the misspelling of it.

Anyway, me and Cee, we're tight like a kite.

"You wanna ditch class?"

"It's the first day of school."

"Exactly. We ain't gonna be doin' nothing anyway," she said as she checked her lipstick in a small mirror she pulled from her purse.

"What happened to startin' fresh?" I asked.

"Yeah, maybe you right," she said puckering her lips. "After all, when you're lookin' as good I am, you owe it to the people to let 'em check you out a bit." Cee-Saw shut her mirror with a *bap*, then smacked her butt with a *thwap*, proud of the way she had squeezed her curvalicious booty into her new pair of jeans.

Everyone wore new clothes on the first day of school. Even the poor kids.

"You know I'm zesty," she added with a *pop* of her gum.

Dang, that girl made me laugh.

Class started to fill up with all sorts of folks I hadn't seen since last June. In real life three months ain't that long to not see someone, but in high school, three months can be an eternity. Peeps my age can change a lot over a summer, both mentally and physically. For example, Estephanie Martinez quietly laid low last

3

year in ninth grade with a flat chest and curly hair. But this year, Estephanie strutted into World History wearing a tank top cut off at the midriff, showing off her silver belly-button ring and sprouting breasts. She'd had what's known as a "developmental growth spurt" over the summer.

And don't think all the boys didn't notice.

"Check out the Hoochie Mama!" Franklin de la Cruz cracked as Estephanie jiggled by.

"Shut up, Stanky Franky," she fired back. "You so ugly, you couldn't get a girlfriend with a Lexus and a record deal!"

Franklin's knuckleheaded buddies broke out in big laughs.

"Aw, she busted you ba-a-ad, homie," one of them commented as Estephanie wiggled to the other side of the room.

"Whatever, dude. She wants me."

Franklin's crew laughed again.

"Yeah, right."

Cee-Saw bobbed her head up and down, watching all the folks fill the room. "Some good stuff gonna be happenin' this year," she said to me. "Good stuff."

"Dat's straight up, girl," I answered back as we traded another *slap-slap-bump* high five on the down low. "Dat's straight up."

My life is weird. It's like I speak two languages. In my head I talk a normal kind of English, but when I chat with my friends or any of my peers I rap to them in this kind of ghetto slang. It's like I purposely mispronounce words and disobey all them rules of grammar. Like, I never say "with." I say "wit'." And I don't say "that." I say "dat." And I sort of slur my "what's up" too and turn it into "wuzzup." One of my favorite things to say to my friends is, "Wuzzup wit' dat?" It makes me sound cool.

Actually, it makes me fit in. And fittin' in 'round here is *huge*. Your clothes got to be fresh, your attitude has to be stylin', and if you talk too proper, you might get jumped by a crew of four or five. That's because people will think you're trying to act white. They'll take you down for that. We got all kinds of unspoken rules like this around here and people who violate them end up paying the price. It may not make sense to an outsider, it may not be reasonable or rational, but it is what it is and only stupid people don't play along.

And I ain't stupid. At least not like that I ain't.

Hmmvvvzzz! Hmmvvvzzz! Hmmvvvzzz!

That's the bell at our school to start class. It sounds like a penitentiary alarm. You couldn't find a more ugly noise to greet the students if you tried.

5

But like most smacked-up things around here, you get used to it.

"Excuse me, why aren't you people *sitting down?*" boomed a voice. It sounded like one of those marine sergeants in the movies who make people do three hundred million push-ups in the rain for not shining their belt buckles.

A whoosh of students scrambled to their desks. In the Honors classes, people actually listened to their teachers. Only in the Honors classes, though.

Cee-Saw, slower than most to scramble, didn't move quickly enough to sit next to me and ended up one row over and one seat up instead of directly across. *Dang! That girl never thinks ahead.*

"I'll say this one time. When the bell rings, I expect you to be in your seats and ready to work. Do we understand?"

No one responded. I guess that meant we understood.

So far my classes seemed like they were going to be pretty chill, even though my teachers were a bit whack. But all teachers are whack, if you ask me. I mean, who chooses to work in a school other than a complete loser?

Losers make for good nicknames though. Some rips

are obvious. Mrs. Carter was Mrs. Farter, Mr. Veliz was Mr. Toe-Cheese, and Mr. Kochs, well . . . he was just, Mr. *Kochs*. But the good cracks, like for Mrs. Horton, the geometry teacher, those are the ones students live for. See, Mrs. Horton once got caught doing the missionary position with Mr. Lincoln, the science department chair, in the teacher's lounge right before Thanksgiving break. Now we call her the "Turkey Baster."

Like I said, nicknaming teachers is downright dope.

"And be forewarned," came the booming voice again, "this is a college preparatory course. Your days of copying off other students' tests and doing no homework on the weekends are over."

The man in front of us was the only teacher on campus who did not have a nickname. Kids had tried for years. The Punisher. The Jailer. The A-hole. Nothing had stuck. He was simply Wardin. Mr. Wardin.

"This curriculum is designed for pupils who plan on going to reputable four-year universities. Students who do hold such ambitions, and I already know that very few of you in here are even remotely qualified to do so, should be aware that kindergarten this is not. Now take out a sheet of paper. We're having a test."

A test? It's the first day of school.

"And you are *not* to write on the paper I give you. Use your own. I am an educator, not the Office Depot."

As Wardin passed out the tests I checked him out. Not checked him out like *checked him out*, just kinda checked him out. He was tubby, balding, had crooked teeth on the bottom row of his mouth, and probably some gorilla-looking hair on his back, too. Pretty much standard stuff for a teacher, nothing out of the ordinary. Nothing except for these sickeningly thick fingers. They were plump and round and thick and looked like undercooked sausages. And his fingernails were itsy bitsy and jagged, as if they'd been chewed and gnawed and spit out like gerbil food a thousand times over.

Plus, he was always licking them.

Gross!

"But what's this test based on?" asked Amanda Hardison, the second-smartest student in tenth grade, with a 4.87 GPA.

"You'll raise your hand if you wish to speak!" Wardin snapped in response. "For the most part, the only voice I want to hear in this class, unless there is a fire or you need clarification of an assignment, is my own." He licked his sausage fingers and handed Amanda an exam. I guess that answered that.

Jesús García looked at his test and crinkled his forehead. *Cite three reasons why the Etruscan Empire was vanquished.* "I mean, we ain't even read no books or nuttin' yet."

Wardin spun around. "Excuse me, is there a deficiency in your auditory aptitude? Maybe you need a three-page typed paper to better understand classroom procedures?"

Thirty-eight nervous teenagers turned around to stare at Jesús. He responded by looking down at his Oakland Raiders sweatshirt and avoiding eye contact with all of us, his brown skin turning red. Jesús would never speak again in here without raising his hand, that was for sure. Matter of fact, he probably wouldn't speak in here again *ever* and we were only three minutes into the first day of class.

Wardin paused. The silence was thick. Thick like his fingers.

"That's what I thought," he said, continuing to move up and down the rows of students, passing out tests. "And for your information, the summertime reading was posted on this class's Web site in July."

"But," said Paula Johnston. Wardin spun around, but Paula raised her hand before he completely turned and acted like her hand had been up the whole time.

"Yes?" said Wardin, all impatient-like.

"What if we didn't know this class had a Web site?"

"Then you weren't properly prepared."

"But I just got my schedule changed into this course this morning," she offered, as if that might be a good excuse for her not to take the test.

"Well then, welcome to Honors World History, tenth grade," Wardin said. And he slapped a test down on her desk.

What a punk.

When Wardin handed me my paper I scoped out his wedding ring. It looked kinda cheap, like it was only thirteen-karat gold or something. I wondered who in the world would marry a guy like him. His wife probably had buck teeth, eight toes, and a glass eye that needed Windex to clean the smudges off it every night.

Explain the role of the Tigris and Euphrates in the societal development in the region known as the Fertile Crescent.

Huh? My eyes wandered around the room.

Most teachers' walls were decorated with goofy inspirational junk like, YOUR MIND IS LIKE A PARACHUTE— IT ONLY FUNCTIONS WHEN IT'S OPEN, or, THE ONLY STUPID QUESTION IS THE ONE THAT NEVER GETS ASKED. Lady teachers usually had rooms with plants, posters, and framed photos of their loved ones, too.

Wardin had nothing. Not even a bell schedule. Nothing but four white walls and fluorescent lights on the ceiling. It felt like a hospital room.

Actually, he did have one thing. It wasn't even a poster, though. It was just a plain white sheet of paper with some words printed on it in black ink that looked like they came out of a crappy typewriter. It read, GOOD THINGS HAPPEN TO PEOPLE WHO TRY. That's all. No color. No inspirational photo of a rock climber ascending Mount Everest. No nothing.

I read it again.

GOOD THINGS HAPPEN TO PEOPLE WHO TRY.

Yeah, right. I looked back down at the test.

As Indo-Europeans moved into southern Greece, what two aspects of their—

Bap!

What the heck?

A small, folded-up sheet of paper landed on my desk, startling me. I looked up and saw Cee-Saw peeping out of the corner of her eye at me and immediately understood. It was a note.

Was she crazy?

I quickly covered up the paper with my left hand and scanned the room for Wardin. My shoulders got tense.

I spotted him. Then he spotted me spotting him. Terror raced through my blood and I quickly looked back down at my paper.

Oh my gracious, what if he saw?

Apparently he hadn't, because he didn't race across the room and come chew me a new butt-hole.

Cee-Saw peeked back at me and nudged me with a flip of her head. *Go on, read it.*

I glanced up again to make sure it was safe. Wardin prowled the other side of the room like a jungle cat. I secretly unfolded the piece of white paper and read what had been written.

Wutz #3? HELP!! ☺

Oh my gracious, was she crazy? Did she want me to cheat eight minutes into the first day of class?

Dilemma is a good word to know for the SAT. It means, "confusing problem." I'd been trying to improve my vocabulary for the SAT so I could one day get into a good college. *Dilemma* was one of those big words that stuck with me. There's like a zillion words a student needs to know for that dumb test, and the truth is, I don't ever think I'll be able to learn them all—and I'll probably bomb the damn thing when the time comes—but at least I'd already been trying to expand my vocabulary and learn a few big words so I could have a bit of a chance.

Dilemma was one of them. And I was in one.

I mean, if I didn't hook up my homegirl with some knowledge, I'd be acting like a punk. And getting a rep as a punk is a bad thing in high school. Jeez, what kind of friend doesn't help out another friend in a time of need? That's just wrong.

On the other hand, if Wardin busted me, I was sure he'd be so pissed, fire would shoot out of his ears. Plus, I needed to do good in this class to go to college.

But if I got busted Wardin would bring the pain— *big time.*

Punk or pain? Punk or pain? Punk or pain?

Like I said, I was in a real dilemma.

Wait a minute, I thought. *Maybe I don't even know the answer to question three?* That would get me off the hook. I looked down at the test.

List three contributions to our modern society attributable to the ancient Persians.

Damn! I knew the answer. At least part of it.

I looked up at Cee. She glanced back with a gaze that said, *Yo girl, hook me up.*

I scanned the room again for Wardin. He cruised in and out of rows of students, watching us all like a sniper on a rooftop.

There was no way. But still I had to try.

Persians invented algebra, abacuses, and chess, I wrote on the note.

And then I wrote something else.

Got a tamp?

In all the excitement of dressing for the first day of school—I mean, you just *had* to look fresh on the first day—I'd forgotten to pack up my necessary supplies. And having an "accident" in class, the kind that boys could never understand, could be so catastrophic, I might have to transfer high schools.

Cee would hook me up, though, 'cause our cycles were pretty much the same. Plus, I was hooking her up with knowledge. It was a fair trade.

I folded up the note and prepared to toss it back. Getting it to Cee would be tricky, but we'd been passing notes to one another since third grade, so I wasn't sweating it too bad. Unfortunately, however, due to her lack of hustle at the start of class, she wasn't in an ideal note-tossing position. Whatever, I thought. All I needed was the right opportunity.

I scanned the room for Wardin. He continued to weave through rows of desks on our side of the room. I began writing an answer to test question number four as he cruised by.

The history of the Greek empire had many features that . . .

After looking over my shoulder, he crossed to the other side of the room. I saw my chance.

As if we were sisters with telepathic powers, Cee instinctively looked in my direction. I lifted my hand to make the toss. Suddenly, Wardin turned and gazed directly at me.

Oh my gracious!

I started scratching my head, pretending I had an itch, and lowered my eyes as if I were concentrating on the Etruscans. A tense moment passed without me breathing. After fifteen more seconds, I peeked back up.

Again, he didn't bust me. *Holy smokes!*

Wardin headed to the corner of the room and paused to ridicule Joanna Lipton, a girl with a mole on her nose.

"Pardon me, but how many *l*'s are there in *Constantinople?*"

"*Umm*, three," she replied nervously.

"Are you sure you're supposed to be in tenth grade?"

I saw my chance. *Whi-i-izzz!* I zipped the note.

It buzzed through the air straight for Cee-Saw's arms. She stuck out her hand to catch my perfect toss and—

15

Intercepted by Rickee Dunston.

What? No-o-o-o!

Oh my gracious!

Rickee Dunston was a football god who had started at strong safety for varsity even though he was just a sophomore, which was a pretty big deal, because we were a regional powerhouse. But Rickee wasn't all that smart. Matter of fact, the only reason he had a seat in Honors classes was because this was where the "good kids" were, and his coach knew that if he placed Rickee in regular classes, he would screw around with all the other screw-offs and misbehave so badly that he would end up flunking every one of his courses. And Rickee flunking would be bad because Principal Watkins cared more about the football team than he did about the Debating Society, Calculus Club, and Science Olympiad all rolled into one. Basically, our principal knew we needed a strong defense to be competitive in league play, and Rickee Dunston hit like a sledgehammer.

In other words, I was screwed.

Rickee smiled like Satan. The first chance he got, I knew he was going to read my note. He might even read it out loud.

Camel crap!

Wardin made his way back toward our end of the class. Rickee quickly hid my note in his left fist. Every student within ten feet of me knew what was going on, but we all sat in anxious tension, pretending to be thinking smartly about history questions we had had no idea we were going to be tested on. My anxiety was so extreme, I thought I was gonna burst.

And bursting in high school would be cataclysmic.

Cataclysmic is a good word to know for the SAT. It means "horribly bad."

Double camel crap!

Suddenly, the door to the classroom swung open with a long squeak. It was Mr. Jamison, the vice principal.

"Sorry to interrupt, Mr. Wardin, but might I have a word with you? It's quite important."

"Most certainly, Mr. Jamison." Wardin turned around and addressed the class in a threatening tone. Really threatening. "Continue the test. Do not talk. I'll be right back." He headed for the door and exited. It was quiet for a moment.

Then he popped back inside.

"And dare not cheat!"

The door closed behind him. There was total silence.

Two seconds later I shot out of my chair and jumped in Rickee's face.

"Wuzzup wit' dat?" I shouted, reaching for the note. Rickee laughed like the evil, mean, jerk of the century he was and held the note out of my grasp in a teasing way. With his free hand he shielded me from grabbing it. Though I tried to get it hard as I could, Rickee was an all-state safety probably looking at a college football scholarship one day. There was no way.

"What's it say, Tee-Ay? Somethin' bout how you love me?" Rickee slid away from Cee-Saw so she couldn't snatch the note from behind. The double team was on.

"I hate your guts, you African pig!"

"Bet that's not what the note says," Rickee taunted.

"Give it to us, fool!" Cee-Saw shouted, trying to climb over her desk to get it from him. But Rickee had faced two-on-ones far worse than me and Cee before. For him, this was playtime.

"Gimme it, punk boy!" I yelled, trying desperately to get it. If any of us spoke a drop louder, Wardin might hear. Then again, I didn't care. I needed that note. Good thing our school didn't have any of those windows in the doors so Wardin could see inside the classroom from out in the hallway. Otherwise, we'd all have been cooked.

But there was no way. Rickee was just too quick and too strong and one day he was going to get a fat paycheck for it. He laughed at me again. This was his kind of fun.

Triple camel crap!

"Hey-hey, Tee-Ay—does this note say who you are going to—"

Bap!

Rickee's white smile vanished. He quickly spun around, not knowing what had just happened. Standing there was Devon Hampton.

That's right, Devon Hampton had snatched the note.

Remember how I said Amanda Hardison was the second-smartest student in tenth grade? She was second because Devon Hampton was first. It wasn't even close. Devon Hampton had earned straight A's on every report card he took home since first grade. It musta been some kinda record. But Devon wasn't a dork. He was cool and had a good personality, pretty much always easygoing and friendly. Ain't nobody never said nothing bad about Devon. He was the type of person that students liked, parents liked, teachers liked, principals liked—heck, even the old white people who occasionally came down to our school to do charity-type "reach-out" stuff liked him. Devon was always put in front of them as if he were the exact representative of all young black men in our school. Rickee, on the other hand, was always kept far from sight. But Devon wasn't like any other person in our school, black or not. Matter of fact, he was the only person in our school who could "talk white" and not get jumped for it. All the homeboys respected him. Devon was unique.

And now he was holding my note.

Rickee's face glowed like blue ice.

"Don't be messin' with me, fool." Rickee glared at Devon with a cold killa stare. "Give it back."

Devon didn't budge.

"Last chance, fool."

Devon still didn't budge.

Oh, there was one other thing about Devon Hampton. He knew karate. Shaolin kung fu. Devon had been taking martial arts classes after school every Tuesday and Thursday since he was six years old. Tactics of the Dragon Warrior were his specialty.

Holy shit, this was going to be a good fight!

2

I know, I know, I shouldn't use language like "holy shit." It's just that sometimes this wild, electric sizzle races through my veins and I just can't control myself. Especially when two boys are about to throw down *big time* over me. It's tough, too, 'cause bad language is everywhere 'round here. I mean the entire school moves to the groove of an X-rated vocabulary. Hip-hop without profanity is like chili cheese fries without the chili cheese—it just don't have no flava.

But still, I should watch it.

Anyway, silence filled the room. Rickee glared at Devon with a burn. Devon stared back, holding firmly on to the note, but calmly, not with a look of hate. I wasn't sure why Devon had even gotten involved in this whole note-stealing mess. It wasn't his beeswax. I guess he just felt it was the right thing to do. Devon was weird like that.

Suddenly, *sque-e-eak*, the door opened. Everyone raced back to their desks. Wardin reentered.

My heart pounded. My stomach rolled. I was so freaked I thought I would puke.

And puking in the middle of class was *not* the ideal way to start off a year.

I looked down at the test and contemplated the situation. *Contemplate* is a good word to know for the SAT. It means, "to think really hard about something." My note now sat in the hands of Devon, which was better than Rickee having it but worse than Cee-Saw, and Wardin seemed to be even more pissed off than when he had left the room in the first place.

I glanced at the test in front of me. It said something about the Byzantine empire.

Sweat. On my forehead. In my armpits. On my thighs. I hoped my mascara wasn't ruined. It took me thirty-seven minutes to do my eyes and hair that morning. You know, first day of school, you gotta look hot.

"If I've told you people once, I've told you people a thousand times, you have got to make good choices in this world. *You!*" Wardin snapped as he pointed to skinny Jayleen Wilcox. "Out of that chair and into that seat right there. Yes, that one right there."

Skinny Jayleen looked confused but grabbed her stuff and did what she was told.

"That back chair will remain empty for a few

months. It seems one of your classmates won't be joining us for a while on account of inanity and senselessness."

The dumb look on most of our faces must have let Wardin know that nobody understood what the hell he was talking about. Wardin explained it to us like we were a bunch of three-year-olds.

"Your classmate Miguel Zalvalza has been shot."

Huh? I thought. *Li'l Zigzag got blasted? No freakin' way!*

The class buzzzzed with a mixture of shock, awe, and fear.

"I don't believe it!"

"Who did it?"

"Is he all right?"

We were all stunned. Miguel Zalvalza, aka Li'l Zigzag, had got capped. Details. We needed details.

"It appears," Wardin explained, trying to get us all to settle down, "that he took a bullet in the stomach last night at three A.M. and had his spleen removed before I finished my breakfast at six-thirty. Can anybody please tell me what in the world an honors student would be doing out on the street at three A.M. on a Sunday evening before the first night of school? How can I be expected to do my job when— *What is that?*"

23

The entire class followed Wardin's eye . . . to Devon Hampton.

Oh my gracious! The note.

In all the excitement, Devon forgot to keep the small piece of paper concealed. *Holy horsehairs!* Wardin had spied it.

Tension crunched up the nerves in my neck as I watched the teacher advance toward Devon. Wardin licked his fat little sausage fingers, extended his hand, and glared. "Hand it over." The class froze.

"I certainly hope these are *not* test answers."

Wardin unfolded the tiny piece of paper. No one in the room took a breath. Wardin's forehead wrinkled as he read the note. He gazed up at Devon with a small look of confusion on his face. Then he read the note a second time. Then he paused. Finally, he looked at Devon with laser-beam eyes.

"Who wrote this?"

Oh my gracious, Devon Hampton, the smartest kid in the school, was about to go down in flames and it was all my—and Cee's and Rickee's—fault.

I looked at Rickee. Damn if he was gonna say nothin'.

I looked at Cee. Damn if she wasn't praying Devon wasn't gonna say nothin'.

I looked into my own heart.

"It was me," I said, rising from my chair. "He didn't do anything. I dropped it and Devon picked it up. The note is mine."

The class gasped. _Gasp_ is another good word to know for the SAT. It means "to take a sudden and shocking breath."

My whole, entire universe gasped.

Wardin slowly turned.

"You realize, it's the first day of class, Miss . . ."

"Anderson," I replied, lowering my eyes. "Theresa Anderson."

"Theresa Anderson," he repeated slowly as he looked me over like he knew me from way back when or something. "Was your older brother . . ."

"Andre Anderson," I said, filling in the rest of the sentence.

"_The_ Andre Anderson?" he asked.

"Yes," I replied, my eyes still down. "That's him."

Wardin paused and crossed his arms.

"And where is Andre now?" he asked me.

"At Stanford University, studying journalism," I answered.

Wardin recrossed his arms, rubbed his chin, and moved into the center of the room.

"Tell me, Miss Theresa Anderson, do you know

any answers to the questions on this preliminary assessment exam?"

I looked up.

"For instance, do you know the answer to question three?" he asked.

My throat dried up like a swimming pool with the water sucked out. I looked down at the test and read the question one more time. *List three contributions to our modern society attributable to the ancient Persians.*

Sweat poured from every inch of my body.

"Well, I'm waiting, Miss Theresa Anderson."

The class stared at me like I was a rib roast for Wardin's weekend barbecue being torched over the fire pit.

"Miss Theresa Anderson!" he barked. "Do you know the answer to—"

"The ancient Persians discovered algebra," I replied. "And chess and the abacus, too. Abacuses helped make their businesses grow and advance their society."

The class remained silent. Wardin didn't say a thing. I didn't know what to do.

So I continued.

"I guess we don't really use them anymore. Abacuses, I mean. But we do still play chess and algebra. I mean, we don't *play* algebra, we study algebra. Oh yeah, ancient Persians are now known as Iranians."

The class continued to stare. Nobody could believe I had done the summertime reading.

Actually, I hadn't. I'd learned all that stuff from watching TV. Sometimes the History Channel could be cool.

Right now, though, my TV habits had tossed me into a huge pot of boiling oil. Why couldn't I just watch cartoons like everyone else my age?

Wardin picked up the test off my desk.

"I am impressed with your knowledge, Miss Theresa Anderson."

Ri-i-i-ip! He tore the exam in half.

"That will be an F."

Damn! I knew it.

"And a six-page typed paper."

Double damn! I knew it.

"And three weeks of Saturday school."

Triple damn! I didn't know that was coming.

"Now tell me," he asked, "who is your accomplice?"

What? I thought. *He wants me to rat out Cee?*

I paused. The class stared at me even harder. I could feel the heat of their eyeballs.

"I asked you a question, Miss Theresa Anderson. Who is your partner in fraud?"

Oh my gracious!

I had stepped up and fessed about the cheating. I had humiliated myself in front of the entire Honors Program. I had basically screwed myself for the rest of tenth-grade World History just eighteen minutes into the first day of class. And now he wanted me to punk out and roll over on my homegirl? Why was he doing this to me?

"Let's make that five weeks of Saturday school, Miss Theresa Anderson. Now, who is your accomplice?"

I sat there frozen. What was I supposed to do?

"Six weeks of Saturday school."

I looked down at my shoes.

"Seven weeks of Saturday school."

I started to go numb. Even if I wanted to talk, I wasn't sure that I could.

"Miss Theresa Anderson, let me be clear. This is a direct question and I strongly suggest you respond with a direct answer. Now, for *eight* weeks of Saturday school, a *ten-page* typed research paper and a *parent conference with the principal of this high school*, please tell me, who is your accomplice?"

I looked up with tears in my eyes. My hands shook with fear. There was no saliva in my throat, but I opened my mouth. I had to say something. Cee would understand, I know she would.

"I can't tell you that, sir."

Silence. I looked back down. A long, soft "Oooooo . . ." rolled through the class.

"Come with me," Wardin ordered. I followed him to his desk.

Wardin opened his drawer, took out a yellow sheet of official-looking paper, and began to write. A moment later he tore the sheet from its pad, folded it over, and handed it to me.

"Being a former military man myself, loyalty to one's comrades is a quality I greatly admire. You'll get an F on the test, do a three-page typed paper on the ancient Persians, and no Saturday school. Karma will take care of your accomplice. Here."

He handed me the yellow sheet of paper. Confused, I took the note.

The entire class took its first breath in about ten minutes. Not me, though. I still waited.

"And no parent–principal conference."

I let out a sigh. Wardin looked me in the eye.

"You have big shoes to fill, Miss Theresa Anderson. Make good choices, please."

I opened the note. It read: *Pass to nurse, then to restroom—G. J. Wardin.*

The nurse? I thought. *Oh,* I realized, *for tampons.* They'd be the crappy kind, but at least they'd get me through the day.

"Get yourself together, Miss Theresa Anderson. Everyone else, back to work."

I lowered my eyes and walked out of the room. When I reached the hallway a little spark of vomit shot up in the back of my throat, but I was able to keep it down and not yak all over the recently shined floor.

3

Of all the smacked-up things about my first day so far, the thing that most killed me was that Wardin brought up Andre. I mean, what could be worse for a person than having to follow in the footsteps of a successful older brother? And to boot, my older brother was the Hoopster, a semifamous former student of Wardin's who was brutally attacked by a bunch of racists for an article he wrote on tolerance and bigotry for some stupid magazine. It just wasn't fair.

"Why can't people just move on?" Sonia replied with a shake of her head when I told her the whole story later that day at lunch. Sonia Rodriguez was my other best friend in the whole wide world. And so what if she was Latina? What law says black people can't be best friends with Spanish people anyhow? Some folks are just haters at this high school, that's all. Ignorant haters. Sonia and I shared french fries.

Actually, Sonia and I had this whole tradition we had followed every lunchtime during our freshman year and our plan was to continue on with it through all four years of high school. I would go buy us a Diet Pepsi and a bag of chips from the vending machine while she would wait in the cafeteria line for french fries and then we'd meet at the bench near the library to share lunch, gossip, and talk about boys. Truthfully, I did a lot more of the talking about boys than Sonia. She was kinda the responsible one. She'd do homework and plan out her schedule and stuff.

"What do you think Jimmy Gomez looks like naked?" I asked.

"I don't want to think about that," Sonia replied, not looking up from her math book.

"I bet he has pimples on his butt."

"*Jesucristo*, I'm eating, Tee-Ay!" For a fifteen-year-old, Sonia sometimes spoke like a church-going grandmother instead of my tied-for-number-one best friend. But I liked her for it. She neatly dunked a french fry into the perfect little mound of ketchup she'd created and went back to her geometry problem.

I know, I know, our lunch sounds like it ain't healthy—and it ain't—but if people saw what the food looked like at the school cafeteria, they'd be eating the same things we did. School food is not real food. The cheese tastes like ass and the turkey like glue. A girl I know named Josephine once bit into a chunk of meat loaf and spit out a Band-Aid. It's the nastiest, funkiest, most disgustingest stuff ever—so gross that most of the people on the Free Lunch Program don't even eat it. They'd rather pay for something else. The only fools who do eat it are the freshman boys, which proves how stupid they are.

Oh, yeah, the teachers love it. I guess when you get paid nothing per year to work as a "professional educator" lunches that cost $1.60 a day including a roll with butter are hard to pass up. Maybe that explains why so many of them are tub-of-goo fat.

But the fries are safe. And with plenty of ketchup and cooked real well-done, they taste pretty good. Perfect with salt and Diet Pepsi.

"I guess we could eat from the salad bar," Sonia once said to me, referring to our school's "Healthy Cuisine."

"You crazy? I heard people put boogers in the lettuce."

"That's nasty," she said with a shake of her head. I wasn't really sure if people made snot sandwiches with the school's lettuce, but I did know that eating from the salad bar would break up Sonia and mine's lunchtime tradition, and neither of us wanted to do that. After all, in high school, traditions are everything.

"Would ya look at how Cyndy Rantell is mackin' down with Justin Wyatt by the flagpole. Ain't she going with Chi-Chi Castenada no more?" I asked.

"She's a ho," Sonia replied without raising her eyes. At first I thought Sonia wasn't even going to look up and check out how they were sucking and slurping on each other's face, but curiosity got the better of her and she spied 'em out as they macked down hot and heavylicious.

"Yep, she's a ho," Sonia confirmed and went back to her schoolwork.

"Get a room!" I shouted and turned my head as if it wasn't me yelling. Sonia stuck her head further into her math work. Their tongues didn't even flinch.

I scanned the campus for Rickee or Devon, wondering how that situation was going to work out. Maybe they had planned to fight after school behind the Taco Bell. There were always fights behind the Taco Bell after school.

"Yo, yo, yo," came a voice from behind us. It was Jaxson Edgars, a tall, semicute guy I had been friends with since second grade. Once Jax and I played Truth or Dare when we were about eleven at a birthday party at Geena Collins's house, but no one ever dared us to do nothing, so we had never kissed. I always thought that was weird, 'cause we were the only two black people at the party, but still no one called for us to hook up, so we didn't.

"Wass' up, my ladies?" Jax said as he strutted up, thinking he looked much better than he really did in a pair of red pants that were the same color as a fire engine. I didn't want to hurt his ego by making any cracks about his outfit on the first day of school so I let it slide. But if he wore them things next week, he was gonna be hearing some stuff, *fo' sure!*

"Who you think is your lady?" I said, giving Jax a hug as he crossed around in front of us. Jax was a bomber, the best damn graffiti artist in the whole high school, if not the whole city. I mean the kid had mad skillz, a true gift with spray paint. As a result of his talent, he'd spent much of his freshman year on suspension or doing Saturday School, wiping down blasts he had created during the week. Jax got so good—I mean his work was just too, too excellent—he couldn't ever work the campus again. Not a school bathroom, PE locker room, or teacher's desk—nothing! "Only Jax could scratch like that," the principals would say, easily distinguishing Jax's work from anyone else's. The blessings of his talent had resulted in the curse of his being banned from using it.

I guess he could have toned down his blazes so that no one would know it was him doing the bombing, but Jax had too much pride. Like I said, Jax had mad skillz and damn if he was going to water them down just so he wouldn't get caught. His goal was to get better, not worse. The ironic part was that the campus was a cleaner place because of it.

Ironic is a good word to know for the SAT. It means "all opposite-like"—like when what you expect and what you get are totally the opposite, kinda like this weird mismatch type of thing.

Now, if those french fries had been mine, I knew Jax woulda grabbed about eight of 'em and started stuffing them in his mouth. But they were Sonia's, too, and she was all the strict Latina about people touching her food, so Jax kept his distance.

"Hello, Sonia," Jax said politely, leaning his head in front of her notebook.

"Hello, Jaxson," Sonia responded, flashing a set of beautiful white teeth. She had just gotten her braces off two weeks before and her mouth was perfect. Took 'em long enough though. Sonia had been wearing braces for three years.

"Ya'll hear bout Li'l Zigzag?" Jax asked.

"Who hasn't?" I responded. In high school bad news circulated faster than stolen tests with the teacher's answer key.

"They say he's gonna be okay, though," Jax informed us. "I don't even know why a person be needing a spleen anyway. A dude's gotta have a heart, but a spleen? Isn't that an organ kinda like your tonsils, that can be taken out no problemo?"

"It's not no problemo, Jaxson," Sonia snapped. "I mean he doesn't get to have all the ice cream he can eat afterward, like with tonsils. He got shot with a real gun and real bullets and I am sure it did some real damage, too."

"What you getting all mad at me for?" Jax replied. "It ain't like any of us were really even tight with Li'l Zigzag."

"Maybe I'm just upset that a fellow student was a victim of violence."

"Well, don't trip on me, girl, 'cause it'll probably happen much more times 'round here before the year's over," Jax said matter-of-factly. "This ain't Beverly Hills, you know."

"That's a crappy attitude," Sonia responded.

"I'm just keeping it real," he replied. "Every year people get blasted. Li'l Zigzag's story probably won't even make the newspapers, 'cause he didn't even die."

Jax's words hung in the air and, for a moment, neither of them spoke. There were supposed to be counselors on campus to help us students deal with "issues" like this, but the budget cuts the year before were so brutal that our school now only had one guidance counselor per every 836 students. I think mine was named Mrs. Lincoln, but I wasn't too sure, 'cause I had never met her. No one I knew had.

"Aw, don't be like that, Sonia. I know you still love me," Jax said, finally breaking the tension. He reached over and tickled Sonia's rib cage.

"Don't you touch me, you red-pant wearer," Sonia responded. "*¡No me toques!*"

"No may toh-kess!" Jax said, tickling her again. Sonia tried not to, but she grinned. I guessed the issue between them was resolved. However, what Jax said was true. You had to die at this high school to make the newspapers. Teenagers were getting capped more and more and nobody was doing nothing about it.

Suddenly to our left, a group of peeps started flowing flavored beats by the fence in their own little lunchtime ritual. The way they could stream, gush, and run rhymes right off the top of their head was amazing. I mean some of those fools had real talent. I swung my legs around in the other direction so I could hear better. I just loved listening to 'em. Undoubtedly, we had the most gifted crew of hip-hoppers and beat-boxers ever assembled on one high school campus. Ever.

Especially MixMaster Mytch.

I swear that boy had a tongue like a serpent. His skillz were downright hard and there was no doubt in everyone's mind that one day he was going to be bringing home the big dollar bills. The only people who didn't know it were the teachers. He had an 0.64 GPA, but the MixMaster didn't give a damn. His eyes were on the prize of a record deal. Coming to school for him was all about the ladies and keeping his mom off his back until he got a recording contract.

And judging by all the girlies around him, his plan seemed to be working.

A group of us listened in, bobbing and weaving and thumping and beating as he flow-flow-flowed. In my heart I was jealous. How in the world could I ever get a guy like the MixMaster to notice me? Especially when there were junior and senior girls running three-deep ready to go on a date with him—and do more than that—anytime he asked.

I wished I had talent. Maybe if I had some kinda skillz, the MixMaster would notice me, maybe ask me for my digits or something.

"Yo, Tee, I gots to rap wit' you 'bout something," Jax said to me as the beats were busting along.

"So rap," I answered.

"Aw, come on, girl. Not here. It's private-like."

"Oh, you want me to get up from where I be all comfortable?" I asked.

Jax looked at me with puppy dog eyes as the flows kept coming from the crew by the fence. The scene grew larger with some Latino dudes in long, white T-shirts battling rhymes with some African boys wearing fresh new basketball jerseys. Everyone was smiling and spittin' out their best stuff. Hip-hop was the one thing in our community that didn't divide the races. Instead, it brought us together. I loved hip-hop for that. Music, rhythm, and rhymes made it all good no matter what 'hood you came from.

Jax pulled my sleeve, tugging me to walk away with him.

"Aw, wuzzup wit' dat?" I replied, putting down my Diet Pepsi and standing up.

"It'll just take a sec," he responded. "Good-bye, Sonia."

"Good-bye, red-pant wearer," Sonia answered as she went back to her math problem, which involved finding the area of a right triangle. Boy, did her teeth look good.

Jax and I took a few steps to the left.

"So, wuzzup wit' your girl, Cee-Saw?"

"What you mean, 'wuzzup'?"

"You know . . . *Wuzzup?*"

"Oh, you like her?"

I never got why guys didn't go straight to a girl when they were interested in them. They always went to the girl's best friend. It's stupid. Us ladies *love* attention. More than flowers or chocolate or diamond earrings. Well, maybe that ain't always true, 'cause I ain't never owned no diamond earrings, though I do got those cubic zirconium ones they sell at the mall. I bought them last Easter for a really good price. But girls do love attention, that's for sure. The only sensible explanation I ever heard came from Mrs. Rogers, my eighth-grade English teacher, who was so old she smelled like brown paper bags.

"Boys are stupid," she said. "And it don't matter what age you get them at, they're all stupid."

Seemed like a good explanation to me.

"So, what's the 411? You think—" But before he could finish his sentence, Jax spied Cee-Saw approaching with a bounce in her step. "Damn, here she comes. Do me right, Tee," Jax said as he rushed off. "Do me right."

And before I could respond, Jax dashed off.

I walked the few strides back over to Sonia as Cee-Saw approached. A glow lit up her face. "I got the best plan ever!" Cee said to me. "Oh, hey-hey, Sonia."

"Hey-hey, Constancy." Sonia never called anyone

by their tag names. She was more formal than that. Except she did call me Tee. Go figure.

"I'm talkin', this is a Plan with a capital P!"

Though I was best friends with both Sonia and Cee-Saw, Sonia and Cee-Saw were not best friends with each other. Don't get me wrong, they got along, but we weren't the three Mouseketeers or nothing like that. They were just regular friends who shared me in common.

"What plan?" I asked in a sour tone. I was still kinda bent on her about all the trouble she'd caused me earlier.

"You mad at me?" Cee asked in an innocent way.

"What makes you think dat?" I responded.

"Aw, Tee, don't be a hater. It was all stupid Rickee's fault."

She was kinda right. If that fool Rickee hadn't messed with us in the first place nothing ever woulda happened.

"And if the tables were turned, you know I woulda had your back. You my peeps, Tee-Ay. Me and you, we're tight like a kite."

I didn't say anything.

"Aw, come on. We cool or what?"

I wasn't sure how to answer.

"What's this 'Plan with a capital P' you talkin' about?" I asked.

"You're gonna join me for tryouts on the cheerleading squad!" she exclaimed as she reached to grab a handful of french fries. And no, she didn't ask.

"What I want to try out for the cheerleading squad for?" I replied.

"That's how you get Rickee. I know you like him."

"Girl, shut up," I snapped back as I looked around to make sure no one else could hear. I had never told no one I liked Rickee, not even my best friends. It was too secret a secret.

"Ain't nobody like Rickee," I said all casual-like.

Sonia looked up from her math book and rolled her eyes at me. Did everyone know?

"Girl, I know your fantasy is to give it up to him one day."

"Shut up, Cee!"

"Well, a girl got to lose it sometime."

"What you talkin' about? You're a virgin, too," I said.

"Yeah, but nothing lasts forever," Cee answered with a mischievous smile.

Sonia remained quiet as a mouse.

Cee-Saw, fired up with energy and excitement, grabbed a few more french fries and messily dunked them into the mound of ketchup, completely destroying the neat, red circle Sonia had carefully constructed. Sonia noticed her creation being squashed but didn't say a word. She did, however, finish solving her geometry problem. I'm sure her answer was right, too.

"I shouldn't really be eating these if I'm gonna be a cheerleader," Cee-Saw said. "I can't be fat."

Then she grabbed three more.

"Yo, Amy!" Cee-Saw shouted across the courtyard as if she was amped up on diet pills. "Girl, I got some stuff to be telling you." Cee-Saw grabbed her backpack and planned a quick exit.

"Tryouts are next Tuesday after school, Tee. All you gotta do is shake your ass a bit and Rickee's gonna come a runnin'."

"Shut up, Cee!" I said, and I was serious. She was playing around too much now.

"We gonna be the most popular girls in high school," she assured me with the hugest of smiles. "Later, ladies! I gots ta' bounce." And she dashed off.

It was silent for a moment, then Sonia spoke. "Rude," she commented, folding up her books. And she was right. Goodness, I loved Cee-Saw, but *damn,* sometimes that girl made me so mad. I mean, the least she coulda done was offer to help me write the three-page paper or something.

I reached for my backpack. Only two minutes remained before the end-of-lunch bell rang. Suddenly, Devon Hampton appeared.

"Oh . . . Hey, Dev," I said, greeting him nervously.

"Hi, Tee," he said with a soft smile. "Just wanted to say, *muchas gracias*."

"Back at ya," I replied.

"Naw, girl, you really saved me. That man was looking to scalp me."

I wanted to ask about Rickee. I wanted to tell him thank you for snatching my note. I wanted to find out why he did what he did, how long he had been studying karate, who he was going to take to Senior Prom in two and three quarter years, and if he liked old-school hip-hop artists like Tupac and early LL Cool J. There were a thousand things I wanted to ask him.

"Happy I could help," I said.

Happy I could help? What a freakin' dork! No wonder I could never get a date for Valentine's Day. Not that I could ever land a man like Devon Hampton—some boys are just out of my league—but still, *Happy I could help?*

"Hey, wuzzup, Dev?"

"Wuzzup, Rickee?"

Rickee!

I spun around expecting there to be an immediate

throw-down with fists, punches, body blows, and kung-fu karate chops flying everywhere. Instead, Rickee blasted me with an ear-to-ear grin and stuck out his long, nasty tongue.

"*Bla-a-ah!*" he zapped at me, then walked on.

I spun back around and looked at Devon. Confusion filled my face.

"But . . ."

"We cool now," he responded. "I straightened it all out."

Huh?

I turned back again to look at Rickee and watched him cruise up to Principal Watkins and give him a big, cheerful high five.

"I don't get it," I said.

"Don't sweat it, Tee, it's all good," Devon reassured me. "It's all good." Apparently, Dev had gone into the boys' locker room all by himself and apologized to Rickee in front of about fifteen football players, saying he meant no disrespect but was just trying to be chivalrous. *Chivalrous* is a good word to know for the SAT. It means "all noble," kinda like one of those knights in King Arthur's court. But no matter how much Shaolin kung fu Devon knew, surviving fifteen football players all alone in a locker room wasn't gonna happen if they wanted to beat him down like a punk. Rickee knew that. Devon knew that. And that's why Rickee appreciated the major props in front of all his boyz.

Anyway, that's how things got cool between them again.

Hmmvvvzzz! Hmmvvvzzz! Hmmvvvzzz!

"Well, time for class," Devon said as he walked off toward Algebra II/Trig. "Much, much *gracias* again, Tee."

"Yeah, sure," I said as he walked off. "Ain't no thing, Dev." But I was still a bit confused. The only clear thought I had as I watched Devon make his way to the most advanced math class a sophomore could take was, *Dang, he's got a nice butt.*

4

My emotions bounce around on the inside of me like a Ping-Pong ball juiced up on Starbucks espresso. And I mean every day. One minute I can be sky-high happy without a problem in the universe and ten minutes later I can be feeling like the loneliest skunk on the planet, as if the world is made up of nothing more than black smoke and fog.

And these mood changes hit me out of nowhere all the time. Up, down. Up, down. Up, down. Happy, sad. Happy, sad. Happy, sad.

Maybe I'm broken on the inside. Does everyone feel like this?

Like when Devon Hampton thanked me and walked back to class, I felt like life was better than chocolate-chip ice cream on a fresh-baked waffle cone. I knew the dude was solid and having solid peeps in your life always makes you feel good. To tell the truth, my experience with Devon left me exhilarated.

Exhilarated is a good word to know for the SAT. It

means "*really* happy and excited." Sometimes I feel like this.

Sometimes I don't.

Like fifteen minutes later, when my biology teacher Mr. Kim started boring me with a lecture about DNA, I glanced over at Lizbeth Ruiz and realized she had prettier eyelashes than any other girl I had ever seen. I was so jealous. Why couldn't I have pretty eyelashes? Why couldn't I have a pretty nose? Why couldn't I have thinner earlobes? My earlobes are chunky.

I became bummed. I didn't even know any fancy SAT words for the word *bummed*. My chunky-earlobe butt is worthless.

Up, down. Up, down. Up, down. Happy, sad. Happy, sad. Happy, sad.

I must be broken—fo' sure!

"Yo, Tee-Ay, did you tell her?" Jax asked when I saw him in the hall after Biology class. Since I was sad about having chunky earlobes, I lied.

"Yeah, go for it, Jax." Besides, Rickee was never gonna be interested in me anyway, even if I did become a cheerleader, which I wasn't going to do, so what difference did anyone else's love life make? "Totally go for it, homie."

"All right!" Jaxson exclaimed with glee. *Glee* is a

small word for "happiness," but it's good to know for the SAT.

Why do I know so many happy words? As I walked home from school I realized I need to look up some sad ones.

I entered my house, tossed my backpack on the couch, and grabbed some pretzel nuggets and cream cheese. Pretzel nuggets dunked in cream cheese are the best after-school snack ever.

"Gimme the remote, I wanna watch!" my brother Teddy screamed as he busted through the front door twenty minutes after I had gotten comfortable. The local middle school was a shorter walk from our house than high school, but since it let out thirty minutes later, I was always home before him. This means I always had the power of the remote control.

"No chance, Stankbutt," I replied. Teddy is only eleven.

"Then make me something to eat!"

"Sure thing, loser."

He watched me not move an inch and became more angry.

"Then gimme some pretzels and cream cheese!"

"Touch a pretzel and you die!" Being four years older meant I could kick his little butt, even if he was a boy.

"My name is Teddy *Bear*! *Arrrggghh!*" he growled as he flexed his tiny muscles. "You shouldn't mess with the *bear*."

I laughed.

"You *suck!*" he shouted as he stormed off to the kitchen. "And you'll pay, too!"

"I'm telling Mom!" I shouted back, too lazy to get up and punch him.

Teddy disappeared. Ain't nobody made me his African slave, that's *fo' sure!* I wondered what was on the Discovery Channel.

Two hours later my mother walked in the front door and saw me lying on the floor watching TV.

"How was the first day of school?"

"Fine."

There was a pause.

"Is that it? Fine? How are your teachers?"

"Fine," I replied again. "Except one. He's a jerk." I switched the TV station to the channel with the good war footage. Those black-and-white pictures of tanks rolling through the streets of Europe are pretty cool.

My mother stared at me.

"What?" I asked with an edge in my voice.

"You know, you have a real attitude problem, Theresa."

"Why are you gettin' all over me? I ain't done

nothin'," I said as I folded up the bag of pretzels and put the lid back on the cream cheese, as if that counted for doing something productive.

"Done *nothing* is exactly right," she answered.

"Well, it ain't like I got any homework or anything. It's the first day of school." Actually, that was a lie. I did have homework. In three classes. But it was small stuff and I could copy off somebody else in the morning.

Of course telling her about the three-page paper in World History would be downright Stoo-pid with a capital S.

"You need to learn that life does not work like this."

"Like what?" I snapped back.

"Like this," she said as she spread out her arms and pointed to the way I was lying about the room. "Your brother understood—"

"Oh, don't start on me with Andre. I already know he's perfect and I'm defective," I said as I got up and made my way to the kitchen to put back the pretzels and cream cheese. Maybe that would get her off my back.

"Don't you get mouthy with me, Theresa!" she replied, following me into the next room. "If you think I work this hard at the bank only to get attitude when I walk in the front door of my own house from—Lord have mercy, what happened here?"

We both entered the kitchen at the same time. It was like a bomb had gone off.

Cabinets open everywhere. Crumbs splattered all over the counter. A jelly knife sticky side–down on the microwave, a cereal box knocked over on the table, an ice tray not put back in the freezer, and a container of milk not put back in the refrigerator—the very same fridge whose door had not been shut, letting every bit of food inside get warm and spoiled.

A quiet *hmmmmmm* filled the room. It sounded as if the refrigerator door had been open for at least forty-five minutes.

"You cannot be serious."

"It was Teddy," I quickly answered. "He must have run off to hang with his little crew."

"And how long have you been home now?" she said turning to me with a mad, mad, mad look in her eye.

"But it was Teddy!" I answered again.

"Theresa! What are you thinking—"

"Why I always get blamed when someone else—"

"You just expect to come home and watch television—"

"It's not fair! I always get in trouble for things that weren't even my—"

We blasted away at each other, shouting and screaming and yelling, neither of us hearing a word the other said. Then we paused, like two wild animals on the Nature Channel who stop in the middle of their fight to stare at each other and catch their breath before they attack again.

Suddenly, my cellie rang. *Thank goodness!*

I crossed to my backpack and checked the caller ID before I answered. Not that it mattered. I would have answered a call from Mr. Wardin to chitty-chat about Etruscans to get away from my mother at that point.

"Hey-hey, girl," I said into the phone. "Hold on a sec. . . ."

I turned to my mom. "It's Cee-Saw. May I be excused?" I spoke as if it were the President of the United States on the line.

My mother shook her head. "Girl, you got nerve like I ain't never seen before." She turned away from me and started to put on her orange cleaning gloves. I took this as a *yes* and walked out of the room.

One thing about Cee-Saw, she always had good timing.

"Wuzzup, homegirl?" I said into my cellie as I flopped on the couch.

"Zero-zero. Wuzzup wit' you?"

"Just my moms givin' me grief."

"Why for?"

"I don't know. She always be trippin' on me," I

answered. But this was another lie. I knew good and well why my mother was always tripping on me.

It had started when I got busted smoking weed with some former friends just over two years ago. Drugs are *everywhere* at my school and practically everyone has tried them. You can get bud, blow, speed, acid, X, shrooms, or smack if you ask around. But when I got caught with a little sack of weed, like only two joints' worth, things got Ugly with a capital U around my house.

Just for one little baggy of chronic my daddy was going to ship me off to a camp. But not a fun camp, like a summer thing with canoes and tents and kickball. It was one of those juvenile work camps where people wake you up at 5 A.M. by smashing garbage can lids against your head and make you pick up trash on the side of the highway all day long to build your character. I might have gone too, it was close, but there was a report on the news about how some teenage girls were being forced to have sex against their will at these places, so I was let off the hook. *Thank goodness!*

But that's not why I stopped smoking dope. Nobody can really make you stop smoking pot if you don't want to. I don't know why parents don't get that, but they don't. I stopped smoking because I didn't want to become some loser, dropout, brain-dead fool like I had seen more and more of nowadays walking around my neighborhood. No job. No education. No future. I mean, it's crazy how things have changed 'round here. There used to be a few white kids at our school, but they're all gone. There used to be a few real businesses in the 'hood too, like a place that sold stationery and a pretty cool bicycle shop. But they're gone as well. All it seems like we got left now is black people, brown people, a few poor Asian people, and a bunch of liquor stores and doughnut shops that sell Chinese food. I always thought that was a weird combination. Who eats fried rice with glazed buttermilks? People are freaky.

But naw, no one made me quit smoking chronic. I simply decided to chip it off, just like that. I mean, I wasn't like a pot addict or anything. You can't even get addicted to pot. Cigarettes yes, but they stink up your breath and your clothes and make your lungs turn into cancer bubbles. Pot? No. I just chipped it off.

My mother, however, still doesn't trust me. She might not think I'm doing drugs right now, but she does think I might go back to doing them, so she's worried. But she's worried about *too* many things.

She scared I'm gonna get pregnant, drop out, have no job, get arrested, and end up homeless on the streets rolling around babies in a stolen shopping cart or something. I mean she gives me no credit at all. Last year at the end of ninth grade I ended up getting one A, two B's, one B minus, and two C minuses. So what if the A was in PE? That's still an A. And I didn't even try real hard. I know some girls who got all F's and D's, not even any C's—like Cee-Saw, for one. But no matter what I do, it's never good enough for my mom and she always be yelling at me. I mean, do I look that stupid?

The truth is—and I've never really told this to anyone—when I graduate, I want to go to the University of Southern California. That college is tight! Since my brother goes to Stanford—there's no way I'm going there—I want to go to a West Coast school that is just as big-time but with a football program that will year in and year out beat the crap out of Stanford. That way I can call him on the phone and punk him. The Trojans of USC are my dream. Not just 'cause of football, though—they got great academics too. I know this 'cause in sixth grade our school took us on a field trip to their campus and I remember eating delicious cheeseburgers right by this building that had the biggest library I had ever seen. There was a fountain with a ton of flowers around and all these young people walking about, looking like they were having the best time ever. They have all kinds of intellectual things you can study, like engineering, anthropology, business, medicine, law, and on and on and on. That's what I want. I ain't gonna be no homeless prostitute drug addict with seven babies rolling around in a shopping cart. One day, I'm gonna be something. I'm going to be something good.

This is why I tell myself I'll even deal with a punk like Wardin. If he's going to help me get into USC, I can handle him, even if he is a moron. I'm gonna do what I gotta do to become a Trojan. I just ain't gonna tell anyone, because my life is full of haters trying to bring me down. Like my mom. She don't have no faith in me.

Plus, Steven Spielberg went to USC. Maybe I'll become a movie director like him and make a film about hip-hop. That sure beats being a dumb journalist like my brother, even if he does go to Stanford.

Naw, USC is my dream, but it's also my secret. I'm just not gonna tell anyone. Not until I get accepted.

"My moms ain't even home," Cee-Saw continued without any real emotion in her voice. "Don't know where she be either. Guess I'll just make me a potpie for dinner."

"Theresa! Are these your pretzel crumbs I see on the floor by the TV?"

"Uh-oh," I said. "Here we go again."

"Wuzzup, she trippin' some more?" Cee-Saw asked.

"Theresa, you'd better hang up that phone, grab a vacuum, and start making our house look the way you know it ought to look. *Now!*"

"My mother hates me," I said. "I'll holler at ya later, girl."

"Peace out, homegirl," Cee-Saw said as we hung up.

"*What?*" I shouted at the top of my lungs, getting up from the couch. "What did I do now?"

5

Copying Sonia's homework was tricky for me because she is such a solid student. If I wrote down the answers exactly the way she had written them, we might both get busted. She's just too good. I learned that the hard way in Mrs. Pinkett's fifth-grade class when we both got three weeks of Saturday school for cheating. Sonia hadn't even done anything, other than give me her answers, but still she had to pay the price for her part as "an accomplice." Teachers and police ain't ever happy nailing just the perpetrators, they always want to bust the accomplices too. In my opinion, it's total BS, but Sonia never complained.

Now whenever I copy, I make sure to change some words around and miss a few questions, too. That way nobody knows. Yeah, it sucks having to miss answers on purpose, but it's better than doing the work myself. That's *fo' sure!*

"You know, Tee," Sonia said as she watched me turn a correct answer into a wrong one, "you're smarter than me."

"No duh," I replied with a smile.

"No, I'm serious. You're smarter than all of us. You need to be doing this on your own."

"Shut up, Sonia," I replied.

"You could be the best English student in the entire tenth grade. Better than even Amanda Hardison or Devon Hampton if you tried." Sonia searched for an unbroken chip to munch in the bag of Doritos we were sharing for lunch. She only liked to eat the ones that were perfect triangles without any broken corners.

"Stop lying," I said as I scribbled down another combination of right and wrong answers. "And gimme the geometry stuff."

"You know, you're gonna need to know geometry for the SAT," she remarked as she passed me her work.

"Whatever, Mom," I responded as I copied down her answers. "Is that a one or a seven?"

"It's a Stick-It-Up-Your-Butt," she snapped as she snatched her work from me.

I looked up. Sonia was mad. Real mad.

"No more homework for you," she barked. *"Nada más!"*

"Whatever . . ." I looked away.

"And I mean *nunca*. Don't even ask," she added.

Goodness, she was serious.

"Chill, Sonia. No need to freak," I replied as I put

my stuff away. At least I had written down enough to get credit for the day's assignment. Well, half credit. Whatever, she'd be cool by tomorrow, so I let it roll.

Speaking of rolling, that's what school was doing, *rolling*, just like most years. There were scandals, fights, gossip, girls hooking up with guys, guys hooking up with girls, and teachers whose only purpose in life was to make us students totally miserable. Though we were only a few weeks in, I was already failing Wardin's class. So were about fifty percent of the other people in tenth-grade Honors World History though, which made me feel better about my own efforts. The crazy part was I did more work for him than for any other teacher on my schedule and I was still getting an F.

What a punk.

"Hey-hey, Tee-Ay!"

"Wuzzup, homegirl? Where you been?" I asked. Cee-Saw approached with a smile so big it looked like she had just won the lottery.

"Just chillin'," she replied as she sat down and searched for a french fry. Too late, we'd already eaten them. "Chillin' with Angie and Stephanee and all of the other *cheerleaders* that is."

"Ooooh, girlll, yes, you made it!" I shouted as I jumped up and gave her a big squeeze.

"Congratulations, Constancy," Sonia said with a smile and a smaller hug of her own. Even though the cheerleaders were always snobby to her, Sonia was happy for Cee-Saw because she knew how badly Cee wanted to make the squad. I mean Sonia wasn't mean-spirited or nothing like that. Plus, she knew that to be a cheerleader meant you had to keep your grades up because they checked for things like a C average and stuff. Since Constancy was a friend, Sonia thought cheerleading could be good for her. After all, Cee-Saw needed something to help motivate her in school. Her grades were terrible.

"Oh, you shoulda done it with me, Tee-Ay," Cee-Saw said with sunshine in her eyes. "It's gonna be so fresh."

"Naw," I replied. "This your thing, girl." The truth is, I thought long and hard about becoming a cheerleader, but I was too scared to wear the uniform. Not 'cause boys would always be trying to look up my skirt—all cheerleaders know that is going to happen. It was because people might see that I have really ugly kneecaps. Not my thighs or my calves, they're fine, just my kneecaps. It's tough to spot, but when I bend my leg a certain way my kneecaps looked like big-headed alien skulls. No joke, they have eyeballs and everything. Ever since I was eleven, I've hated both my earlobes and my kneecaps. I could never be a cheer-leader with alien-skull kneecaps.

"Well," Cee continued, "at least ya'll can come to the . . . *par-teeeeee!*" she shouted. "Party! Party! Party! Party! Party!"

About fifty people turned to see what the commotion was all about.

"Girl, you crazy," I said rubbing my ear.

"It is gonna be a rage-fest, homegirl! Football players. Cheerleaders. A lack of adult supervision," she added with a sly twist of her mouth.

"No parents?" I asked.

"What fun is a gig with parents?" she responded. "I mean, it's gonna be so fresh. See, Angie's folks are out of town for the weekend so there ain't gonna be no *regulations*, if ya know what I mean." Cee-Saw was bouncing up and down so much I thought she was going to wear out her sneakers. "You gonna come, Sonia? I'm sure you're invited. Like a hundred million people are going to be there."

"I don't think so," Sonia answered softly.

"Oh, come on, girl, it's gonna be a blast!"

Sonia bowed her head and lowered her eyes. All three of us knew she wasn't going to show. Parties weren't her thing.

Cee-Saw turned to me.

"I know you gonna be there."

Right then I realized how much I hated my mom. I was on a two-week punishment for breaking the earpieces of Teddy's new headphones when we were fighting over who got to sit on the good part of the couch—I was there first—and I knew that there was no way she was going to let me go out this weekend. Especially to a cheerleaders' party where there would be no adults.

"I don't know. My mother been on my case something big-time lately," I told her.

"You gotta be kiddin' me. Rickee's gonna be there."

"So, what I care about Rickee?" I said, acting all casual. But on the inside I was burning.

"Girl, you need to stop frontin' and figure out a way to get to this party on Friday night. It is going to be the bomb."

My mom was Darth Vader, evil ruler of my universe.

Suddenly, Jaxson Edgars cruised up wearing a dark black turtleneck that made him look kinda *GQ*. It also made him look kinda like a scarecrow that had robbed a department store, 'cause the sweater was way too big for his narrow frame. But at least I had to give the boy points for trying.

"Yo, Cee-Saw, can I get a rap a minute?" he asked, all smooth.

"Oh, yes you can," Cee-Saw replied enthusiastically. "I been waitin' to rap with you all week."

Jax paused and seemed surprised. Pleasantly surprised. So was I. Maybe Cee-Saw did like him after all. I mean a graffiti artist as talented as Jax probably attracted the interest of lots of ladies, even if he was so skinny you felt like feeding him every time you saw him.

"Walk me to class?" Cee-Saw asked with a flutter of her eyelashes. Cee-Saw had just turned sixteen, but by that age, most all girls know how to flutter their eyelashes to attract a man. Some nights we even practice in the mirror.

"Don't you know it, girl," Jax answered as he smoothed out his sweater. "May I carry your books?"

"Aw, look at you tryin' to go all nineteen-fifties on me," Cee-Saw said with a grin.

Jax picked up Cee's backpack as she called out, "Later, ladies!" to us.

"Yeah, later, ladies," Jax added as he readjusted his turtleneck.

They walked off arm in arm. Sonia and I traded a look.

"Seems to me we got what's known 'round here as a . . ."

"Dee-vel-o-ping sit-u-a-tion!" we both finished aloud at the same time with a shared giggle. Girls in high

school like me and Sonia love watching love bloom. I mean, what could be more pure than high-school romance?

Hmmvvvzzz! Hmmvvvzzz! Hmmvvvzzz!

I grabbed my backpack as MixMaster Mytch finished spitting his hard rhymes by the fence. Forget spring—lunchtime is the most romantic season of the year, and if you knew where to look, romance happened every day in high school.

Fifth period bored me as usual, and in sixth period we had a sub who picked his nose for half the class. I finally caught up with Cee-Saw in the hall right before seventh.

"Hey-hey, Tee-Ay."

"Wuzzup, homegirl?"

We gave each other a *slap-slap-bump* high five on the down low.

Since Jax and I both had Spanish II in seventh period, I was gonna find out all the juicy details about what had happened between him and Cee in less than three minutes anyway, but since I caught Cee in the halls, I figured I might as well find out what went down from her point of view before I found out what had gone down from *his* point of view.

After all, when it came to "dee-veloping situations," a person couldn't know too many points of view.

"You rap with Jax?"

"Sho' 'nough," Cee replied. "Told him how much I wanted him to hook me up with Devon."

What?

"Yeah, Jax and I rapped and I asked him, 'So, wuz-zup wit' your boy?' At first he didn't know what I was talkin' about, so I spelled it out for him again, like 'You know, *Wuzzup wit' dat?*'"

I gulped.

"And . . ." I slowly asked, "what'd he say?"

"He kinda didn't say nothing . . . *Yo-yo! Wuzzup, Steph-a-nee!*"

Stephanee, too cool to actually respond verbally, just kinda nodded a *Wass'up?* to Cee-Saw, cheerleader style, as she crossed the hallway. Cee-Saw nodded in the same cool way in response and then turned her attention back to me.

"I think Jax may kinda like me, but I got no time for boyz like him. Not when one of the hottest dudes in the tenth grade is on the market."

"You told him that?" I replied in shock.

"Hell, no," Cee replied. "I kinda let him feel like he's got a chance with me even though we both know he don't. Ya never know, maybe he'll buy me an expensive present or something one day. After all, a girl can't have too many admirers."

"Are you crazy, Cee-Saw?"

"Yeah, *cra-zzeeeeeee!*" she answered, flashing a twisted grin. *"Hey-hey, Pauley Zee!"*

"Hey-hey, Cee-Saw!"

"So, what'd Jax say?" I asked, scared to hear the response.

"He said he'd do me right," she said with confidence. "He gonna *doo—mee—right!* Look, I gotta bounce. Me and Samantha Hines gonna ditch last period and go grab a latte. You wanna come?"

"Naw, I'm straight," I replied, still somewhat in shock.

"Well, we gotta skate outta here before security does their sweep. Otherwise, it's more detentions, and you know I already gots me too many of those," she said with a laugh. "Peace out, homegirl."

Slap-slap-bump, we high-fived on the down low.

"Yeah, peace," I said softly as I turned and headed for Spanish II.

Dang, what had happened to the "dee-veloping sit-u-ation"?

"Hey-hey, Jax."

"Naw, I ain't hearing none of that."

"Jax, I didn't know."

"What you mean you didn't know? That's your girl."

"I swear. I—"

"All you girls is whack, you know that? I mean, something is seriously wrong in y'all's brains. Bitches just be playing with dudes, like we some kind of entertainment or something."

Though I hated when guys referred to girls as bitches, he was right. Girls loved to mess with the heads of guys, and right now, Jax's head was being spun and scratched and flipped and jammed like a piece of vinyl on an old-school turntable.

"So, you gonna rap to Devon?" I timidly asked.

"I would never sell out my boy to a hoochie like that! Devon's a man's man and you girls is whack. Especially your stoopid-crazy-nutcase girl Cee-Saw."

Jax stormed off to the other side of class. I didn't follow, but I felt really bad for him. Cee-Saw had punked him and it was all my fault.

Plus, and this was like *so obvious*, he still had a crush on her—big-time.

6

Friday night came, and instead of slamming it up at the party of the century, I was helping my youngest sister Tina braid her hair. Don't ask me how much I loathed my mom. The way I saw it, she was ruining my life.

Loathe is a good word to know for the SAT. It means "to totally, totally not like." It's a really strong vocabulary word.

Not strong enough if you ask me.

Bing-bong! Our doorbell rang.

"Was that the television?" Pops asked. My father was hard of hearing from an accident he had when he was younger. I think he fell off a ladder.

"No, it's the doorbell," answered my mom as she came out of the kitchen to see who it was.

"Hi, Mrs. Anderson, is Theresa home?"

Oh my gracious, Cee-Saw. I jumped out of the chair and bolted toward the front door, leaving Tina's hair sticking up in all kinds of crazy directions like she had just stuck her finger in an electric socket.

"Hello, Constancy," my mother said with a suspicious look. My mom knew Cee-Saw must have known that I was on punishment, but, not wanting to be rude straight off, my mom played along with Cee's little game of acting nice and being overly polite. "How are you this evening?"

"I'm fine, Mrs. Anderson. And you?"

"I'm fine, thank you. Is school going well?"

"Yes, very well. I'm on the cheerleading squad now."

"Congratulations," said my mother. "And how are your classes?"

"Fine," Cee answered.

Gulp. Couldn't Cee have said something other than "fine"?

I arrived at the door wearing pajama pants.

"Hey, Cee," I said softly, trying not to alarm my mother, who I am sure felt cause for alarm. "I wasn't expecting you."

I was telling the truth. I had no idea Cee had planned to come over. I doubt my mother believed that, though. She didn't believe anything I said these days, even when I was telling the truth.

"Well, this was kinda spontaneous," Cee answered, trying to be delicate. "You see, my moms and I are going to the movies and I was hoping Theresa could join us."

Cee stepped back from the door and pointed to her mother, who was waiting in her lime-green Lincoln Town Car at the edge of the driveway with the engine running. Ms. Sawyer's car oozed white exhaust from the tailpipe and had a couple of rusty dents in the passenger-side door. In the distance she waved a small *Hello*.

My mom half waved back.

"I'm sorry, Cee, but Theresa is on punishment this weekend for—"

"Who's at the door?" Pops interrupted as he walked up, scratching his belly. "Oh, hello, Constancy."

"Hi, Pops," Cee-Saw answered with an even brighter, more eager smile.

"Why's everybody standing out here? Come in, people. You're gonna let out the warm air."

"Thanks, Pops, but I don't have time. Our movie starts in about half an hour," Cee-Saw said.

"Oh, I didn't know you were going to the movies tonight," my father said, looking at me.

"Theresa's *not* going to the movies tonight," my mom replied. "She's on punishment, remember, dear?" It's like I was the bug and my mom was the boot and *squish* was the music of our life.

"Aw, honey, let's give the girl a break. You know as

75

well as I do that Teddy starts stuff all the time with her just as much as she starts with him."

"The girl is on punishment," my mother insisted.

"Baby, don't get crazy."

"Don't you tell me not to get crazy!"

"Ya see, you're getting crazy. It's just a movie."

"I don't care what it is. There are some things about life that this girl just needs to know and she ain't knowing them the way she needs to. I mean, she can't be as stupid as she's been acting!"

Ouch!

It got quiet.

I looked down at my fuzzy slippers and my eyes became watery. Did she really need to say that? Especially in front of Cee. I mean, I hadn't even done anything.

"Oh, I don't know . . ." my mother added a moment later, apparently aware that she'd gone too far.

That small opening was all I needed.

"Please, Mom. Please! Please! Please! *Please! Ple-e-ease!*" I begged, trying to make her feel guilty.

"What time does the film end, Constancy?" Pops asked.

"We should be home by eleven, sir," Cee answered. "Eleven-thirty at the latest." Boy, sometimes I wished I knew how to think on my feet as fast as Cee did. Just like that she got me an extra half hour if we could only pull this off.

"*Ple-e-e-ease*, Mom? I've learned my lesson. I'll never, ever, *ever* do it again."

I had no idea what I'd "never ever" be doing again, but for the chance to go to a movie with Cee on a Friday night, I'd swear to pretty much anything.

Mom glared at Pops. He shrugged his shoulders.

"It's called positive parenting. Theresa will be a better daughter for it."

"Positive parenting?" my mother asked.

"Yeah, I heard about it on CNN," Pops said, reaching into his wallet. "Make sure you bring me the change."

Next thing I knew I was holding a twenty-dollar bill. Oh my gracious, I *loved* CNN.

Beep-beep!

Cee-Saw's mom tooted the horn, impatiently signaling us to hurry up.

"Do we have any ice cream?" Pops asked, drifting off to another topic. "I got me a taste for some chocolate chip. Maybe I'll take the new car out and get some—"

"With your cholesterol up as high as it is, you are *not* having any ice cream tonight. And you're definitely *not* taking my brand-new car to the store to get it either. And you," she added, turning to me with darts in her eyes. "If you're not home by eleven thirty-one P.M.—"

"I promise, I promise, I promise," I said, dashing off to my room to change clothes quickly before she even finished.

Oh my gracious! I was going out!

"What should I wear? What should I wear?" I frantically asked as I threw open my closet door.

Cee-Saw reached into my closet, grabbed six different outfits with four pair of shoes and jammed them all into a bag. "You'll get changed at my crib," she said, pulling me by the arm out of the room.

"But I don't have any underwear," I said.

"You won't need it," she replied as she yanked me along. A bolt of lightning raced up my spine.

What? I thought.

"Hold on a sec, Cee, I gotta get me some panties."

I turned, opened my underwear drawer, and began to look for the perfect pair. *Should I wear blue flowers or pink stripes or—* Suddenly, Cee's hand reached into the drawer and pulled out a black lace G-string. It was the sexiest thong underwear I owned. My mother didn't even know I had it.

"Well if you're gonna wear something, wear these."

She crammed my G into the clothing bag and we darted out of the house.

"'Bye, Mrs. Anderson. 'Bye, Pops," Cee-Saw said, leading me out toward the car.

"Thanks, Mom. Thanks, Pops," I added, as I climbed into the lime-green Lincoln with the rusty dents.

"Theresa Anderson, you'd best hold up your end of this agreement," my mother warned.

"I will!" I shouted back. "I wi—" Cee-Saw slammed the car door before I even finished speaking. The next thing I knew, we had driven away.

Holy penguin piss, I'd been sprung from Alcatraz!

"Hi, Ms. Sawyer," I said, a gigantic grin plastered on my face.

"Hi, Tee," said Ms. Sawyer, making a right at the stop sign. "It's good that ya'll will be working on your project at the apartment tonight. Girls your age should be studying on the weekend. School's important."

Project at the apartment?

Cee flashed me a fiendish grin.

"Uh, yeah . . ." I responded. "We have a lot of work to do."

"I mean ya'll know how I really don't like to be leaving Cee home alone too often if I don't have to," Ms. Sawyer continued as she made a left on Oak Street.

"But I got plans tonight. After all, it's Friday, and on Friday nights it's good to go out and let off some steam."

"Yeah, you deserve it, Momma. You work hard."

"Truth to that, girl," Ms. Sawyer replied as she lit a cigarette and rolled her window down a crack for the smoke to escape. "You speakin' the truth to that."

Cee-Saw's grades may have stunk, but nobody could deny that there weren't perfectly good reasons for Constancy Eloina Sawyer to be in our school Honors Program. Time and again she demonstrated wicked smarts.

When we arrived at Cee's apartment. Ms. Sawyer didn't even turn off the engine.

"You girls have a good night and behave," she said, dropping us off by the front of the apartment building. "I should be home by two. Two-thirty at the latest."

"We will, Momma. Have fun," Cee said, exiting the car. Ms. Sawyer flicked her cigarette out the window and waved. The next thing I know, the lime-green Lincoln with the rusty, dented doors had driven off with white exhaust oozing out of the tailpipe.

"Well, come on, homegirl. We gotta get fixed up."

"What movie are we seein'?" I asked.

"Movie?" Cee-Saw laughed. "We're going to the fiesta at Michelle Baxter's."

"Michelle B's?" I said with a puzzled look. "But I thought the party was at Angie Hamilton's."

"Naw, her folks canceled their trip so the gig got moved to M. B.'s crib."

"But that's only a block and a half from my house," I replied.

"Don't sweat it, girlfriend. Everything's gonna be chill. Now come on, get changed. If you ain't home by midnight, your Momma's gonna trip."

"Eleven-thirty!" I said.

"Yeah, that's what I meant," she answered as she dug through my bag of clothes. "Wear that," she commanded, pulling out the shortest dress I owned. "Rickee's gonna love that."

Everyone had always said high school would be one of the most memorable times of my life. I guess that was because of nights like the one I was about to have.

At some high-school parties the hosts set out a few bowls of chips and other snacks so the kids can have a chance to nibble on tasty goodies. They play decent music, have plenty of ice for the soft drinks, and serve some type of dessert toward the end of the event, like a chocolate layer cake with a side bowl of vanilla ice cream so everyone gets a good taste of sweetness to make their night complete.

As soon as I walked up to the front of the house, I knew that this was not that kind of party.

We entered the door through a cloud of smoke. Cigarettes. Marijuana. Cigars. Incense. I even think I detected the sweet funkiness of cloves. Those things are unmistakable.

About a zillion teens had taken over the house. None of them looked familiar.

"This is the bomb," Cee-Saw remarked as she led me deeper inside. But instead of feeling good about things, I felt nervous.

"Follow me," Cee said.

Was something wrong with me? I mean, wasn't I supposed to be feeling fine, too?

Just chill, Tee, I told myself. *It's all gonna be chill.* And I followed Cee.

Fresh tunes bumped on the sound system and a DJ with two dope turntables was spinning vinyl like a sorcerer. People grooved all over the place. The couch had been moved over by the window so that a dance floor could be set up, but the sofa was pressing against the curtains and tearing the seams at the top. No one seemed to mind, though. Especially not Michelle B.

She greeted us after we passed through the first wave of people in the doorway with a vodka drink in her hand. Every word out of her mouth was a slurred shout.

"Yo! Cee-Saw, my girlfriend! Wuzzup?"

"Sweet party, M. B."

"Aw, you know it, bitch! Wuzzup, Tee-Ay?"

"Hey-hey, M. B. Where're your folks?"

"They *died,*" she said with a snorting laugh, as if it were the funniest thing she had ever uttered. "No, just bullshitting. They're in San Diego with my sick grandmother. She's really bad in the hospital with—"

But before Michelle B. could explain her grandmother's disease, Eddie Morton circled around behind her and stuck his tongue deeply into her mouth. I don't even know if Michelle realized who was kissing her, but that didn't stop her from kissing back.

"Let's do this," Cee-Saw said. "Let's do this right."

We *slap-slap-bump*ed a high five on the down low, but I was still feeling a lot of trepidation. *Trepidation* is a good word to know for the SAT. It means, "anxiety, edginess, tension." SAT words, however, didn't strike me as being too important to too many peeps at this party, that was for sure. Then again, I couldn't be positive, 'cause I had never been to a party like this. It almost seemed as if there was too much freedom. The inside of my stomach danced.

Cee-Saw, on the other hand, strutted her way through the crowd as if this was home turf. She bobbed her head from side to side and wove like a major player through a maze of homeboys and homegirls, all of 'em dressed in super-dope clothing. Bouncing through the room like the new force to be reckoned with in this new world we were now entering, Cee-Saw walked with a thump I had never seen in her before.

As for me, I kept my gaze low and avoided eye contact with most everyone. During the times I did look up, I noticed guys and girls hooking up all over the place. Even though I hadn't taken any drugs, I still felt a bit dizzy. Laying low seemed like a good plan.

"This is livin' right here," Cee-Saw said with a huge

smile as she led me deeper into the house. "I'm sayin', this is what it's *all* about."

I didn't answer.

We came to the kitchen and I finally saw a few faces I recognized. Seeing school friends outside school always shows you people in a new light. Boys who you think are kinda quiet and goofy suddenly turn out to be Marlboro smokers who play poker. Loners, I discovered, actually have some friends and all of them play guitar. Athletes, however, turned out to be predictable. They gulp beer, exaggerate every story they tell, and use profanity each time they open their mouths.

But all guys—jocks, stoners, wannabes, posers, and players—all of them share one thing in common. They all hope to score on a chick. And all the ladies know it.

That's why we come dressed in clothes our mothers don't know we own, wearing makeup that makes us look about five years older than we really are. As I walked through Michelle B.'s crib, I realized that most of the girls' deepest goals were to make every guy in this house wish he could have sex with them that night. And every girl's deepest fear was that the one guy she *really* wanted to *want* her would not even notice she was alive. It all made for a lot of sexual tension and at this party—the wattage boomed off the hook.

"I'ma go get us some drinks. Chill here a sec and wait for me," Cee instructed and before I could answer, she slipped through the crowd and disappeared.

The last thing I wanted to be right then and there was alone, but I refused to show my fear, so I bobbed my head to the music and grooved a bit to the beat as if it was all chill.

Wearing a black lace G-string did nothing for my self-confidence, though. It felt downright weird to be in such a short dress with dental floss running up my butt. I was scared that the whole world could see my goodies.

"*Yo, yo, yo,* you wanna hit this one time, sugar?"

I looked up. "Who—me?"

"Yeah, baby, go ahead," said a dude with a green bandanna wrapped around his forehead, offering me a pipe. "It ain't gonna bite ya."

"Nah, I'm straight," I replied.

The green-bandanna dude stared at me like I was a freak. His glare made me feel uncomfortable.

"Whatever, girl," he finally said and then took another puff off his pipe and went to find someone else to smoke with.

I decided to head toward a different part of the house. Maybe I'd run into someone I knew, like Devon Hampton. He knew a lot of SAT words.

Naw, a guy like Dev would never be at a party like this.

I cruised through the dining room and saw some big senior from the football team on his knees guzzle down a beer bong. He swallowed all the liquid through a hose as if it were being shot down his throat from a cannon. I had no idea how a person could handle that much fluid at one time being rammed past their tonsils, but after taking it all down in three huge swallows, he rose to his feet in glorious triumph.

Bu-u-urp!

It was the biggest, most disgusting belch I'd ever heard. The crowd, however, went crazy.

"Yeaaahh! Whoo-hooo! Do another!"

"Bring it on, *bay-beeeee!* Bring it on!" The football player dropped right back down to his knees and someone reloaded the beer cannon.

Gulp! Gulp! Gulp!

Bu-u-urp!

The crowd went crazier.

Where in the world is Cee? I turned and decided to walk over toward the—

Bump. I ran into someone.

"Excuse me," I said, not looking up.

"Well *excu-u-uzzze* me," came the reply.

Oh my gracious, Rickee Dunston.

"Wassup, Tee-Ay?" Rickee said with glistening, red eyes. "I ain't know you wuz coming tonight. Gimme a big ol' squeeze."

I gave Rickee a hug. A long hug. His rock-hard muscles made me feel as if I were embracing a piece of iron surrounded by chocolate flesh.

"Lemme get you a drink. Whadya want?"

I really didn't want anything, but I couldn't say that.

"I'll have what you're having."

"Cool," he responded. "Come on, follow me." He took me by the hand. I didn't resist.

We wove through about a thousand people, but instead of feeling more nervous at seeing Rickee like I thought I was going to, I started to feel a bit better. Maybe I was getting somewhat adjusted to the atmosphere. Maybe having Rickee hold me by the hand made me feel more secure. Maybe I did really belong at a gig like this. After all, I was a sophomore in high school. It was my time, right?

Shit, this is what hip-hop was all about—parties, dancing, hookin' up. I grooved a little more to the beat and squeezed Rickee's hand a bit tighter. Yeah, it was my time.

Rickee led us back to the kitchen, where I found Cee-Saw at a breakfast table doing tequila shots.

"Well, look who it is," said Cee, standing up

awkwardly to give Rickee a hug. "I see you found my girl, Tee-Ay. You treat her right, you hear?"

"Oh, I'ma treat her right," Rickee responded.

"Yeah, you better," Cee-Saw warned. "'cause that's my homegirl right there. Girl, gimme some love, Tee-Ay."

Cee-Saw circled around the breakfast table, knocking over somebody's can of Budweiser.

"Hey, watch it."

"Screw you, fool."

She gave me a *huge* squeeze.

"I love you like a sista, homegirl."

"I love you, too, girl," I responded. "I love you, too."

"Now, did I do you right tonight or did I do you right?" she asked.

"I gotta admit," I replied, "you done me right."

"Word to that. I'm a major player with major schemes!"

Slap-slap-bump, we high-fived on the down low.

"Now have some fun, girlfriend, 'cause tonight it's all green lights. Green freakin' lights." Cee spun around.

"Gimme 'nother, fool!" she snapped at Paco. "I gots to wet my whistle."

Over the course of the next two minutes I saw Cee-Saw slam three tequila shots. She was a funny drunk.

"Now pour one up for my girl, Tee-Ay."

For me?

"Naw, I'm straight with this," I said, smelling the orange concoction Rickee had handed me. *Concoction is good word to know for the SAT. It means, "a mix of all sorts of ingredients."*

Oh, goodness gracious, couldn't I just let all this SAT crap go for a night?

"Yo, wuzzup wit' dat, Tee-Ay? You gots to do a shot wit' your homegirl," Cee-Saw insisted.

My stomach started to dance at the thought of it.

"Tee-Ay! Tee-Ay! Tee-Ay!" Cee-Saw started to chant my name. A few other folks at the table joined in even though they didn't know me.

"Tee-Ay! Tee-Ay! Tee-Ay!"

More and more people started calling out my name. It quickly became embarrassing and all I wanted to do was shut them up.

"Tee-Ay! Tee-Ay! Tee-Ay!"

But there was only one way to shut up the crowd. I lifted the tequila glass and sniffed. It smelled like an oil rag.

Rickee sprinkled a taste of salt on his wrist and lifted his arm to my mouth.

"Lick this first," he instructed.

I paused and looked around.

"Go 'head," he instructed me. "It's how ya do it."

"Do it, girl! Do it!"

"Tee-Ay! Tee-Ay! Tee-Ay!"

I licked the salt off Rickee's wrist, then—*bam!* I slammed the shot of tequila. Three seconds later, I felt the fire.

Suddenly, someone jammed a lime in my mouth. The cool juice helped me not vomit.

Barely.

"Yea-a-a-ah! Bay-beee! Whoo-hoooo!"

Whatever I had done, it pleased the crowd enough for everyone to go back to doing whatever it is they were doing before they had learned my name.

I gulped again and hoped I wouldn't puke. No more tequila shots for me, no matter who chanted my name, that was *fo' sure!* That stuff was just downright nasty.

"Way to go, girl. We partying tonight!" Cee-Saw stuck her finger in Paco's ear. "Homie, you need a Q-tip."

Everybody laughed. Cee-Saw was hammered.

"Come on," Rickee whispered in my ear. I felt the warmth of his breath on my neck.

"Where are we going?" I asked with a small, seductive smile.

"For a walk," he answered.

"A walk where? We goin' for fresh air?"

"Naw," he said through red eyes. "We just going for a walk."

I looked over and made eye contact with Cee-Saw. She grinned.

"Uh-huh!" Cee said. "You go, girl!"

Turns out our walk wasn't that far at all. Just up the stairs.

8

Michelle B.'s parents lived in a pretty big house, considering that our neighborhood wasn't really all that upscale in the real estate market. Some of the homes were built during the early 1930s and back then they built them big and spacious. By my count there were at least three rooms upstairs.

Rickee led me into bedroom number two and closed the door.

"Have a sip of your drink, girl," he said as he crossed over to the window and closed the blinds. We were in a boy's room, that much I could tell. I would have guessed the kid was probably around seven from the baseball designs on the bedspread and the Little League trophies spread about the room. Where this little boy was during the party, I had no idea.

"This drink's strong," I remarked.

"Naw, it's good for ya," Rickee said as he approached me after turning out one of the two lights. "Drink up."

I faked taking a sip. The thing was nasty.

Next thing I know we were kissing. Rickee had a big tongue. I could smell the alcohol on his breath.

My head started to spin. I couldn't wait to get back to school on Monday and walk hand-in-hand down the halls with Rickee Dunston. We'd have lunch together, write love letters in class, and walk home with one another after I watched him kick some butt at football practice. He was going to be my first real boyfriend—not none of that middle-school crap—someone I could share time with, someone I could tell my problems to, someone who would buy me chocolates and flowers and mysterious romantic presents on Valentine's Day. Valentine's Day had always made me feel sad and lonely, but this year would be different. I couldn't wait. I was the luckiest girl in the whole school.

Rickee and me were going to be a "couple."

Then I felt a hand on my breast. Then another reaching under my dress. We'd been in the room less than eighteen seconds.

"Yo, there," I said, gently pushing him away. "Slow down a bit, baby."

"Wuzz' the matter, girl? That's what we're here for," he said, smoothly reaching in for another kiss.

I kissed him back. He might have had a big tongue, but he had wonderfully soft lips.

Two seconds later I had to stop his hand from reaching under my skirt again.

"What's the rush, baby?"

"Oh, come on, Tee-Ay," Rickee responded. "I know you like me, girl."

"And how 'bout me?" I asked.

I waited for an answer. He didn't seem to understand the question.

"How about you what?" he asked me back.

"Well . . . do you like me?" I repeated, feeling kinda stupid that I even had to ask.

"Oh yeah, I am all into you, girl," Rickee said, reaching in yet again for another kiss. This time he didn't put his hands anywhere. All we did was kiss. It was nice.

Suddenly Rickee's hand quickly unzipped the back of my dress in a speedy swoop that had my outfit almost all the way undone before I had a moment to react.

"*No-o-o, no, no!*" I said, backing away. Rickee's eyes scanned down to my black bra and he licked his lips. "You are moving at time-traveler's speed," I said.

"Come on, Tee-Ay," he said, moving closer. "If you really liked me . . ."

Rickee reached in for another kiss. I backed up.

"And if you really liked me, you'd . . ." I replied.

"I'd *what?*" he barked angrily, then pushed me against the wall, causing my left foot to fall out of my shoe. I looked into his eyes. There was anger.

"I do really like you," he insisted.

A vein pumped in Rickee's forehead as he stared at me. I trembled. The strength of his muscles pressing me up against the wallpaper was overwhelming. Rickee was five-eleven and one hundred ninety-five pounds of pure athlete. Physically, there was nothing I could do to resist him.

My skin started to tingle with panic. He glared longer. All I felt was fear. Time stood still.

What was happening?

BAM! Rickee suddenly swatted a Little League trophy off the mantel.

"Aw, girl, you trippin'!" He backed away and headed for the door.

"No, Rickee, wait!" I yelled as I reached out and grabbed his elbow.

He yanked his arm away.

"Girl, you ain't nothing but a tease," he snapped as he stormed out. I tried to follow him.

"No, Rickee, wait!" I shouted again as I exited the bedroom, zipping up the back of my dress while trying to put my shoe on at the same time.

"Wait!" I screamed as I burst into the hall.

But Rickee wasn't in the hall. Or at least he wasn't alone. Four other people were in the hall with him, including our school's star quarterback, our school's star running back, Stephanee Campbell, and Angie Hamilton, the dynamic duo of cheerleading. Their conversation froze mid-sentence as they stared at me. I lifted my dress back over my shoulder to cover up my bra.

Silence filled the air. Another moment in time stood frozen.

Our school's star quarterback broke the silence by raising his beer.

"Hey-hey, I see someone got a taste!" he blurted out, lifting up his drink to salute his football teammate. "Way to freakin' go, Dunston!"

Rickee gave the quarterback a high five and disappeared down the stairs. "I need a beer," he said and he was gone.

Gone forever.

The star cheerleaders quickly whispered something into each other's ears and giggled at me. They didn't even try to hide it.

I finished zipping up my dress and clumsily put on my shoe. I had to step over the four of them to make my way back downstairs. They didn't even move to let me by.

Oh my gracious. What had just happened?

Time to go. Time to go. That's all I could think about as I cruised through the downstairs crowd of drunk, stoned, sexually hungry teenagers. *Gotta find Cee, time to go.*

But of course, I couldn't find her anywhere. Holy jeez, this party was mobbed. More so than I remembered.

Maybe she is still in the kitchen?

"Hey, Paco," I said, trying to squeeze my way toward a table filled with homies playing drinking games. "Paco! You seen—"

"Yeah, bay-beeeeee!" one of the players suddenly shouted, as if he had just hit a buzzer-beating three-pointer to win the NBA Championship.

I mean how much skill does it really take to bounce a stupid quarter off a table into a cup filled with beer?

"I pick you, fool!" The crowd laughed when the guy pointed at Paco. Paco slumped his head in agony.

"Paco!" I said again, trying to get his attention. "Paco, have you seen Cee-Saw?"

Paco lifted his head crookedly and looked at me with foggy eyes.

"All I see is *cerveza*." And his head slumped again. He was wasted.

I spun around, wondering where I was gonna find—

"Oops. Sorry, babe . . ."

Oh, jeez. Don't tell me this nappy-haired freak just spilled his drink all over me.

It took a second. Then I felt the wetness leak through my dress.

Damn!

"Didn't see ya comin', girl," he said. "But wish I had. *Dang*." The guy took a step back to check out my breasts, then my ass. "Wuzz yo' name?"

This fool spills a drink on me, scopes me out like I'm some sort of ho, and then expects to get a rap in?

I walked off, my dress soaked with alcohol.

This whole night was a freakin' disaster. At least I could still make it home by 11:30. *Where the hell is Cee?*

I crossed into the next room. The gig was bumpin' off the hook. Peeps were groovin' everywhere—and I mean *everywhere*. I couldn't hardly see nothing. Screw it, I thought. I should just bail out on her and walk home.

I decided to give it one last chance and did a final cruise through the living room. Suddenly, we made eye contact—me and Rickee.

He glared at me with hate. Just then a boy who

was dancing accidentally bumped his elbow, almost causing Rickee to spill his beer.

"Sorry, homes."

"That's right you sorry, bitch!"

Bam!

Rickee busted the dude in the jaw with such a ferocious punch, it sent the guy flying into the wall, knocking down a framed portrait of Michelle B.'s family. It fell to the floor with a *smash!*

"Aw, hell no!" shouted one of the boy's friends. He jumped over a chair to bust some ass for his pal who had just been knocked out.

But Rickee was too quick. He dodged a wild punch and tossed the guy over his left shoulder.

Ba-bam!

Rickee blasted him so hard, a piece of his tooth got chipped off.

Then a bottle got thrown, a girl got tripped, and twelve people started scrapping in the middle of the room. Punches flew everywhere! I tried to bolt out of there best I could, when all of a sudden—*bash!*

The whole party stopped. Someone had thrown a chair through the plate-glass window. A freakin' chair! That was gonna be thousands of dollars in damage. A moment later the brawling resumed.

Where the hell was Cee-Saw?

"Cops are on the way!" I heard a voice shout. Like a herd of buffalo, everyone started rumbling toward the front door in between punches and kicks. I saw one fool take a boot to the face. *Da-dumph!*

Screw this! I gotta get out of here!

I climbed past a dude who was bleeding behind his ear when suddenly I heard a cry from the stairs.

"Tee-Ay! Tee-Ay, is dat you?" Cee-Saw sat slumped on the stairs, unable to stand. "Dat you, Tee?" I fought my way through the mass of people heading for the door and ran to her side.

"Come on, Cee, get up! We gotta go. The cops."

"I'm spinning, Tee-Ay. The whole world is spinning."

"Oh, come on, girl, you gotta get up!" I said, trying to lift her. "The po-po are gonna be here any second."

But she was too drunk to stand.

For a moment, I have to admit, I thought about leaving her. The whole reason I was in this mess in the first place was because of her. Of course I wasn't gonna, but the idea did cross my mind. Self-preservation, that type of thing.

It took me all of my strength to lift Cee-Saw up and carry her down the stairs. She was heavy. Too many french fries. I tried to get a better grip 'round her waist, but accidentally dropped her.

Thump. She landed on her head.

"Ow!"

"Sorry."

The next thing I knew, red and blue lights were everywhere.

It didn't take long for the cops to take complete control of the situation. After all, there must have been about a zillion of them. Jeez, it was only a high-school party. With all the po-po on the scene a person might have thought there was a bank robbery or something.

The officers made all the kids they caught line up on the sidewalk and sit on the curb while they "sorted out the situation." Truthfully, I think they did this not only to restore order but to humiliate us. That's because with all the cop cars that had been called, traffic had to be rerouted into a single lane that just so happened to get to drive slowly past all the neighborhood delinquents.

How convenient. We were like a freak show of teenage criminals on display for all the world to see. It was so unnecessary.

Each person in every car drove by at about one mile per hour, staring at us like we were a bunch of mass murderers. I guess if I were in one of those cars, I would have stared the same, too. However, since I had to sit on the sidewalk, I was mortified.

Mortified is a good word to know for the SAT. It means "severely embarrassed." I was mortified that the cops were showing us off to the local traffic like a bunch of thugs headed for a penal colony. I mean, where did they get the nerve to—

Oh my gracious!

He looked at me at the very same moment I looked at him. It was the worst eye contact I have ever made. Worse than Rickee ten minutes earlier. My stomach sank.

I thought about getting up and running. Maybe a cop would shoot me in the back. Dying, it seemed to me, was a much better alternative right then to facing my father. That's right, Pops, driving my mother's brand-new car, had just cruised by.

Oh no! Please don't. Please don't. Damn!

Yep, he put on his turn signal and parked across the street.

Oh my gracious!

Should I still run? Would the police shoot an unarmed girl? What if I asked them to?

After a conversation I could see but not hear with one of the lead officers, my father "took custody" of me and Cee. No charges were to be brought against us. Apparently, my father convinced the police that his court of law would be harsher than theirs. For the first time in my life, I wished I was being sent to the big house instead of my own house.

We got in the car, me in the front, Cee in the back. She was so drunk, my father had to swing her legs around to close the car door for her.

He started the engine. The silence was spooky. I smelled like booze. There was a paper bag on the floor containing a pint of Häagen-Dazs chocolate-chip ice cream. *Unbelievable!* Pops had snuck off in the middle of the night to satisfy his sweet tooth and, as fate would have it, he had run into me.

Maybe he wouldn't tell my mother about me and the cops so that he wouldn't get busted himself for eating ice cream, with his cholesterol so high.

Yeah, right.

I shook my head. It couldn't possibly get any worse.

Bla-a-ah!

Cee-Saw vomited all over the floor of the backseat of my mother's new car.

It had just got worse.

9

Though I didn't have to wear handcuffs, I was under full house arrest. No this. No that. No nothing! And no discussion. Chores and school were like a blessing.

The idea of camp was seriously discussed again, but when Teddy got busted later that same week for cracking the encryption codes on his school's mainframe computer, our parents' attention was temporarily off me. It turns out that once inside the school's main brain, Teddy had sent three thousand letters out to parents informing them that the vice president of the United States would be coming to campus and invited all of them to a formal talk in the auditorium regarding the state of public education. The letter asked them to wear their best clothes, be patient with security, and bring a gift of steamed Brussels sprouts for the vice president because they were his favorite vegetable.

Thousands of parents took the day off from work. They showed up in coats and ties and elegant dresses, holding container after container of steamed Brussels sprouts. The principal had no idea what was going on and was forced to hold an emergency assembly to explain how it was all a practical joke. The parents got angry.

And the whole auditorium smelled like farts. After all, when you steam thousands and thousands of Brussels sprouts, that's what happens.

When they finally figured out it was Teddy, he was suspended for two weeks with an additional three weeks of cafeteria cleanup detention tacked on once they let him back in school. Additionally, the principal forced Teddy to show the school's computer guys how he had cracked the encryption codes so that they could prevent security breaches like this in the future. Teddy was reluctant, but Pops was so furious, there was no debating the matter. Teddy was forced to reveal his secrets. Once he showed his tricks, all these supersmart adults started talking about intelligence measurement and aptitude analysis and the next thing anyone knew, Teddy was being put through a whole series of IQ and aptitude tests.

I don't know why. I could have saved everyone the trouble and told 'em what was plainly obvious: my brother was a mental midget.

No one asked me, though. They never did.

At that point my parents were ready to send two kids to camp, but after a long discussion, they chose to pound us themselves. It was Punishment with a capital P, the worst I had ever known.

Cee-Saw got put on punishment, as well. For two weeks. But her mom wasn't around to ever really enforce it and three days later she got to go to the mall. Life just ain't fair.

I mean, I was even put on academic probation, meaning that every period of every class of every day of every week I had to get each of my teachers to sign a stupid sheet of paper saying that I had come on time, participated, done all my homework, and behaved in a satisfactory manner.

"It's so embarrassing," I complained to Sonia after taking a sip of Diet Pepsi. "But my mom checks the slip every night and I know if I screw up even just a tiny bit, she's gonna kill me."

"You didn't hear about Constancy, did ya?" Sonia asked, nibbling a perfect chip.

"What, that she got to go to the mall and didn't hardly get but a slap on the wrist?"

"Not just the mall, but the movies."

"Oh, with her new *cheerleading* friends?" I asked sarcastically.

"Uh-huh. And they ran into Devon."

"Devon Hampton?" I asked, not sure where Sonia was going with this. "What about him?"

"Now, you ain't heard this from me, but from what I know, Constancy ended up fixing it so that she and Dev sat alone in the back of the theater and before the film was over he had a hickey the size of Texas on his neck. They a couple now."

And just as if I were watching a movie myself, along came Cee-Saw walking arm-in-arm with Devon through the center of campus.

"You mean, he's her man?" I asked.

Sonia didn't answer. She didn't need to. The way Cee was hanging all over him made it clear to me— made it clear to everyone—that Cee-Saw had landed one of the hottiest dudes on campus.

Repulsed is a good word to know for the SAT. It means "disgusted, severely turned off." And I was repulsed by the sight of Cee hooking up with Dev.

Yeah, she was my best friend, but still, I could tell right away that this wasn't right. Dev wasn't some trophy to show off to all the other girls on campus during lunchtime, but that's how she was treating him. Touchin', huggin', smoochin', right in the middle of school where everyone could see, while wearing her stupid little cheerleader uniform that let everyone spy her milk-chocolate, no-alien-kneecap legs—it just wasn't right.

They cruised up to us like honeymoon lovers. I tried to play it chill.

"Hey-hey, Tee-Ay."

"Oh, hey-hey, Cee," I said, as if I hadn't noticed them approaching. "Hi, Dev."

"Hi, Tee."

"Wuzzup wit ya'll?"

"Just chillin', ain't we, Dev?" Cee leaned over and planted a huge kiss on Dev's lips. I watched her put her tongue in his mouth.

Ugh!

Dev pulled back. Yes, he kissed her, but he didn't seem to be all into the touching, feeling, squeezing, and groping that Cee was into. I mean, he held her hand, but he wasn't ready to do the newlywed cuddle thing in the middle of lunchtime in front of five thousand other students the way Cee was ready to, that was for sure.

Cee didn't seem to notice his reluctance, though. Or care. She hugged him close.

Just then Jax walked by holding a sketch pad. I am sure it was filled with all kinds of dope new drawings.

Usually he would have stopped and shown them to us. Instead, he passed right by, hunched over, glaring angrily at the world.

"You wanna ditch sixth period wit' me?" Cee asked Dev in a girlie-girl way.

"Naw, I can't miss Chemistry."

"We could have some fun," she added in a seductive voice.

Devon smiled uncomfortably. "I really can't. Matter of fact, I have to go see Mr. Fryer early before class. Catch ya later, ladies."

"Bye, Dev," Sonia and I said at the same time.

"Want me to come with ya?" Cee asked.

"That's all right. We'll see each other later."

"Promise?" she asked teasingly.

"Yeah, promise," he responded.

Cee then gave Dev another giant kiss with even more tongue. It was like she wanted to stick it as far back into his mouth as she possibly could. After a moment, Dev pulled away and left. Cee then scouted the scene for a french fry and took a seat. I stared at her. She must have sensed it.

"*Wut?*" she asked.

"Why you tryin' to corrupt Devon with ditchin' class?"

"Why you care? He's my boyfriend."

"I just don't want to see him mess up in school."

"*Shee-it,* he ain't gonna mess up. My Devon's smarter than most of the teachers."

"*Your* Devon?"

"Damn, Tee, what's up wit' all these negative vibes I'm feeling from you lately?"

"Ain't no negative vibes you feelin' from me."

"There sure is, girl. You been hatin' on me something fierce lately."

Just then, I realized Cee was right. I had been hatin' on her. But I had good reason. She had got me in the worst trouble of my life, she was abandoning me for a crew of conceited cheerleaders, and she had pretty much been actin' like an inappropriate, arrogant bitch/punk/ho.

Of course, I couldn't tell her that.

"Hatin' on you?" I responded. "Why would I be hatin' on you?"

"Girl, you blamin' me for things I didn't do. Why don't you try growin' up and taking responsibility for your own actions? I can't help it if things didn't work out with Rickee."

"Rickee?" I responded. "Rickee ain't got nothin' to do with this."

"Oh, I think he do. You're jealous 'cause I got a hot new man and you ain't got nothin' for yourself."

I turned to Sonia for support. She lowered her eyes, quiet as a library.

"You think I'm jealous of you?"

"Thought you could put it aside, though, 'cause we all supposed to be tight like a kite. But I understand. I mean, just look at me and look at you."

"And what's that mean?" I replied.

"It means I'm wonderin' where you come off havin' such attitude with me when things in my life are *going on* and things in your world just ain't. I mean, I am zesty, girlfriend!" *Bap!* she smacked her rear-end. "Zesty with a capital Z."

Hmmvvvzzz! Hmmvvvzzz! Hmmvvvzzz!

"Don't be a player hater, Tee. You're supposed to be happy for your friends when good stuff happens for them."

And with that she wiggled off, her little cheerleading outfit swishing as she walked away.

I was stunned, totally shocked. Sonia packed up her books and mumbled something. *"Qué monstruo."*

"Huh? What's that mean?" I asked.

"What a monster."

Two days later I walked up to Wardin's class ready to kick butt on a quiz we were scheduled to have on

Egyptian gods. I had totally studied. Then I saw Cee-Saw weeping.

Good, maybe someone poisoned her goldfish.

"Tee . . ." She approached with tears streaking down her face.

"What?"

"Devon dumped me."

The nerve of her.

"Look, now ain't a good time to . . ."

She broke into hysterical sobs. The kind with the shakes, hiccups, loss of breath, all that. I was still so mad at her, but watching her bawl like that . . . well, it just broke me down.

"Damn, Cee, I can't do this right now. We're having a quiz in Wardin's class today and I totally studied for it."

"No man is ever going to love me."

"That's stupid. Don't talk like that."

"It's true. I'm nothing but a piece of shit."

Why am I always in situations where I don't know what to do? I mean, pissed as I was at Cee, she was still one of my best friends for years and years and here she was in a time of *huge* need. How could I bail out on her?

On the other hand, ditching Wardin's class would

be nuclearly stupid. And with only thirty-seven seconds before the bell rang to start class, I didn't even have time to really think through my options.

I got it!

"Check it out, Cee," I said pulling her to the side. "I ain't gonna ditch Wardin's quiz, but I will agree to be late, all right? I'll give ya like five minutes right now and then we'll work it all out in full later. Cool?"

"You'd do that for me?" she asked through another wave of tears.

"Come on, let's bounce before I get seen." And we took off to behind the art room.

Five minutes turned into nineteen. Cee moaned and whined and cried and wept about all kinds of stuff that truthfully, I thought was kinda stupid. Maybe it's 'cause my attention wasn't really focused on her the whole time. The vision of a pissed-off Wardin kept creepin' in on my thoughts.

Finally, after it seemed like Cee had gotten a lot out of her system, I stood up.

"Look Cee, I *must* go to Wardin's class to take that quiz. Let's meet at the flagpole after school. We'll rap more then."

"At the flagpole?" she asked shakily. "You promise?"

"I promise, at the flagpole right after school. But,

girl," I said scooping up my backpack, "right now, I gotta go."

"Good luck," she said as I took off. "See ya after school."

I raced up the stairs and opened the door a bit out of breath.

"Do you have a pass?"

"There was an emergency that I had to—"

"I asked if you had a pass, Miss Theresa Anderson."

"But—" I paused. "No."

Wardin grabbed the daily academic parole sheet that was in my hand and scribbled *absent*.

"Absent?" I replied when he handed it back to me. "But I'm here."

"Twenty-seven minutes late to a fifty-five–minute class is not what I call tardy, Miss Theresa Anderson. It's absent."

Oh my gracious, my mother is going to kill me.

"Can I at least take the quiz?" I asked.

Wardin walked to his desk, picked up a quiz, scribbled *F* across the top and handed it to me.

"Make sure you put your name on it."

But I studied, I thought as I took a seat at my desk. I studied.

When I looked up, Rickee Dunston was laughing

at me with one of those big old grins you only see on baboons that live in the rain forest.

"I don't know why you're chuckling, Mr. Rickee Dunston. You haven't passed a quiz all year."

The smile disappeared from Rickee's face. I sat in my chair and stared at my Daily Academic Parole Sheet.

My mom is going to kill me.

Later that afternoon, I waited twenty extra minutes after school by the flagpole. Cee never showed up.

Turned out she went for nonfat iced lattes with the cheerleaders. Apparently, she felt much better.

10

I got two more weeks of Punishment with a capital P added on for failing a quiz I totally knew the answers to. With the way things were going, I'd be lucky to get out of the house again by my senior year . . . of college.

Speaking of college, I knew I had to start getting more real about it. With all my "free time"—meaning, I had no social life whatsoever—I'd been *engorging* my vocabulary with *recalcitrant* SAT words spoken only by *gregarious* persons. I wasn't even sure if I was using all my new words correctly, but at least I was trying. Andre showing up at the house during a four-day weekend he had off from school made me realize how far I still had to go if I wanted to go to a university myself one day.

"I mean, I never understood Picasso, with all those noses in the place where an eyeball should be, until my professor explained Cubism. It's about multiple points of view. Now, when I go to a museum, I understand why Picasso is considered a master."

Though I had no idea what the hell he was talking to my father about—and I still hated him—I had to admit, my bro looked good. I don't think he'd grown any taller, but he had added a bit of thickness to his body that made him look more mature and handsome. With the extra muscle, I bet he was a better scorer in the low post, too. Despite all this brainy chat, I knew he hadn't given up hoopin' it up. Once hoops is in your blood, it never leaves.

Andre talked with Pops about social justice, the need to vote, and a whole lot of other smart stuff. I looked at him closer. I mean, he'd always spoken well, but there was an extra confidence and sophistication to his whole way of being that going to college seemed to be giving him. Hip-hop always talks about the benefits of "elevating your mind." Andre was living proof.

And as his mind expanded, I understood how he was gaining more and more of an advantage over so many of the other nineteen-year-old black dudes from our 'hood. It was almost unfair. I mean Andre was gaining a lead in a life race that other peeps his age would never, ever be able to catch up to. Did they know this? Did they care? Were they doing something to help their own selves out other than complaining about how "the shit just ain't fair"?

Aw, forget those dudes, Tee, I thought. What're you doing for you?

When I asked myself this question, I was forced to ponder my situation. *Ponder* is a good word to know for the SAT. It means "to think deeply about something." I pondered my situation.

My freshman year in high school was like a blur. Lost in the halls, "big" kids all around, sex everywhere. I mean people were doing *da Freak* all over the place. Me, I was just amazed that there were soda machines and candy for sale everywhere. The fact that no one gave a damn if I had a Pepsi with a bag of Skittles for breakfast at 7:05 A.M. in the morning blew me away. Maybe the reason ninth grade had flown by so fast is because I was all drugged up on sugar the entire time. I ended up with a 2.68 GPA.

Naw, that ain't great. If I had gotten a few more B's instead of C's, I might have hit a 3.0. For some reason, that's like the magical number to be above for college. If only I woulda given just a little more effort. *So stupid.*

That's the one good thing about being on punishment for so long—there ain't nothing to do but homework. My grades for the first semester of tenth grade improved.

A–	Honors English
B–	Honors Geometry
B–	Honors Biology
B	Art
D+	Honors World History
A–	Spanish II

Overall, not bad. Except for World History, of course.

Devon Hampton earned an A in World History. He was the only one. Well, three other students earned an A–. But forty-three percent of the class failed and another twenty-two percent earned a D of some sort. Wardin likes to think of his class as a "collegian weeding-out process."

Everyone else thought of it as bullshit.

I mean I definitely deserved higher than a D+. In my heart I felt I had done enough for a C+ or B–, maybe a C at the worst. But a D+?

I wondered if that whole cheating thing on the first day of school had hurt me. *Whatever.* In my book, Wardin was a punk.

Some kids think Devon Hampton got a good grade just because of who he is, but that wasn't true. I knew Devon worked his butt off. He always had his homework, always studied for his tests, and always made an extra effort to succeed. Like the time he did an extra-credit eight-page typed report on socialism. Or the other time for his oral presentation when he earned bonus points for adding a PowerPoint presentation that compared Socrates to Aristotle to Plato, all set to classical music. It was amazing.

I mean, sure he was smart. But the dude worked harder than anyone else in the class. I didn't care what the haters said, Devon had earned his A.

I ended up with a 2.92 GPA for the semester.

Not a 3.0. Not anything remarkable. Not good enough for college.

Ouch! Pondering can be brutal.

"So then we all stripped down to our underwear to have our picture taken on the Golden Gate Bridge in San Francisco. My butt was literally freezing."

Pops smiled ear to ear as he listened to Andre's stories about the weekend trips he got to take with his buddies at school. Funny how he wasn't mentioning the fact that USC had slaughtered Stanford 48–3 that year in football.

I smiled all that Saturday long. Stanford was lucky to have kicked a field goal.

Let Andre ponder that.

• • •

Weeks later I saw Cee-Saw in the halls popping off to three cheerleaders about she had really been the one who dumped Devon Hampton, and not the other way around.

"He just didn't have enough game."

All of them laughed.

"Hey-hey, Tee-Ay," she said as I walked past.

"Hey-hey, Cee," I replied. But there was no *slap-slap-bump* high five on the down low.

"To boot," Cee continued, the louder, the better, so everyone around her could hear, "he was all brokenhearted when I said 'Sayonara, sweetheart.'"

I kept walking. It was hard for me to handle Cee these days. Real hard.

All she ever thought about was boys. I mean, I think about boys all the time, too, but she flirts with all of them. More than flirts, even.

Like during the Black History month assembly in the performing arts building, Cee-Saw macked down with two different guys during the course of two different MLK assemblies and then got busted for ditching class by Mr. Horner, an older black teacher who runs his senior Economics class in a way students describe as tough but fair.

Mr. Horner's one of those old-school black men, the

kind who believe that individual determination means a lot and ebonics is a bunch of garbage. When he took Cee aside he, needless to say, wasn't happy when her first words to him were, "Yeah, what you be wantin'?"

The whole way Cee had told me this story about her and Mr. Horner was weird, too. It's like she wanted me to be agreeing with her, but I found myself agreeing more with him.

"And then he said to me," Cee had explained in an exaggerated voice, "'Young lady, don't you see? You are Dr. King's dream.'"

"I just popped my gum, not really wantin' to be hearin' all about that power-to-the-people mess. Old folks like him ain't realizing times have changed."

Cee-Saw thought she sounded impressive. I thought she sounded ignorant. Just goes to show how much we'd drifted apart.

Our drift, however, didn't really bother me the way I would have expected. I guess I just found her act to be all played out. Yet, there was one thing that did bum me out about the difference between our lives— Cee's world was exciting, mine was boring. She was full of stories about girls losing their virginity. My brain was bloated with vocabulary words.

Bloated is a good word to know for the SAT. It means "overly filled."

Like I said, *boring*.

I made my way to Wardin's class and took my seat like a tired old dog.

Hmmvvvzzz! Hmmvvvzzz! Hmmvvvzzz!

After a minute, an Indian dude walked in with a funny accent.

"G'd morneen, class. I am Meester Sanjiraj. Meester Wardin is out today."

"You our sub?" Cee-Saw asked, rising from her desk.

"Excuse me, meess. Would you please seet down?"

"Aw, hell naw," she said, laughing at his accent. "You know I got better places to be."

And Cee headed for the door.

To survive at this high school, a person had to know how to stand up for themselves. Don't matter if they're an adult, either. It was one of those unwritten rules: getting punked in public without standing up for yourself meant you would continue to get punked for the rest of your days.

Thirty-seven teenagers stared and waited for the sub's response to Cee-Saw's challenge. He was being punked.

None came.

"Peace out, fool," Cee-Saw said as she walked out. The door closed with a *thud*.

For a moment there was total silence. The sub

pushed his eyeglasses up his nose, took a pencil from behind his ear, and called the first name off the roll sheet, trying to pretend nothing had happened.

"Berry well, ees there a Sylvester Adams here?"

People immediately started busting out headphones, cellies, and candy bars. Four more students walked out, claiming they were going to the nurse, library, restroom, and "his momma's house." Although this Indian dude's day had just begun, it was already Over with a capital O.

And the rest of his time at our high school was gonna be hell, too. Subs like him got eaten for lunch. Once the word was out about "Meester Sanjiraj," there was no way to bring it back.

"I said, ees there a Sylvester Adams here? People, seet down. I must take roll."

An assignment had been written on the board. I crossed the room and took a seat next to Devon Hampton. He already had his book out and was answering the first question.

"It's just busywork," Dev explained to me, referring to the assignment. "It'll only take me ten minutes to bang this out."

"Naw, that's cool," I responded. "I'm gonna do it too. I mean, you know Wardin's gonna be hot tomorrow."

"Like a flamethrower," he answered.

I grinned and took out my book. Dev finished number one then, moved to number two.

I watched him for a moment in silence. All the students around continued to screw off. Devon handled his business.

"Yo, Dev, lemme ask you something."

"Yeah?"

"Why you ain't say nothin' when you know Cee-Saw is spreading false rumors about you being dumped by her? I mean, why you don't set the record straight? Your rep is gettin' totally trashed."

He didn't look up from his book.

"Reputations aren't everything," he replied.

"Oh," I said. It was as good an answer as any. I took out a sheet of paper and wrote my name and date across the top. "Besides," he added, "I don't give a shit."

I tried to make eye contact with him, but he wouldn't look at me.

Devon went back to finishing the assignment. I nodded my head and did the same. A few minutes later, we had finished.

Over the weekend there was a raging party that all the cheerleaders went to. I, of course, wasn't invited. Not that I would have been able to go, but still, an invitation would have been nice.

Particularly since a *"dee-veloping situation"* had emerged. Seems my old best friend had landed a new boyfriend. Rickee Dunston!

"I can't believe she would do that to me," I complained to Sonia as she sipped a Diet Pepsi. "How could she go out with a punk like him?"

"Keep your voice down. Here she comes."

I spun around. "So, let her come."

"Hey-hey, Tee-Ay."

"Don't hey-hey me, Cee. Wuzzup wit' you and Rickee? How could you sell me out like that?"

"Aw, don't be a player hater, Tee. You wasn't wit' him no more and things just kinda happened."

" 'Kinda happened'? I thought me and you was tight like a kite."

Cee-Saw took out a nail file and started fixing her tips. She didn't respond.

"Ain't you gonna say nothin'?"

"They told me this was gonna happen."

"What was gonna happen? Who?"

"They told me it happens to all cheerleaders. People hate on them for being good-looking and popular."

"Damn, girl!" I shouted out of frustration. "Don't you know that Rickee is only after one thing?"

"Well, you should know."

"What the hell is *dat* supposed to mean?"

"Oh, stop it, Tee-Ay. All the cheerleaders know you performed oral on him that night in the bedroom."

What?

"The whole school knows," she said matter-of-factly.

My stomach sank. *Huh?*

"I can't believe you never even told me you did that. I thought we were friends, Tee-Ay. How could you keep a sweet secret like that from me?"

I shook my head in disbelief. No, it couldn't be true.

The next thing I know Rickee walked up, threw his arm around Cee and gave her a giant kiss on the lips.

"Is my girl ready to bounce?"

Cee-Saw looked at me and paused, waiting for a response. I couldn't even raise my eyes.

"Let's roll," she answered. They walked off arm in arm.

As they cruised away I heard Rickee ask, "Yo, wuzz-up wit' dat?" in reference to me.

"Whatever," Cee replied. "I have moved on."

They smashed lips.

Hmmvvvzzz! Hmmvvvzzz! Hmmvvvzzz!

11

Finally, after about three hundred months, I was let off punishment. However, it was like being set free in a desert. What was there to even live for?

High school really sucked. I wasn't cool, smart, athletic, pretty, talented, loved, sociable, or exceptional in any way whatsoever—except when it came to screwing up. My teachers were lame and totally hated me, I had torn apart a bond with my father, which I didn't think he'd ever forgive me for, and my mom gave me grief all the time for the smallest and stupidest of things. Matter of fact, I think the only reason she let me off punishment was so that she could find another excuse to put me back on punishment at some later date. It seemed her biggest thrills in life came from grounding me.

If it hadn't been for Teddy getting into more and more trouble all the time and shifting the attention off me, I'd have run away. He was becoming a monster.

It turned out the tests he was forced to take came up with something. Teddy wasn't a mental midget at all. Just the opposite. He was a genius. Like a real, certifiable genius. Supposedly he had an IQ that was in the upper two percent of all Americans, with a capacity for abstract thinking beyond anything the test givers had ever observed in an eleven-year-old before. They wanted to pull him out of school and put him into some special genius academy in Maryland, but my parents didn't want him moving to the other side of the country all alone.

None of it made sense to me. I mean, he never even got straight A's.

"Call me 'Einstein,'" he said to me with a swagger after finding out the test results. *Swagger* is a good word to know for the SAT. It means "to have a cocky bounce in your step, like a strut."

"Okay, Einstein, what's the word *swagger* mean?" I asked.

"It means 'accidentally demagnetized,'" he answered.

"Not even close, peckerhead."

"Oh, I must have been talkin' 'bout your cellie. That's what happens when you leave things carelessly lying around in potentially scientific areas."

Huh? I looked at my cell phone sitting on the kitchen table next to the new science kit my parents had just bought Teddy to give his "geniusness" something to do.

"You busted my cell phone?"

"Naw, I think it still works. My guess is, just the memory card was erased. You probably lost all your contact lists and phone numbers."

What?

I raced to my phone and scrolled through the address book. There wasn't a single name or number to be found.

"I'm gonna kick your little ass!"

"Mom! Theresa's messing with Super-Genius!" he shouted, running into the kitchen before I could grab him. My mother was seasoning a chicken.

"Now cut it out, you two."

"But he erased my cell phone."

"She used the word *ass*."

"I said, *cut it out!* Any more fighting and you're both gonna spend a week without electricity. No telephone, no TV, no computer—nothing. I may even make you go to the bathroom outside as if you were using an outhouse."

I glared at Teddy, ready to strangle him.

"Theresa, I'm warning you. I'm tired of all this."

"But he—"

"No buts. Am I clear?"

I stormed out of the kitchen, snatched my cellie, grabbed my headphones, and slammed the front door behind me. *Bang!* It was so unfair.

There was only one place to go. After all, I only really had one real friend left in the universe and I hadn't even seen Sonia in three days.

Her house was about a half-hour walk from mine, but I had hip-hop to keep me company. Beats bounced through my brain, rhymes rocked with raw rhythm, and the whole way was like a slo-mo flow of a dope, dope show.

"Throw your hands in the air and holla, 'Yo-yo-yo!'"
Yo! Yo! Yo!

By the time I knocked on Sonia's door I felt better. That's because hip-hop understands me. Sometimes it understands me better than I understand myself. Hip-hop is magical that way.

It wasn't like Sonia to miss three days of school in a row. Her phone being disconnected for the past three days wasn't much of a shock though, because her family had a history of having their phones disconnected from time to time when they couldn't pay their bills, so I didn't sweat that. Unfortunately, she couldn't afford a cellie, so I didn't have any direct number where I could contact her. But not answering e-mails, either? I had to see what was up.

I knocked on the door. Sonia's mother answered.

"Hola, Señora Rodriguez."

"*Venga, Theresa. Venga,*" she said, motioning me to enter. I had to turn sideways to get past her. She was pregnant again—this time with twins.

"*¿Está bien?*" I asked Sonia's mom as I made my way past. I knew she'd been bedridden a lot lately.

These next two children would be numbers six and seven in the household. Sonia was the second-oldest child, but the eldest daughter, which basically meant she was kinda the servant of the entire family. They made her do everything. Cook, clean, wash clothes, feed siblings, read mail written in English—you name it, she did it. I mean, her oldest brother coulda done something, but he had dropped out in ninth grade and believed that doing stuff around the house was "a woman's job."

Rodrigo's "job" was washing cars at an automobile dealership, but he only worked part-time for minimum wage. Basically, he played a lot of video games.

"*¿No puedo llorar por que quién tiene orejas para mis problemas?*" Sonia's mom said to me in her rapid-fire Spanish. I had no idea what the heck she was talking about, so I smiled politely, not wanting to be rude.

"*Muy bien,*" I responded. All those years of Spanish class were paying off, kinda.

How people could live their entire life in the

United States without learning English was something I never really understood. I mean, it seemed crazy. Sonia's mother had been in America for more than nineteen years, but if she wanted to order a turkey sandwich for lunch, hold the mayo, she had no way of doin' it.

Then again, she always bought her turkey sandwiches with no mayo from people just like herself who didn't speak English either. 'Round here, Sonia's mom had everything she needed: her own stores, markets, shops, restaurants, and turkey-sandwich makers—you name it, she had it. In some places it was the English-speaking people who struggled.

At times it felt like our neighborhood was two different countries. I don't mean that in a bad way though, 'cause Hispanic folks are pretty much cool peeps if you ask me. Lots of them own homes and go to church and are trying to do better in society. Sonia's dad is a perfect example. That man had *two* jobs. Hard ones, too. One as a day laborer on a construction site, where he mixed cement. Then at night, after lifting all those bags and sweating with all those shovels, he went to a fancy sports gym to clean racquetball courts and wash sauna towels for seven hours. Sonia told me he left the house at 5:30 A.M. every morning and didn't return home until 12:30 at night, six days a week. And once a month on Sundays, he sold mini palm trees at the local Swap Meet starting at 4:30 A.M. That's how he paid for Sonia's braces.

Once Sonia mentioned to me that her father woulda been home by 11:30 P.M. most nights, but he didn't have a car, and the bus ride took one hour and forty-five minutes each way. He had to make two transfers.

Some black men in our neighborhood didn't have no jobs and some Hispanic men had two. Why is that? I wondered. But before I could come up with an answer, two plump boys raced past me with toy guns, almost stepping on my foot. They were playing shoot 'em up.

Pow-pow! Pow!

"*Sonia! La puerta.*" Sonia's mom disappeared into the bedroom to watch one of her favorite *telenovelas* on TV.

Sonia appeared from the back of the house with a tired smile on her face. She was perspiring from whatever she was doing. "Hey, Tee," Sonia said.

"Yo, girl, I thought you had evaporated off the planet," I responded, happy to see her.

"No, I just have some stuff to do around here."

Sonia closed a door that separated the back of the house from the front so we could be alone in the living room. I could tell this was the type of home that didn't really allow much alone time for anyone. Sonia checked over her shoulder, then spoke softly.

"My uncle's back."

"Again?"

"Uh-huh."

Sonia's uncle had popped in and out of her life for years, always living with them "temporarily" for months at a time. He drank a lot of tequila, spoke no English (of course), and lost at cards all the time.

"Why doesn't your dad give him the boot?"

"He's my mom's brother. Plus, his wife left him for a tow truck driver."

"That was, like, five years ago."

"What can I say? He's family."

"So?"

"*Tu no entiendes 'familia,'*" she replied. "We do things differently."

None of it made sense. I mean, in order to help out her mom, who already had more babies than the family could afford, Sonia was throwing away her own future while her uncle got drunk, slept all day, and borrowed cash from her dad that he'd never be able to pay back. It was crazy.

"What about doing for you?" I asked.

"We do for each other."

"How's that fair?"

"I told you, Tee. It's family."

Suddenly, her uncle opened the door. Though it was two o'clock in the afternoon he looked like he was just waking up. His face was unshaven, his greasy hair flew around in all kinds of wacky directions, and I was sure his breath stank like the butt-hole of a sweaty marathon runner.

I stared at him with abomination. *Abomination* is a good word to know for the SAT. It means "a lot of hatred and disgust." Pure abomination.

He looked back at me as if I weren't even a person. I know the fact that I'm black meant that I was nothing but *una negra* to him, the racist pig.

But he wasn't just a racist pig. Sonia had told me stories about how the last time he was in town she felt he was leering at her in her pajamas.

Leer is probably a good word to know for the SAT, too, but I don't need to define it. Every girl knows what it means to have an older man *leer* at you. But when it's a family member—*ugh!* What could be more creepy?

Freakin' pervert.

"*Oye, Sonia. ¿Qué pasa?*" he said, looking at me suspiciously.

"*Nada. Todo está bien, Tío.*"

Her uncle paused, scratched his chin, then turned around and wandered into the toilet. I heard a loud fart.

"That just ain't right," I said, shaking my head. Sonia didn't respond.

I hated the way Sonia's family kept her down. She was smart enough to go to college. A good college, too. But not if she kept missing school the way she'd been doing lately. If she was a boy, her parents would have done everything they could to support her education. But Sonia was a girl and girls weren't expected to have brains and win college scholarships. They were expected to win husbands and have babies. The smacked-up part about the whole thing was that Sonia didn't even fight it. She didn't even stand up for herself. The more I thought about it, the madder I got.

"You gotta represent for yourself, girl."

"You just don't get it, Tee. You just don't get it."

"You know what, Sonia?" I rose to my feet. I was so mad on the inside I felt like I was about to say something which might break off our friendship forever. And then I realized I didn't want to do that, so I changed up my thoughts and simply grabbed my backpack. "Aw, I'm just gonna bounce."

"But you just got here."

"Yeah, I should go. I only stopped by to bring you

some schoolwork so you wouldn't get left too far behind."

I reached into my backpack and tossed some papers on the table. Sonia scanned through the work, then smiled.

"What?" I replied angrily. "You screwing up in school ain't funny, Sonia. It ain't funny at all."

Sonia lowered her eyes. "I already did it."

Huh?

"Yeah," she said, looking through the papers I had tossed on the table. "Tomorrow's, too."

Turns out Sonia had anticipated where the teachers would be going in all of her classes so she worked ahead a few pages in each of her books after she'd cleaned the dishes, folded the laundry, and put the younger kids to bed. She might have been absent from school, but she wasn't behind in her classes. I shook my head and laughed.

"What a dork!" I told her and we both smiled.

"Wanna share some *papas*? I'm kinda hungry," she said. It was nearing three o'clock in the afternoon and this was the first chance she'd had to eat.

"Absolutely," I answered, putting down my backpack. We crossed into the kitchen.

It may not have been the bench by the flagpole, but

sharing french fries—well, Mexican fries—with Sonia made us both feel good.

She even had a Diet Pepsi in the fridge. Perfect.

"*Sonia, tengo hambre,*" her uncle declared when he entered the kitchen fifteen minutes later and smelled the food. "*¿Qué tenemos?*"

Sonia looked at me, then lowered her eyes. Her break was over. Time to cook her uncle lunch. Or breakfast. Or whatever it was in his world. Freakin' pig!

"*Puedo hacer huevos y papas con salsa ranchera si tu quieres, Tío.*"

Her uncle paused to think about it.

"*Está bien,*" he responded and exited to the den.

Obviously, he expected Sonia to call him when his food was ready.

"*Pero, apúrate. Tengo hambre.*"

12

Nine weeks, four days, three hours, and sixteen minutes had passed since I last exchanged words with Cee-Saw. I know because I wrote down the date and time of our big fight on my school planner.

I also wrote down the date and time we started speaking again, 'cause that was memorable, too. I mean how could I ever forget Cee's first words to me in more than two months?

"I'm pregnant."

The words just sat there like a wet newspaper.

Rickee had dumped her, her mom was gonna kill her, and damn if she could tell the cheerleaders a freakin' thing.

"What am I gonna do?" she asked with tears in her eyes.

But Cee-Saw wasn't really asking me a question. She had already made up her mind. She just needed my help.

"I'm going to have an abortion."

Whoa, I thought.

"Tee, I know you hate me right now. I hate myself, too. But you're my best girl in the whole wide world. Will you please come with me to the clinic?"

I said the only thing I could.

"When?"

We walked down the sidewalk by the front of a gray building that didn't have any signs on the wall.

"Are you sure this is the place?"

"This is the address, right here," Cee-Saw answered, looking at a sheet of paper. "Nine-two-oh-five Wiltworth Drive."

I don't know what I was expecting, but this certainly wasn't it.

"I mean, I don't imagine they'd be posting huge banners saying 'Abortion Clinic—End Your Baby's Life Here,'" Cee added, trying to make a joke.

I chuckled nervously.

Cee pressed her face up to the glass door and tried to peek inside. All of a sudden there was a *buzzzz!*

Security had let us in. I guess they saw us coming.

The waiting room was cool from air-conditioning. And quiet. I didn't see a person anywhere.

A moment later, a woman appeared from behind a door. She smiled.

"Hi, I'm Janet, a counselor here at the clinic."

Janet was a smart-looking, thin, thirty-something-year-old white woman who wore a sweater that looked very comfortable. Matter of fact, everything in this room looked very comfortable. The walls were creamy beige, the couches looked soft and cushy, brand-new magazines lay on the table, and pictures of landscapes and gardens and waterfalls decorated the walls. It seemed as if someone had spent a lot of time trying to make this place feel warm.

But still it felt cold.

"You must be Constancy," Janet said as she approached. "We spoke on the phone earlier." She handed me a stack of forms and sat down. "Here, let's start with these."

"It's for her," I answered. "Constancy is right there."

"Oh," Janet replied. She looked at Cee, then back at me. There was an awkward moment of silence. I passed Cee the forms.

"I'll need you to—" Janet stopped midsentence. Apparently, the pager she wore on her belt had started vibrating, because she looked down, read the text message, then stood up.

"If you could just give me one second, and fill those out, please, I'll be right back."

"Sure thing," Cee answered as Janet disappeared behind another door. I turned to Cee-Saw.

"I can't believe she thought I was pregnant," I exclaimed as soon as Janet left the room. "That's it. No more cookies for a month. I must be getting fat."

"You're not getting fat, Tee-Ay," Cee-Saw snapped. "*You're* not getting fat at all, so quit worrying about it." Cee-Saw zipped that last part in a tone that kinda meant, *Yeah, but I will be.*

I shut up. I had forgotten where we were for a moment.

Cee-Saw filled out the papers in silence. I tried to wait patiently. All I could think about was my mom. If it had been me sitting where Cee-Saw was and my mother sitting where I was, well . . . that would *never* happen. My mother would sooner be sitting in a funeral home grieving me than sitting in an abortion clinic comforting me. That was *fo' sure!*

It took Cee a long time to check off all the little boxes that needed checking off. Usually, she'd asked me to help with stuff like this, but this time she didn't. Matter of fact, it was almost as if she was covering up her answers like one of those kids in class who's doing well on a test and doesn't want anyone cheating off them. I just sat there quietly. I was gonna reach for one of those brand-new magazines, but I didn't know if that would be rude, so I didn't.

Where was Janet already?

Cee kept checking off boxes on the form. There must have been ten pages' worth of stuff. Finally, Janet returned and called Cee into a room for an interview. I stood up to go with her.

"Sorry, only Constancy."

"I can't come in?"

"No, just Constancy," she told me.

"Okay," I said, sitting back down. I guess I'd get to read a magazine after all.

"If she don't come in, I ain't coming in," Cee-Saw suddenly blurted out.

Neither Janet nor I were prepared for the force in Cee-Saw's voice. Janet tried to calm things down before they got unruly.

Unruly is a good word to know for the SAT. It means, "all wild and out of control."

"It's just an interview, Constancy."

"I don't care what it is. No Tee, no me."

"But we have a policy that says—"

"Maybe you ain't hearin' me so good? I said, *No Tee, no me!*"

After a moment to weigh the situation, Janet stepped aside and motioned for both of us to enter. I didn't know if she was breaking any rules or not by letting me come in too, but it was clear to all three of us that Cee needed me with her. *"No Tee, no me"* was the rule of the day.

We moved to a room behind one of the doors. It was comfortable.

"I see you're wearing loose-fitting clothes," Janet observed. I think that meant Janet understood that Cee was ready to have the procedure today.

"Yes, I called a few days ago and found out a bunch of information."

"A few days ago? Funny, I didn't see a file on you this morning when we spoke." Janet turned around and pulled open a drawer in a big filing cabinet and started looking through the vanilla-colored folders.

"Let's see . . . Sawyer," she said. "Sawyer . . ."

"Oh, uhm, no, there wouldn't be no file," Cee responded after a moment of watching Janet look through the folders. "I gave a fake name."

Janet stopped. "A fake name?"

"Yeah," Cee-Saw said, lowering her eyes. "I didn't want anyone to know who I am."

"I understand," Janet said in a kind way that put us both at ease. She grabbed a pad of paper and a pen from the desk. "Why don't you tell me the fake name so I can make sure it gets removed from the system.

We don't want anybody doing unnecessary extra work. We're already so overworked as it is."

Cee-Saw paused. "Do I have to?" she asked.

"If you wouldn't mind."

There was another long pause. All this waiting around was getting on my nerves.

"Just tell her the damn name, Cee," I ordered. "You don't want them doing extra work for nothing."

"Theresa Anderson," Cee-Saw blurted out.

"*What?*" I shouted. "You gave 'em my name?"

"I was scared. I didn't know what to do."

"So you gave them *my* name?"

"I couldn't think."

"*Oh my God! Oh my God! Oh my God!*"

"Relax, Theresa," Janet said to me. "Everything is confidential. Nobody can ever find out anything without a patient's written approval."

"But you got to erase my name from your files, ya hear? I mean zap it good—forever. If my momma finds out that I'm in an abortion clinic, she'll kill me. She don't play that stuff like that. I mean she'll . . ."

I stopped talking and looked up. Both Cee and Janet were quiet. I guess it sounded like my mom was better than Cee's mom, which wasn't what I meant to say, but still, I think it kinda came off that way. However, I didn't care. There was just no way I could have my name on file in a place like this. No way!

"Just erase it," I said sitting back down. "Erase it good."

I watched her write down my name on the pad of paper. Now my name was written down twice in this joint. *If my mother*—I tried not to think of it 'cause I was too afraid of what might happen.

Janet started going over the forms Cee had filled out, double-checking to make sure everything was correct.

"Have you had anything to eat within the last twelve hours?"

"No."

"To drink within the last twelve hours?"

"No."

"To smoke within the last twelve hours."

"No."

"Have you taken any drugs within the last forty-eight hours?"

"No."

"Are you wearing any jewelry?"

"No."

"No bracelets? No rings? No necklaces?"

"No."

"No belly-button rings? No nose rings?"

"No. No."

"No nipple rings? No genital piercings?"

"Genital piercings?" Cee replied.

"Yes, you know, jewelry worn—"

"Yeah, I know, I know, but I ain't into all that freaky stuff."

Janet lowered the forms. "It's not my job to judge, Constancy. Just to ask."

"Well, the answer is no," Cee replied. "No."

Janet explained that the whole procedure would take between two and three hours. Then she turned to me.

"Are you going to accompany Constancy home?"

"Uh-huh."

"What is your method of transportation?"

"The bus," I answered.

"And your form of payment, Constancy?"

"The person on the phone the other day said I could pay with cash." Cee-Saw reached into her purse and removed $325 in a lump of wrinkled, unorganized, messily folded-up bills.

Where did she get all that money? Not from her mom. Did Rickee help pay?

This wasn't the time to ask.

"Do you want general anesthesia or local?" Janet asked.

Cee looked confused. "I don't know. What's the difference?"

"If you choose local anesthesia the nurse practitioner will numb the cervical area before you go into the surgical suite," Janet explained. "If you chose general anesthesia you will go directly to the surgical suite, where you will be sedated entirely."

Cee still looked confused and it was clear she still didn't understand. Janet patiently re-explained it again in a more simple way. "You can be knocked out or remain awake with only your pelvic region numbed for the process."

Cee-Saw paused and said, "Uhm, I don't know," then looked to me for the answer. I didn't know the right choice either.

"Could you explain it a little more?" I asked. "I'm still not sure we get it."

"Sure," said Janet, never running out of friendliness or patience. I had to admit, she sure was trying to be friendly, but under the circumstances, well—let's just say that this wasn't really a sociable kind of environment, like listening to hip-hoppers flow fresh rhymes by the chain-link fence. To tell the truth, this was about a million miles away.

Janet made sure to speak clearly. "A licensed CRNA

will administer anesthesia and a licensed medical doctor specializing in gynecology will perform the procedure by gently removing the contents of the uterus by vacuum aspiration. The actual surgery will only take about five to seven minutes."

"Well, five minutes or not, I don't think I want to be seeing this," Cee-Saw responded, understanding much better now. "Knock me out. Knock me out good."

"That would be general anesthesia," Janet answered, checking off a box on the chart.

"I can't believe how professional ya'll are here," Cee said with a sigh of relief. "I mean, this ain't at all what I expected."

"Yes," agreed Janet, looking about the room. "The process has come a long way. Years ago, American women didn't have the options they have today."

"I heard about that stuff," I said. "Like people crossing borders and dirty coat hangers and women dying and stuff like that."

Cee-Saw's eyes got as big as basketballs.

"Dirty coat hangers and women dying?" she exclaimed.

Maybe I shouldn't have said that?

"Relax," Janet said with a smile that calmed both of us. "Unsafe procedures used to be a tremendous

problem, but that was years ago, before *Roe v. Wade.*
Nowadays, the health and safety of the woman patient
is our number-one concern. You'll be fine, Constancy."
We could tell she meant it too. This place was all about
sterility and safety.

"Will it hurt?" Cee asked with fear in her voice.

"A little," Janet replied honestly. "You'll be uncomfortable for about a week."

Blam! All of a sudden I realized something.
Something huge! Janet wasn't just an employee. Janet
was experienced in these matters. *Oh my gracious,*
Janet had once had an abortion. I quickly looked at the
floor and shut my mouth. *Holy smokes!*

"Well, that pretty much covers it," Janet said, standing up. "And remember, there will be a mandatory
follow-up in two weeks to make sure that you're feeling well and your body is healing properly."

I looked up. Cee was stiff in her chair.

"Don't worry, Constancy," Janet added. "You'll still
be able to have kids one day if you should want to and
no one will ever have to know."

"I know," Cee answered, holding back tears.

I felt like I was gonna cry myself. Janet reached
over and put her arm tenderly on Cee-Saw's shoulder.
"How do you feel?" she asked. "You all right?"

Cee straightened her posture and replied with lots of confidence. I was really impressed with how brave she was. "I feel perfectly fine."

And then she vomited all over the floor.

Green-brown puke shot out of Cee's mouth as if an alien had been living in her stomach. My first thought was, Ooh, that's definitely gonna stain the carpet.

Janet didn't seem too shocked, though, and went to get stuff to clean it up, but Cee beat her to the door and dashed into the lobby's waiting room.

"Let me outta here!"

Cee-Saw was gone. More than gone. She was gone-zo. What could I do but follow? She hit the door running, desperate to get out to the street. But the door didn't open.

"Let me out!" Cee screamed. She was locked in. "Let me out!" Cee started to freak. She began pounding and kicking and blasting the door. But it was no use. The door would still not open. "Let me out! Let me out! Let me out!"

No matter how hard Cee smashed, the door wouldn't budge because it was the kind of door that had been specifically designed not to budge in the face of being smashed, pounded, kicked, and blasted. Places like this needed doors like these in order to keep out wacko anti-abortion fanatics who have been known in the past to shoot up clinics with automatic weapons.

This door was not only bulletproof and hammer-proof, it was Cee-proof. The only things that was going to break from all the smashing were Cee's hands.

"Let me out!" she screamed. All Cee needed was a *buzz*. But the *buzz* never came. "Please, let me out!"

Janet appeared, calm and patient like before. "Hold on a second, Constancy. We can't let you leave yet."

Suddenly, a six-foot-three-inch-tall, 320-pound black man entered the room from a door on the other side of the couch. He was huge! Dressed in a hospital gown and tennis sneakers, he approached Cee. "Please," he said grabbing her arms. "Do not do that."

Cee-Saw, weeping and shaking, sank to her knees in fear.

"Let me *ow-owt!*" Her cries were growing weaker.

What was happening? Who was this giant? Where had he just come from and why wouldn't they just open the damn door?

"I can't let you go," Janet said again as she walked up to Cee while the giant black man prevented her from punching the door any more. "Not until I give you this." Janet handed Cee an envelope. It was filled with cash. "You don't want to forget your money," she added calmly.

Buzzzz!

Cee-Saw reached for the envelope with a trembling hand.

"You might want to go home and take a bath," the giant black man said to Cee gently. "Maybe have a cup of hot tea."

Buzzzz! The door buzzed again and the monster in the hospital gown politely held it open for Cee to exit. Cee-Saw rose to her feet, her face wet with tears, a bit embarrassed by her behavior, and exited. I followed.

Outside, we walked in silence toward the bus stop. My plan was not to say a word to her until she spoke to me. I promised myself I would respect Cee's feelings and not engage her in any conversation until she was ready to talk. When the time came, I am sure she would want to chat. Until then, my plan was to let her come to me. Her personal boundaries needed respecting.

We waited for the bus. Eight seconds passed.

"You okay? Talk to me. Let me know wuzzup, girl." I asked, rubbing her shoulder. "You doin' all right? Come on, let me in." So much for promises to myself.

"I'm keeping the baby," she responded, then blew her nose in a tissue. "I'm gonna keep the baby and get back together with Rickee. He'll be a good dad, especially if it's a boy." A glimmer of sunshine returned to her face.

"Oooh, I hope it's a boy, 'cause then Rickee can teach him how to play running back and arm wrestle and play video games. Rickee would be great at teaching a little Rickee how to play video games." She rubbed her tummy with affection. "Yeah, little Rickee."

Cee-Saw then looked at the $325 in cash.

"And with this, I'm gonna open a savings account. It'll be the first deposit toward my baby's college education." She smiled at me. "My baby's gonna be smart and well educated."

I tried to smile back. The bus came two minutes later. There weren't too many folks riding, so we each got to take our own seat. Cee-Saw spent the whole trip staring out the window, full of hopes and dreams. I stared out the window, too, but with a whole bunch of different thoughts and emotions running through my mind.

None of them I felt I could tell to her.

13

" 'To be or not to be.' "

The end of the school year meant Shakespeare in English class. Hamlet was debating suicide. By the looks of Cee-Saw, I had a feeling he wasn't the only one.

"Hey, hey, Tee-Ay," she said without much energy, as she approached me and Sonia, wearing baggy sweats.

Baggy sweats were all Cee ever wore these days. At least, on the days she came.

"Hi, Cee. How you feelin'?" We didn't even give a *slap-slap-bump* high five on the down low. I simply made room for her to join us during lunch.

Two or three days a week in class was the average for Cee nowadays and she was completely lost when it came to *Hamlet*. Me, I was learning how Hamlet's uncle had murdered his father, then married his mother, and was leading Denmark toward glorious defeat. I mean, Hamlet's uncle was having sex with Hamlet's mother. Gross!

Cee-Saw was learning about morning sickness.

It crossed my mind later that night that maybe I

should create a *Hip-Hop Hamlet* for Cee-Saw so that she might understand more of what was going on. It actually might be kinda dope, too. I mean, the story is fresh, even if Hamlet does talk on and on and on about God knows what. But considering it's one of the most famous plays of all time and English teachers have to teach Shakespeare at some point during high school, *Hip-Hop Hamlet* might actually have an audience somewhere.

Plus, it'd be a good reason to get a rap in with MixMaster Mytch. After all, it was impossible to even get that boy to make eye contact with me. This would be a good reason to "collaborate."

Yeah, good idea, Tee.

After all, how many other ladies approach him with a scheme to make millions? Next time I saw him in the halls, I'd chat him up about it, all businesslike. Maybe he'd even ask me for my digits? Wow, if he asked for my phone number that'd be *sweet*. I mean, who doesn't want to date a budding hip-hop superstar?

Yeah, I could become a millionaire and land one of the hottest dudes in the whole school by rewriting the most famous play of all time into a hip-hop show.

I went straight to work. It would start with a little beat and go something like this . . .

To be or not
To be or not
Homie Hamlet thinks a lot
To be or not
To be or not
It is the question
The lesson
That's stressin' and messin' and keepin' him
    guessin'
'Bout what he's destined for—
So much oppression
To be or not
To be or not
Homie Hamlet thinks a lot
To be or not
To be or not
Homie Hamlet got a lot
Of problems

But after those seventeen lines I was tired. Plus, I had math homework. Cee-Saw would have to figure out the rest of the play by herself.

So much for dating MixMaster Mytch. Would I ever have a boyfriend?

Was I being selfish for even asking such a question?

Lately, every time I thought about something I wanted for myself, guilt came over me. After all, one of my two best friends in the whole wide world was totally preggo, completely jobless, and majorly miserable, and here I was complaining about silly little stuff like not having someone to holds hand with or send goofy e-mails to. Was I an idiot? *Jeez,* look where having a boyfriend had got Cee-Saw. But still, I wanted one.

I remembered back to the time when my emotions bounced around like Starbucks espresso shots, *up and down, up and down, up and down.* Nowadays, they bounced back and forth in a different direction, between guilt and confusion. That's all I ever seemed to feel, guilt and confusion.

Guilt, confusion. Guilt, confusion. Guilt, confusion.

Oh yeah, there was depression, too.

Seeing Cee struggle to keep up her deceiving ways bummed me out. Hiding her situation from her mom, the school, and all the peeps on campus was a full-time job. She'd stuff whole bags of Twinkies into her mouth in the back of class when she thought no one was looking. She'd forge notes from the woodshop teacher excusing her from PE so she wouldn't have to change clothes in the locker room with all the other girls. And when her mother went to the store and asked Cee if she needed tampons, Cee-Saw told her yes, to go ahead and pick some up, then threw the entire box away five days later so that her Mom wouldn't discover the tamps she'd bought for her daughter weren't being used. Cee's mom was already pretty much broke and here Cee was, literally throwing her mother's money into the garbage. Didn't she know she'd eventually get discovered? I mean, after all, it was inevitable.

Inevitable is a good word to know for the SAT. It means, "sooner or later, it's gonna happen."

And sooner or later, Cee's secret would be exposed. You just can't hide being a pregnant teen. *Why didn't she get that?*

"You want a fry, Constancy?" Sonia asked on a Tuesday about two weeks later. She had sensed Cee hadn't been doing so hot lately and was simply trying to be nice.

Cee-Saw took one look at the fry and almost vomited. That's when Sonia got it.

I mean, Sonia wasn't dumb. Turning green at the smallest sight of food. Tired all the time. Putting on weight. Come on, Sonia was Latina and they make babies all the time. Her mom was even pregnant—with *twins*! Naw, she didn't have to be Sherlocka Holmes to figure out Cee had a bun in the oven. She just happened to be the first one to do so, that's all. And many others would follow.

Like I said, it was inevitable.

Sonia, being the kind person she was, didn't mention anything and when the bell rang we all went to class. But the next day Sonia came to school with a gift.

"What's this?" Cee asked when Sonia handed her the brown bag.

"Ginger candy. It'll help the nausea."

Cee-Saw turned and shot me an angry look.

"What? I didn't say nothin'!"

Cee-Saw didn't believe me, but it was the truth. Though I had wanted to about a thousand times, I hadn't told a soul.

"You'll also want to avoid spicy foods. And I put some plain crackers in there, too. Saltines help." Cee-Saw looked at Sonia. Her anger turned to tears. "It'll be okay, Constancy. The morning sickness will pass." Cee started crying. Really crying. Sonia gave her a hug. "I know, I know."

It was the closest I had ever seen the two of them.

Across the way, Rickee cruised by with three of his beefy buddies. These big, tough dudes were all wearing their football jerseys for the huge end-of-the-year awards banquet.

Rickee didn't even have the guts to look our way.

"Does he even know?" I asked Cee.

"Yeah," she answered, putting a Saltine cracker in

her mouth. "But I don't want to pressure him. He'll come 'round soon. I'm sure of it."

When Cee wasn't looking, Sonia rolled her eyes at me.

Final exams came. I kinda studied, but I kinda didn't. I guess I did all right for the semester, 'cause I earned a 2.98 GPA. That's not bad. It's not exceptional, either. When am I going to learn that close is no cigar? I need to crack a 3.0.

Wardin gave me a C. What a punk.

At least it was summertime and I was done with Wardin hating on me. However, that didn't mean that I was done helping Cee-Saw deal with her problems. And like her belly, they started to grow.

Somehow, I had become Cee-Saw's *everything*. I brought her food, aspirin, gumballs, potato chips, baby powder, hand lotion, and flavored teas with lots of ice.

Plus, she called me all the time to complain.

"My thighs are swelling."

"My pillow doesn't support my neck."

"Peanut butter grosses me out."

Literally, I must have gotten fifteen calls a day.

"My back hurts."

"I feel nauseous."

"Can you bring me a raspberry smoothie?"

And if the girl wasn't asking me for something, she was burning up my cellie minutes moaning about the smallest and stupidest stuff.

"You know my blue pants with the flower? They don't fit."

"Oatmeal cookies need more raisins."

"Why are cats always tired?"

What I became tired of was listening to Cee-Saw squawk. Then I got my cellie bill. It was $94.63 higher than usual.

Pops was *pissed*.

"No, please don't cancel my phone," I begged. "I swear I won't go over next month."

"Fine, then pay me back," my father answered.

"How am I gonna pay you back nearly a hundred dollars?" I asked.

"I don't know. Why don't you . . . get a job!"

He stormed out of the room, mad at me for about the ten thousandth time this decade. Then I realized, he was right. Maybe I should get a job. But where?

"You could sell your picture at the Ugly store. You'd be rich by the end of the week."

"Shut up, Teddy!"

I put on a nice pair of slacks with a pretty top to match and went to the mall. Two days later I had landed my first real employment—at the movie theater.

I don't know why so many people are always complaining about work. In my opinion, work is pretty dope. I got to see free films, eat all the popcorn I want, and could do other things with my time besides listen to Cee-Saw whine.

Plus, there were a ton of cute guys that came in. I flirted with about two hundred of them a day—three hundred on weekends, when a big new film came out. And I didn't care if they were with another girl on a date. I'd smile at them anyway.

Some folks might say I was acting like a hoochie, but I was simply providing "friendly customer service."

Having money in my pocket that I could do whatever I wanted with felt good too. One Wednesday, I bought three tank tops and didn't even have to ask my mom's permission to do so. I had paid Pops back and had some steady dollar bills rolling in. Maybe, I thought, I could even start to save for a car. *Having my own wheels would be super-duper dope!*

Yep, earning cash felt good.

I just wished Sonia hadn't left with her family to Mexico for nine weeks. Sonia's family always went to Mexico for the summer. They even pulled her out of school eight days early so they could get cheaper airfare. Her mom felt that Sonia missing class wasn't as important as the twenty-two–percent discount they could get off the price of her ticket.

"But why can't you stay?" I asked.

"I gotta go," she explained as she packed her suit-case. *"Es una tradición de nuestra familia."*

It was frustrating not having any homies to hang around with. Sure, I had made some new friends, but homies are hard to replace. Working at the theater meant I could see free movies and, once a week, even bring a friend at no charge. Too bad I didn't really have any friends to bring.

My other peeps from school had stuff goin' on them-selves. Jaxson Edgars got hired to create a wall mural at a local preschool. The pay was virtually nothing, but they bought him all the paint he needed, provided him with a twenty-seven-foot-wide concrete canvas, and told him just "Do your thing." Jax was in heaven.

Devon Hampton had earned an internship to Washington, D.C., through the Georgetown High School Debate Society Outreach Program. More than three thousand students applied. They only selected eighteen. Devon was one of them.

I was so happy for him when he sent me the e-mail telling me the news that the night before he left, I Instant Messaged him to wish him Good Luck with a capital G L.

> Tee-Ay Anderson: Dev, U B good and kik sum
> boo-tay!

168

DevHampt: thx - but gotta admit, I'm nrvus

Tee-Ay Anderson: Nrvus . . . Y?

DevHampt: Cuz I nver bn on an arplane b4

This was gonna be Dev's first time on an airplane and he was nervous. *So cute!*

Tee-Ay Anderson: Neh - dn't swet it.

DevHampt: Y-not?

Tee-Ay Anderson: Cuz u ain't got razrs.

DevHampt: razrs???

Tee-Ay Anderson: Yeh- snce u don't shave, u got nuthin 2 swet frm C-cur-ity

There was a pause in the IM.

DevHampt: Very ☺☺☺

I smiled.

DevHampt: But-wut u talkin' bout? Peeps call mee GRZZLY CHIN!!!

I smiled again. Grizzly Chin, that was funny. Suddenly, my IM with Devon was interrupted by Cee-Saw popping in on me.

Cee-Sawyer: T-A? U on?

Crap, not Cee-Saw! What was I gonna do?

Tee-AyAnderson: Wuzzup, C?

Cee-Sawyer: Dmn, my ankls bee killin me.

DevHampt: U stll here Tee?

Tee-Ay Anderson: Yeah Dev, C-Saw jst poppin' in on me.

DevHampt: Oh . . . U gotta go?

Tee-Ay Anderson: Naw - 1 sec . . .

I quickly shot Cee-Saw an IM.

Tee-Ay Anderson: Cee, cn't yap now - got Dev on b4 he goto Wash, DC.

Cee-Sawyer: Dev? Sweet! Hookus-up 3-way.

Double damn! Why didn't I just make up something else and lie to Cee?

Tee-Ay Anderson: We'ez into smthng, C. I holla at ya L8r.

Cee-Sawyer: Aw, so its lyke dat?

Tee-Ay Anderson: Naw, it aint lyke dat. we jst in-2 sumthin'

DevHampt: T? U on? I stll gotta pck for DC & am
    runnin' L8
Cee-Sawyer: Jus' hookus-up, T. Lemme rap wit'
    Dev 4 a sec
DevHampt: T? . . . U there?

I started typing as fast as I could.

Tee-Ay Anderson: YES . . . stll on?
Tee-Ay Anderson: We'ez in-2 sumthin' Cee
Tee-Ay Anderson: gotz C-Saw poppin in on me,
    dat's all
Tee-Ay Anderson: mee n Dev gotz stff 2 rap
    about
Tee-Ay Anderson: I'm-a bee off wit Cee in
    a sec
Tee-Ay Anderson: wutz up wit the 3rd dgree on
    dat? Cant-ya chill?

The first reply to come through was from Devon.

DevHampt: C-Saw . . . wutz up wit her?

I paused.

Tee-Ay Anderson: Oh . . . nuttin.

171

If he only knew.

Cee-Sawyer: Leest lemme tll Dev Gud Lck b4
he go.

If I did that, she'd yap at him all day. I started to type a reply to Cee when a reply from Dev interrupted me.

Tee-Ay Anderson: Look, C, lemme just holla at
ya a bit L8r when . . .
DevHampt: Can't do the 3-way thang rght now
Tee. gotta bzz off. Peece Out - Hve a ☺
summer!!

Shit!

Tee-Ay Anderson: Jst w8 a half sec, Dev
Tee-Ay Anderson: Dev? . . . U on?

No reply. He had signed off.

Tee-Ay Anderson: Yea- U2 - Hve a ☺ summer, Dev!!
Cee-Sawyer: hey T?
Cee-Sawyer: T . . .

> Cee-Sawyer: U stll on? Wanna go get sum
> i-scream? my moms gav me 5 dolla so
> my treet.

I turned off the computer.

Three minutes later I went back in the room and turned the computer back on to edit my Block Sender list. I checked the box next to Cee-Sawyer.

Then I turned the computer off again for the rest of the night.

When my cellie rang five minutes later, I didn't even check the screen to see who it was. I got nine more calls in the next half hour. I didn't check the caller-ID screen for any of them.

I already knew.

Two weeks later I kissed a boy named Sebastian who worked with me at the movie theater. I think I smooched with him because I liked his name. It sounds regal.

Regal is a good word to know for the SAT. It means, "kinglike and noble." I thought maybe kissing him would help improve my SAT score.

But that's all we did, kiss. And just one time. It was at a bowling alley after a semi-sorta date. Sebastian goes to a different high school and I think he's a bit of a player. A week after we kissed he quit the theater and we never really hooked up again. I guess it was my regal summertime fling. Every girl's gotta have one.

Soon enough, summer was coming to an end and, of course, I had procrastinated doing the summertime reading for next year's English class. We'd been assigned *The Autobiography of Malcolm X*. Everyone I knew was planning on ditching the book and renting the movie. Sounded like a good plan to me. Teachers are so stupid. Don't they know students always check to see if there is a movie before they'll read the book?

"Mom, can I take your car to the video store?" I asked one afternoon.

"You mean my new car?"

"But it's not even new—it's, like, a year old and I have a driver's license."

"Eight months. I've owned the car for just over eight months."

"So."

She didn't answer. I guess my mom felt she worked so hard at the bank earning her promotion that her car was never not allowed to be new. Even in twenty-five years when the bumper was rusty and the headlights were about to fall off, it'd still be her "new" car.

So far I had saved $837.15 for wheels of my own. Essentially, the only thing I could afford to buy was a piece of crap. One day, I'd have a phat ride though. Something totally sweet.

I put on my sneaks, busted out my headphones, and started pounding the pavement for the trip to the video store.

**Put yo' hands in the air
Like U just don't care
Beware!
I'm slayin' MCs everywhere**

Some people walk on this planet. Peeps who have hip-hop and headphones get to float.

I made it to the video place in no time and found the DVD I was looking for. It was the last copy on the shelf. I turned to go to the checkout register and ran into, guess who, Rickee Dunston. He had his arm around a girl dressed in neon green named Ashley.

What a punk.

"What's up, Tee-Ay?" he said to me as if we was all chill.

"Wuzzup?" I responded quietly, lowering my eyes to walk past him.

"Hey, bay-bee, looks like they all out of *Malcolm*

X," I heard Ashley say. Who does she think she is anyway, wearing all that neon green? She looked like she'd been attacked by a lime Popsicle.

Rickee spied the DVD he wanted in my hand and we proceeded to have one of those silent conversations using only eye contact.

His eyes said something to me like, *Since you happen to be in possession of the last copy on the shelf, maybe there is a way we can work something out.*

My eyes responded by saying, *You ain't never gettin' this movie while I am still breathing and my plan is to pay late fees for the next sixty-three months.*

Then our silent conversation was over.

"We'll just get somethin' else, bay-bee, like a comedy." With that Rickee walked away.

"But I thought you needed to watch *Malcolm X* for school," Ashley responded.

"Yeah, whatever," Rickee replied, and they made their way over to another section of the store while I got in line.

Why is it that the people who end up in front of me in line at the video store are always such idiots? I mean, there was only one guy ahead of me, but he was renting six different movies and wanted to hear a full critical review about each and every title.

"Have you seen this? Is it good? What have you

heard? Should I get it? Who's in it?" Then he paused. "Okay, I'll take it. What about this one? Have you seen this? Is it good? What have you heard? Should I get it? Who's in it?"

Oh, come on, dude. Just check them out already.

Frustrated, I turned and saw Rickee and Ashley goofing around and cuddling in the comedy section.

"I am DVD man!" Rickee exclaimed as he put a movie down the front of his pants. "If you want to watch this film, please reach into my player and push the button." Ashley giggled. "And plan to keep pushing the button all night long."

What a punk. I turned back around.

"Have you seen this? Is it good? What have you heard? Should I get it? Who's in it?"

Oh, come on, dude! I turned back again to look at Rickee and Ashley. She was kinda grinding up against him.

"Girl," Rickee said, "tonight just might be a double feature."

I turned back again to the guy in front of me.

"What do you mean I have late fees? I returned that movie on Tuesday. Double-check the system."

"I've already checked, sir."

"Well, check it again."

Just then, something in me snapped.

I mean *snapped!*

I got out of line and rushed up to Rickee.

"You know what, take it!" I pressed the DVD against Rickee's chest. "Yeah, take it." Needless to say, he was shocked. "I'm gonna read the book."

I stormed toward the exit.

"Whatever," Rickee scoffed.

Scoff is a good word to know for the SAT. It means, "to make fun of or ridicule." Rickee scoffed at me.

So what? I put on my headphones and bounced on over to the library. I was sure they'd have the book there.

And they did.

I found exactly what I was looking for in no time flat. Matter of fact, there were four copies.

The Autobiography of Malcolm X: As Told to Alex Haley. Wow, it was a big book. Bigger than I expected: 466 pages. I had never read something that big in my entire life and I only had six days till school started. *What am I, an idiot?*

I dragged my feet up to the librarian.

"Excuse me, do you have the Spike Lee movie *Malcolm X?*" I knew libraries had movies too. Maybe I could get lucky.

"One second," she responded as she typed a search in her computer.

"It's checking," she said after another moment. "Our computers are a bit slow."

"No problem," I answered and turned my head to see the person I had sensed just walk up behind me.

It was a pregnant lady—a young, pregnant lady. I mean she couldn't have been more than nineteen. Wow, she was big. Looked like she was in her eighth month. I smiled at her.

Suddenly, I heard a little girl's voice.

"Momma, can I get this, too?"

Huh? I thought. Ain't no way. A girl this young already has two babies?

"I told ya befo' we came, just one. Now put it back." she ordered. The little girl frowned. "What I said to you? Put it back."

The little girl turned to put her book back and the mother smiled at me.

"Damn kids," she said.

I faked a smile back. *Gulp.*

"No, I'm sorry, miss. The movie has already been checked out. I can put you down on the hold list if you'd like," the librarian said to me.

I don't know if it was the fact that I didn't think the movie would get returned before school started next Monday or if the sight of this young black girl's belly had freaked me out beyond anything I wanted to admit, but something right then and there made me realize how easily it could have been me in this sista's situation.

I made a huge decision.

"I'll just read the book," I said to the librarian, showing her the copy I held in my hand.

The librarian smiled. "You'll like it. It's a good one."

And she was right.

I started that night and couldn't put it down. Malcolm was a thug. Malcolm went to jail. Malcolm got tossed in solitary.

Like I said, I couldn't put it down. At two A.M., I went into the kitchen to get a glass of chocolate milk. Malcolm was so crazy, they had nicknamed him Satan.

And to get nicknamed Satan in jail, you had to be a gangsta.

"What are you still doin' up?" I said to Teddy as I made my way toward the kitchen. He was on the computer in the living room, surfing the Internet.

"Hey, you want to know the Social Security numbers of all the people who work for the gas company?"

I walked up to him and looked at the computer screen.

"What are you doin'? You hackin' into goverment Web sites? Go to bed."

"I can't sleep."

"Why? You don't feel good?"

"Naw, I never sleep. Maybe one hour a night," he said as he continued tapping at the keyboard.

"An hour a night? How long's this been goin' on?"

"I dunno."

"You ain't been sleepin' for more than one hour a night? What are you doing?"

"I scheme."

"You scheme?"

"Yeah, I scheme."

I shook my head and paused. Did my parents know? What difference would it make anyway? I didn't have time for Teddy's nonsense. Malcolm was waiting for me and he had just gotten tossed into the hole.

"Go to bed," I said and exited the room. But Teddy didn't listen and went back to typing on the computer.

I finished the entire book in four days. Plus, I ended up finding a copy of the movie and watched that, too. The film was good, but watching a movie ain't the same as reading a book. No way. And somehow, the experience of reading this book changed me.

I mean, this was the first time in my entire life that a dumb book had ever spoken to my heart. Usually the only books I read were the stupid ones assigned by schoolteachers, if I even bothered to read those at all. Malcolm was a brother and his words really spoke to me and changed my perspective. I mean, if he could go from the streets to jail to solitary confinement to becoming a highly educated and influential man who strived to lead our people out of oppression, then I had to be able do something with my life. Malcolm had nothing and did it all on his own. Me, I had a ton of opportunities available to me. And I mean right here and right now.

Damn, if it wasn't the weirdest thing, but reading had made me feel good.

The next day, two things happened. First, I got my school schedule in the mail. All Honors classes. I was gonna kick some ass. Especially since Wardin wasn't gonna be my teacher no more. I had some new guy named Morowitz for Honors American History.

Hell was over.

The second thing was, I bought a new poster to hang up right next to the picture of Tupac on my wall. That was some sacred space right there.

But my poster of Malcolm looked good.

14

Bing-bong! I pushed the doorbell. It was the right thing to do. And these days, I was all about doing the right thing. Besides, I hadn't seen or heard from Cee-Saw in almost five weeks. Ms. Sawyer answered the door. She didn't even say hello. She was just simmering with anger.

Simmering is a good word to know for the SAT. It means, "almost boiling because of intense heat."

From the moment the door opened I could tell the inside of this household had seen some intense heat.

Ms. Sawyer looked me up then down. "*Shee-it,* least someone can keep her panties on."

She lit a cigarette and walked away, returning to go watch more television.

I could understand why Ms. Sawyer was so pissed. She was only thirty-three and was about to be a grandmother. That's what happens when you were a seventeen-year-old mom and have a daughter who becomes a sixteen-year-old mom herself. And there wasn't a father to be found anywhere.

Babies having babies, all over my community.

Cee-Saw appeared from the back. Wow, she was huge!

"I'm fat, aren't I?"

"Naw, girl, you just . . . well, you know, just . . ."

"Fat."

She looked tired. And old. Plus, her toes were funky. I've always hated funky toes. Cee needed a pedicure.

"Close the door!" came a shout from the other room. "You're letting the air-conditioning out. Air-conditioning costs money, you know." There was a pause. "Diapers cost money, too. But when the Money Fairy comes, I'm sure he'll be bringing both of 'em! Diapers and air-conditioning, courtesy of the Money Fairy."

I stepped inside. Cee closed the door.

"Come on, let's go to my room," she said softly.

I could sense things had been sorta like this around her house for some time now.

Cee-Saw's room was a mess. I tried to pretend as if it wasn't so bad, but it was. I took a seat on the corner of the bed, looking for a nonfilthy spot to sit.

"Your mom's trippin' on you, huh?"

"Trippin' hard." There was a pause. It was awkward. "You're hair looks nice, Tee," she finally said to me.

"Oh, thanks," I replied.

There was another awkward pause. Then suddenly Cee-Saw ripped into me.

"Shit, you are like the only sista I know with two parents who live at home under the same roof. My single-ass mom is the normal one 'round this neighborhood—not yours, so don't be judging the way we—"

"I wasn't judging, Cee. I swear, I wasn't judging at all."

More silence fell on us. Maybe I shouldn't have come. I thought about Malcolm. Oh yeah, Malcolm.

"I brought you a gift." I reached into my bag and pulled it out for her. "It's a copy of *The Autobiography of Malcolm X*. This book changed my life."

I handed it to Cee with the hope that she might get out of it as much as I had. After all, it was never too late to change your life around and make good things happen. Never too late. I mean, Malcolm was in solitary confinement in prison and still found a way to change his circumstances. If he could do it, Cee could too. I was sure of it.

"Well, this book's pretty good, too," she said to me, reaching over to the table by her bed to pick up a copy of *What to Expect When You Are Expecting*.

I took the book from her and tried to pretend I was interested. It was a top-to-bottom pregnancy guide. Me and Cee were living on different planets.

"What's gonna happen with school?" I asked.

"They won't let me come back, so I'm dropping out," she informed me. "But only for now. Then, after the baby's born, I'll take some classes at Gateways."

Gateways was our school district's continuation high school where teens had a last chance to earn their diploma. Adolescents in and out of prison, gangbangers, kids who were thinking about dropping out, pregnant teens—those were mostly the students who went to Gateways. Though a student could take all the classes they needed, the success rate of students who matriculated at Gateways was outrageously low.

Matriculate is a good word to know for the SAT. It means, "to enroll in a school or college."

And even if a person could get in to Gateways, the odds were stacked big and fat against them. Just so many potential cracks to slip through once they're in that type of situation. Better never going there at all than having to try to get out once you're in.

"Then, after Gateways, I can go to community college and eventually transfer to UCLA," Cee-Saw said with hope in her eyes.

"You mean USC," I responded with a grin. UCLA is USC's crosstown rival.

"Naw, UCLA. I'm gonna be a Bruin," Cee-Saw

answered. She had her plans firmly laid out. "Yep, I'm gonna finish my high school diploma at Gateways, enroll at the CC, transfer into UCLA, and become a—*ooh!*"

She winced in pain.

"You okay?" I asked.

"Yeah, just a kick." But I could tell she was still physically uncomfortable. "What was we talking about again? Oh yeah. One day, I'm going to become a Bruin. Excuse me a sec, I gotta pee."

I watched Cee-Saw struggle to her feet.

"I'm peeing about four hundred times a day right now." She exited to the bathroom.

I looked around the room. A part of me just couldn't believe this whole thing. It was just so *real*.

While my room always had one small bottle of water, which I liked to keep by my bed, Cee's room had about a six-pack's worth of empty soda cans lying all over the place. While my room had a laundry hamper for my dirty clothes (I even folded my clothes before I put them in the hamper—yeah, I know it's weird), Cee had dirty undies and smelly socks lying all over the place. While my room had pictures of Malcolm X and Tupac on the wall, Cee had pictures of all these gangsta rappers showing off money, jewelry, cars, and practically naked women—the bling-bling lifestyle. Had our bedrooms always been so different?

I snooped around on Cee's little bedside table. Aspirin. Tums. The phone number to the Suicide Hotline.

The Suicide Hotline?

"What do you think of the name *R. Jay*? You know, like 'Rickee Junior,'" she said, coming back into the room. "I think it's a good name for a boy."

Her voice surprised me and I was startled. Cee-Saw stopped and stared at me. Her eyes scanned the table in front of me and paused at the Suicide Hotline's phone number sitting in plain view. She knew I had seen it. And I knew she knew I had seen it.

"You been looking through my stuff?"

"I just—"

"Yeah, I called. I called 'em three times already. Tell you the truth, they good. They helped me a lot."

All of a sudden Ms. Sawyer called out from the other room.

"Does your friend want to stay for dinner? The Money Fairy is gonna bring some KFC chicken. Does she want some KFC chicken?"

"Naw, thanks, I gotta go. My mom's making a family dinner tonight," I told Cee. "She made us all promise to be there." I don't think Cee believed me. "It's true," I added.

"Naw, she gotta go," Cee called out.

"Figures," her mom said to herself but loud enough for both of us to hear.

I set the book I had brought for Cee down on her table, but for some reason, I doubted she would ever read it. So much valuable information and education was right there at her fingertips, free of charge, too, but I just knew the girl wasn't gonna take advantage of it. It just made no sense.

None of this did.

Our good-bye was awkward. Thank goodness Ms. Sawyer had left before I did so I didn't have to see her again.

When I exited the house, a part of me wanted to scream.

Could I be a worse friend?

I came home to find Pops sitting in his favorite chair, watching a baseball game on TV. The volume was turned up extra loud. All of a sudden I felt tears come to my eyes.

I ran up to my dad and gave him a hug.

"Hey-hey, what's all this about?" he asked. "You want money?" I continued to hug him with all the hugs in my body. "You on drugs?" I smiled. "You're not pregnant, are you?"

"No, I'm not pregnant," I said, wiping tears from my eyes.

"Good, 'cause I thought I was gonna have to whup some little boy's ass."

Pops grinned, meaning it as a joke, but still, I wish he hadn't said that. I mean, sure, he didn't know about Cee, but I was just trying to be warm and his first reaction was suspicion of me. I guess he had a right. After all, I have done a lot of stupid stuff.

But doesn't it ever end?

"About time you're home, Theresa," my mother said to me as she exited the kitchen. "Go set the table and make sure everyone has a sharp knife. They're gonna need it for dinner."

She could have said, "*Hi.*" She could have said, "*Please.*" She could have said, "*How was your day?*"

Then again, I guess after me always responding, "Fine" whenever she asked me how my day was, she had probably stopped trying. Since I wanted to lay low under the radar, I didn't respond with anything but politeness.

"Yes, ma'am," I answered.

I was sick of all the hostility in my house. All I wanted was to get along peacefully with my family. I guess I was fortunate to have one.

Forty-five minutes later I heard Pops exclaim,

"Wow, baby, you really cooked your tail off." We all took our usual seats at the table, a feast of food in front of us.

"How many ribs you want, Theresa?" Pops asked me. I think he was serving me first in order to be nice.

"None, thank you."

"Wass' the matter, you ain't hungry?"

"No, I just stopped eating pork."

My mom froze. After a moment of silence, Pops continued to serve me.

"Don't be crazy, girl. These here are BBQ ribs, your mother's specialty. We'll start you off with two of 'em," Pops said, putting two ribs on my plate.

I quickly pushed my plate away.

"No, thank you, Pops," I said. Everyone stared at me. "Look, I don't mean it as an insult. I just stopped eating pork."

"Since when?" asked Pops, a hint of anger growing in his voice.

This dinner had taken my mother hours to prepare and was expensive. Plus, tonight, being the last night of the summer before school started again, she wanted to send us all off to a new year on the right foot. It was tough enough for my mom that Andre wasn't here 'cause he had stayed up at Stanford working over the summer—and he had always been her favorite—but still, it meant a lot to her for us to have a nice family dinner where everyone got along at least for one Sunday night.

So I am sure she was thinking, Why does Theresa have to do this now?

"Look," I explained calmly, 'cause I didn't want to start no trouble. "I've been doing some reading over the summer and I have decided that I don't wish to put pork in my body any longer."

"Why not?" asked my mother.

"Yeah, why not?" said Teddy, egging me on.

"Shut up, Teddy."

"Mom, Theresa told me to shut up."

"Teddy, be quiet a minute. Now why do you no longer want to eat pork?" my mother asked.

"Well, if you want to know the truth"—I could tell my mom was starting to take offense before I had even said anything, so in order *not* to piss her off, I approached it from a scientific perspective. "It has been proven that pigs can be unclean animals."

The logic of science would help me avoid confrontation.

"What do you mean, 'unclean'?"

"You know, unclean. For example, they sleep in their own fecal matter."

"*Oooggh,*" Teddy exclaimed, pushing his plate away. "This dinner's been sleeping in shit."

"You watch your language!" Pops shouted.

"*Oooggh,*" said my younger sister, Tina, following Teddy's lead. "Poopy!" She pushed her plate away.

Now no one wanted to eat.

"Everybody, eat your food!" Pops ordered.

"If Theresa don't eat, I'm not eating either," Teddy said crossing his arms.

"Oh, Theresa's gonna be eating."

"Why do I have to eat pork? Can't anybody respect my choices?"

"What are you, a Muslim?" Pops asked.

"*Muslim-ina! Muslim-ina!*" Teddy started screaming at me.

"I'm not a Muslim-ina," I shouted back. "I just don't wish to eat pork."

My mother, in order to get this dinner moving along, put a rib, some corn, and a well-done biscuit on Tina's plate. "Here, honey, eat some dinner."

Tina looked up with sad eyes.

"How come I have to eat the poopy?"

"It's not poopy!" Pops said, slamming down his fist. Then he grabbed four ribs, three biscuits, two pieces of corn, and two scoops of homemade coleslaw.

"Fine, I'll eat it all if I have to," he said, reaching for the salt to season his corn.

But my mother grabbed the salt before he could get to it and put it out of his reach.

"*Nuh-uh,* no salt for you. It's bad for your hypertension."

Pops put down his napkin, stood up firmly, crossed the table, picked up the salt, returned to his chair, and put some on his corn.

"A sprinkle of salt ain't gonna kill a person," he said in a commanding voice.

What he really meant was, *I am not a child and this is my house!*

My mother glared at him.

"Can I be excused?" Teddy asked.

"Hell no, boy! Now start eating some damn ribs," Pops answered.

The whole table turned to me. I paused, unsure of what to do. Then I slowly put my napkin on my plate and stood up.

"Just make sure you change the vacuum bag. It's been full for three days," my mother said as I walked away from the table.

One of my best friends in the whole world was pregnant and on the verge of suicide and the only thing my mom cared about was a stupid vacuum bag being changed?

So typical.

I didn't even argue with her.

"I don't care what that girl says, honey. These ribs are dee-licious!" Pops said, licking some sauce off his fingers.

"Why don't you put some salt on them, too?" my mom replied. She was pissed. Teddy laughed.

"And you, Mr. Funny Man, can go vacuum the living-room floor when Theresa's done changing the bag."

"But I wanna eat some ribs."

"Too late," she shot back, taking Teddy's plate away from him. Then she turned to Tina.

"Listen to me, Tina, there is nothing wrong with this food. See Pops over there eating it? Now get some nutrition in your stomach. I want you to eat some dinner."

Tina put a tiny nibble in her mouth, but she didn't really want to eat.

Teddy crossed to me as I changed the vaccuum bag. "Way to go, Muslim-ina."

"Shut up, Teddy."

"That ain't my name no more. Call me T-Bear."

"Oh what, you goin' all gangsta now?"

Teddy pulled up his shirt and flexed every muscle in his torso. Though he was only going into seventh grade, the boy had a six-pack that was pretty ripped. *Damn,* my little bro was growing up.

"My name's T-Bear, *Aaarrrgghh!*" he said with a growl, pounding his chest. "You shouldn't mess with the Bear."

I shook my head, handed him the vacuum and headed for my room.

"There you go, T-Bear."

Nothing I ever do is good enough. I mean, all I'm trying to do is advance my intelligence and move forward in a positive direction. Why were my parents always hating on me? Damn, wasn't I even going out of my way to be nice? So what if I don't want to eat pork, I'm allowed. Heck, if I wanted to convert to Islam, I'm allowed.

Do I want to convert to Islam? I don't think I can. I mean, I believe in Jesus Christ, and if I leave Jesus Christ, my soul is going to burn in hell.

But if I go to Allah, he will save my soul and take me to heaven. *Hmmm,* how's that gonna work? One half of my soul in Islamic heaven and the other half in Christian hell? Or vice versa?

Goodness gracious, how am I supposed to figure all this stuff out? I can't even grasp the hypotenuse of a right triangle, and Algebra II is on my schedule first period this year.

I put on my headphones and looked up at the wall. Thank God for Tupac. Thank God for Malcolm. And a special thanks to God for hip-hop.

I let the fresh beats take me away.

15

I walked through the gate on the first day of Junior year and the first thing I saw was all the beat-boxers and hip-hoppers flowing rhymes by the fence. Damn, they were good.

All the homeboys and homegirls were dressed in their sickest clothes, too. Dope styles ruled the campus outright. That was one thing about the poor kids in our 'hood—they sure didn't look it.

A buzz of electricity ran through the air. It was time to see and be seen. Peeps were chattin' up and down all over the place. By the stairs, near the library, across from the flagpole—wherever I went, scandalous happenings from the summertime floated through the air:

"Yo, yo, you hear 'bout Daniella Weston? She got freaky with Marcel Thompson."

"Yo, yo, you hear 'bout Cecelia Flowers? Her parents kicked her out da house and now she living at Jennifer Belling's grandmother's place."

"Yo, yo, you hear about Frostee Jenkins? He got busted slangin' drugs at the park and the judge slammed him with two years at Los Padrinos."

Hmmvvvzzz! Hmmvvvzzz! Hmmvvvzzz!

Yep, school was back in action.

I showed up to third-period Honors American History wondering what this new dude Morowitz was going to be like. Hopefully, he didn't give a lot of homework.

I entered the room. There weren't any posters on the wall. Maybe he hadn't had time to decorate yet.

Hmmvvvzzz! Hmmvvvzzz! Hmmvvvzzz!

I found an empty desk and sat down. Then I noticed a sign.

GOOD THINGS HAPPEN TO PEOPLE WHO TRY.

Huh? *No way!*

I spun my head around as the teacher walked into class.

Holy shit! It was Wardin.

"Excuse me, why aren't you people *sitting down?* And take out a sheet of paper. We're having a test."

No-o-o-o-o!

Turns out this new Morowitz teacher had heard about all the violence in the community—it had been a growing problem over the summer—and his wife had made him take a job at a different high school in the suburbs. Who could blame him? The pay was higher, too.

But Wardin again—*goodness gracious!* Why didn't *he* go to the suburbs?

"Well, hello, Miss Theresa Anderson. How do you like my new classroom?" Wardin smiled at me in an ominous way.

Ominous is a good word to know for the SAT. It means, "menacing—like something bad is going to happen."

"The air-conditioning works better in here, don't you think?" he added as he passed me my test. I noticed his fingers, his sickeningly thick undercooked-sausage fingers. He licked them before giving me my exam.

Gross!

Not only did Wardin give us a test on the first day, which nobody was prepared for, he gave a monster assignment, too. A five-page typed paper due at the beginning of the next week: *Compare and contrast two uprisings from two different eras in United States history.* Outlines due tomorrow.

"Welcome to Honors American History, a college preparatory course," he said. "Your days of copying from other people's papers and no homework on the weekends are over."

Since I had promised myself that this year was

going to be different, when I got home I didn't have any pretzel nuggets with cream cheese. And I didn't turn on the television. And I didn't fight with Teddy. I went straight to work on Wardin's assignment.

After much thought, I decided to do a paper comparing the civil rights uprisings of the 1960s to modern hip-hop's struggle to rise up against the various forces that hold economically disadvantaged people back in contemporary society.

Wow, that sounds good.

1960s Civil Rights Uprising	Hip-Hop as a Cultural Uprising
Dr. Martin Luther King: A nonviolent approach to rising up **Textual evidence:** *Letter from a Birmingham Jail*	**KRS-One** (Knowledge Reigns Supreme): The value of education and intelligence **Textual evidence:** *The Temple of Hiphop*
Malcolm X: By any means necessary **Textual evidence:** *Malcolm X: The Speeches at Harvard* by Archie Epps	**Tupac Shakur:** Faith in yourself despite long odds **Textual evidence:** *The Rose That Grew from Concrete*
Cesar Chavez: *Sí, se puede.* (Yes, we can.) **Textual evidence:** *The power of the boycott*	**Eminem:** Yes, I can. **Textual evidence:** *Grammy Award–winning lyrics, "Lose Yourself"*

Not only did I do a two-page outline, double the amount required, but I even created a thoroughly researched graphic chart to clearly show where I'd be going with my paper.

When I looked up at the clock it was 1:26 A.M. and I was just finishing up my research on the textual evidence. *Whew!*

I went to the computer to double-check Eminem's lyrics before going to sleep. I discovered Teddy wide awake, surfing the Internet.

"Get up, I need the computer."

"I'm in the middle of something."

I looked at the computer screen.

"No, you're not, you're playing games."

A chessboard was on the screen. Teddy moved one of his pieces. A moment later, words written in red flashed across the IM box across the top.

> **Boris Spunkinov: Congrats, Grandmaster T-Bear. You've beaten me again.**

Teddy typed a response.

> **Grandmaster T-Bear: All night long, Moscow punk!**

"You changed your name to 'Grandmaster'?" I asked.

"Naw, that's my chess status. It's like a ranking thing."

"Who you playing against?"

"I dunno, some dude in Russia."

I stared at Teddy, then shook my head.

"Get off!" I ordered.

I didn't have time for Teddy's foolishness. I needed to finish up and get some sleep. After all, it was only the first night of school.

"Lemme know when you're done," he said as he exited the room. "I'm gonna go take a poop."

"You're disgusting," I told him.

"What? It's Mother Nature."

He left the room and I sat down at the computer. The IM box above the chessboard flashed again.

Boris Spunkinov: You need to learn some manners, T-Bear.

I typed a response for Teddy.

Grandmaster T-Bear: Yes, I know. I am a rude and ugly JERK!

I laughed. A moment passed, then the Russian's reply came.

Boris Spunkinov: LOL—most of the brilliant players usually are.

I hit the X and closed the window on the chess game. "See ya, Mr. Russian."

For the first time in my life I was excited to go to Wardin's class. It was all I could think about in first and second period.

"No!" he said.

"Why not?" I asked.

"Because wearing baggy pants does not make for an uprising."

"Hip-hop is more than baggy pants."

"That's right. It's also criminals, profanity, and misogyny."

"It is not!" I protested.

"Do you even know what the word *misogyny* means, Miss Theresa Anderson?"

I paused.

"No," I admitted.

"Then choose another topic." Wardin grabbed my

paper and wrote NOT APPROVED across the top in bold red ink.

"Next!" he commanded. Sheila Josephson stepped up to his desk with her outline. He read her paper and paused.

"You do know that the French Revolution was a *French* Revolution and that this is an *American* History class, don't you, Miss Sheila Josephson?"

I wandered back to my desk and stared at the words NOT APPROVED. I couldn't believe it.

"So what are you going to do your paper on?" Sonia asked me at lunchtime. Of course we shared french fries.

"I dunno. Probably the Boston Tea Party and Rosa Parks."

"Oh, that's original."

"Exactly! I mean, hip-hop is the voice of the people. Just look at how all the folks our age respond to it."

I pointed over to MixMaster Mytch, who had drawn a pretty big crowd by his usual area. He was spittin' hard rhymes in a way that came from a soulful place deep in his heart, a place that Wardin could never understand.

The past ain't nothin' to me
See, I'm free

Livin' in the land of dee-mocracy
Hip-pocrisy
Makin' a mockery
Of peeps from the streets like you and me be

Classes like Wardin's didn't mean anything to a guy like him. After all, what the hell did the MixMaster care about the Industrial Revolution? Folks like him were staging their own revolution and Mytch didn't care one damn bit if his teachers got it. And his teachers didn't care one damn bit if he got them, either. I guess their thinking was that by the time you're seventeen years old, if you don't understand the importance of education, you probably ain't about to start now, so instead of trying to get the MixMaster to recognize the value of going to school, his teachers had given up. Plus, a new generation of fourteen-year-olds had just arrived on campus this week, and maybe they could be reached. But dudes like the MixMaster, he was long gone.

"Hip-hop's cool, but I like *tejanos* and *boleros*. *Musica Latina* lets you dance."

Sonia rolled her shoulders, then her hips. Latinas sure know how to shake their thing.

Later that night I looked up the word *misogyny* in

the dictionary. Maybe it was a word I needed to know for the SAT.

mi•sog•y•ny: a hatred of women

Well, Wardin hates me and I'm a woman—does that count?

I ended up getting a C+ on my Boston Tea Party paper. Written across the top in red ink were the words *Not much original thought.* No duh.

During the second week of my junior year I realized how much peeps all around me were starting to find their own groove in life. Like Jaxson Edgars— *wow!* He had really made some strides as an artist. The preschool project came out great and a local hip-hop group that had just signed with a small record label asked Jax to scratch their very first album cover. And they were gonna pay him $2,000 to do it, too. *Damn!*

When Jax told us the news I was totally excited for him. Sonia was too.

"So what's' up with Cee-Saw," he asked a little later. "I still ain't seen her yet this year."

Sonia and I looked at each other, not knowing what to tell him. Obviously, Jax was hoping to "get a rap in wit' her."

It was only a matter of time before the whole school found out that Cee-Saw had become a preggo teen and dropped out. But ain't no way that I was gonna be the one to break the 411 on campus.

"She's been a bit under the weather," I said.

Hmmvvvzzz! Hmmvvvzzz! Hmmvvvzzz!

Thank goodness, saved by the bell before I had to explain any more.

Three days later there was a big fight after school. I couldn't see any of the action, but from what I could tell, someone got stomped—and good.

Security tried to clear the crowd.

"That's enough. Everyone clear out. It's all over!"

There was nothing more to watch other than seeing the campus security guards drag the two dudes who had been brawling off to the office, where they would each be given automatic five-day suspensions.

I was standing right next to one of the guards when he grabbed his walkie-talkie and contacted the front office.

"This is unit C11 to Eagle 8. C11 to Eagle 8."

"This is Eagle 8. Go ahead, C11."

"Yeah, you might want to call a medic. One of our forty-sevens got banged up pretty good."

The next sight I saw was Jaxson Edgars being carried off by two guards. His face was *smashed*—I mean pounded like raw hamburger meat. There was blood, swelling, puffiness, and his eye was as big as a softball. It looked like it was going to fall out of his head.

Oh my gracious—Jax!

The next person I saw being dragged through the crowd was Rickee Dunston. There wasn't a scratch on him.

"Fool gonna mess wit' me." Rickee talked trash the whole way to the dean's office, "Shit, dat's a *monsta* mistake."

Turns out, Jax had found out about Cee-Saw and confronted Rickee. I imagine he was trying to be chivalrous.

A "*monsta* mistake" indeed.

Jax spent the night in the hospital. His chivalry had resulted in a broken eye socket with retinal damage. Rickee was back on the football field the next day. Turns out academic suspension didn't mean he couldn't practice with the team. When Jax found out that Rickee still got to go to football practice he immediately dropped out.

"This whole place is BS, a freakin' joke," Jax said. "Besides, I'm gonna be a professional artist."

I'm sure he would be, too. But it'd probably take

him at least six weeks to get going on his new career. That's how long the doctors said he'd be blind in his left eye.

And goodness, the things they were saying about Cee-Saw.

16

I made it all the way to Christmas break without another crisis. I'd pretty much just been laying low and *"doin' my thang."* As a result, stuff was vibing for me. I ended up with a 3.23 GPA for the semester, my best grades yet.

A– Honors English
B   Honors Algebra II
A– Spanish III
A   Computers
C+ Honors American History
B– Honors Chemistry

Yep, I'd cracked a 3.0—and that was with a part-time job and without being put on punishment one time in four and a half months. Inside, I felt good.

Then, just after we got our report cards, my mother called a "family meeting."

I hated family meetings. Something bad always happened at them. But I know she wasn't about to get on me about my grades. Not with a full load of Honors classes and only one C. Actually, it wasn't even a C. It was a C$^+$, in Wardin's class. Of course. Once a hater, always a hater.

Andre, however, had earned a 3.87 for the semester at Stanford and was double majoring in Journalism and English Literature, so any big props for grades went to him. No matter what I did, I was always second place.

At least USC had won 47–10 this year in football. The score would have been worse, but SC fumbled a bunch in the mud. It was a rainy day at Stanford stadium.

Yet still, as we gathered around the kitchen table to have our family meeting I sensed that something bad was coming. But what? I mean, I hadn't done anything.

Or had I?

"We're moving," my mother began.

"What?" I shot back. "We're moving? To where? Why?"

"We're *thinking* about moving," my father said. "Nothing has been decided for sure yet. That's what we're going to talk about."

Essentially, our neighborhood was undergoing what my mother called a "poorification." The streets were getting worse, battles between different gangs were occurring in the community more and more, and general deterioration was everywhere. All in all, our middle-class neighborhood was on an obvious downslope. I think I'd really started to notice it more when my brother Andre's best friend Shawn and his family moved out of the neighborhood. They were the last of the white people. My parents had moved into our house eighteen years before, when our neighborhood was totally and completely middle class. But now, middle class had given way to lower middle class and we were starting to see lower middle class give way to straight-out low class.

And when middle-class people like us live in low-class areas like this, we are forced to mull over whether we should stay or leave.

Mull over is a good expression to know for the SAT. It means to "think something over and consider the options."

My mother had *mulled* things over and wanted to leave.

My father had *mulled* things over and wanted to stay.

Andre had *mulled* things over, but since he had essentially moved out and only lived at home for a few weeks a year—he wasn't even at this meeting, he had returned to school two weeks before—he didn't want to vote.

But I didn't need to mull things over at all. No way

did I want to move. I was right in the middle of trying to do something with my life. Besides, this was my 'hood. I knew my way around and knew how to keep safe. Plus, moving would mean I'd have to go to a new high school right in the middle of my junior year.

"Do you know the kind of social *freak* I'd be?"

"You already are one."

"Shut up, Teddy! We can't move, Mom. We just can't."

"What do you think, Teddy?"

My brother looked up from his Rubik's cube game toy. In the seventeen minutes we'd been at the table he had not only gotten all of the colors on all of the sides to match up, he had then figured out a way to change it and rearrange it so that all the colors on each side matched up a second time except for the center square.

How'd he do that?

"Don't matter to me," Teddy answered. "I'm-a survive wherever you put me."

Thanks, Teddy.

"But Mom, please, we can't move now. We just can't."

And after another half an hour it was decided. We would *not* move.

Yet.

Thank goodness.

But it wasn't 'cause of me, it was 'cause of Pops. Ultimately, he felt he had put too much heart and soul and sweat and blood into this home and he wasn't ready to give it up yet.

Yet, that is. But it was getting close.

"Then some things are going to have to change," my mother said. "Tina, I do not want you leaving the front yard to go down the block with your friends. You hear me?"

"Yes, Mom."

"I mean it. If I catch you walking off, you won't be allowed outside again. I mean ever."

"I heard you, Mom."

"And Theresa . . ."

"I know, I know, no walking alone at night."

"And no more movie theater."

"What? But that's my job."

"The mall's become too dangerous. I mean whoever heard of kids shooting guns by a food court? I tell you, it's time for us to move away from here."

"We're not moving," Pops said.

And there went my money supply.

Funny how hip-hoppers are always rapping about how economic oppression is the means by which the man keeps us down.

What a joke, I thought as I got up from the table

after the family meeting. My momma has become the Man.

On January 2, right after New Year's, I tried to reconnect with Cee-Saw. I took her name off the Block Sender list of my IM and then decided to take it one step further by visiting her. After all, it was the right thing to do.

Not three seconds after I knocked on the door, I wished I hadn't come.

Teen pregnancy is depressing—even more so during the holiday season when your family ain't got no money.

Damn, I felt awkward.

"Hey," Cee said without much energy when she answered the door. My goodness, she was *as big as a house*. I tried not to stare.

Though her mother wasn't home at the time, the house vibed like Ms. Sawyer's negative energy all over the place. The shades were drawn, making it dark in every room, and the only real holiday decoration I saw was a beaten-up piece of green string that said MERRY XMAS in cheap red glitter hanging off a mantel with chipped paint. There was a pizza box sitting on the living room floor. It could have been tonight's dinner. It could have been last night's dinner. For all I knew, it could have been tomorrow's lunch.

Had Santa forgotten to climb down their chimney this year? Maybe he had just avoided it on purpose.

"Come on in," Cee said, lowering the volume on the TV. I closed the door behind me.

"You feelin' all right? How's the baby?" I asked.

"Eighth month now. Totally healthy, knock on wood." She rubbed her belly. "Little Rickee Jr. doin' strong and fine."

"That's good," I said. "That's good."

Uncomfortable silence filled the air. She didn't ask me what I'd been up to lately and I didn't tell her.

"Have you heard from Rickee?" I finally asked. Maybe it was a stupid question, but I didn't know what to talk about.

"Kinda, sorta, but not too much right now," she answered. "But once the baby is born, I know he'll come 'round a lot more."

I wanted to be supportive. I wanted to be encouraging. I wanted to be inspirational and positive and full of hope, happiness, and good vibes for Cee-Saw. But I just didn't know how. I mean, here she was popping off about how Rickee was gonna show up like a white knight and realize the error of his ways and come be some kind of father to this child. What kind of bull crap was she feeding me?

What kind of bull crap was she feeding herself?

Delusional is a good word to know for the SAT. It means "filled with fantasies and not in touch with reality." Cee-Saw was being totally delusional. The question was, how could I, as her friend, sit there and listen to her live in some sort of fantasy world?

She needed to do something, to make some kind of plan. Rickee wasn't going to come around, that was *fo' sure!* Football season had just ended and he had made All State. From what I heard, the dude had girlfriends in high schools up and down the West Coast. Hell, he might have even had other babies floating around, too. The idea that he was going to drop everything, get a job, and come support this child financially and emotionally was crazy. This baby—like all babies—needed to be nurtured and cared for and raised by a father. And Rickee stepping up to do that was never gonna happen. *Never.* How come Cee didn't realize this? As a true friend, I had to tell her.

But I had to start slow.

"Hey, Cee," I began. "What happens if, you know, Rickee *doesn't* come around?"

"Oh, he'll come. How could he not want to see Rickee Jr.?"

"Yeah, yeah, I understand. But I'm just saying, *what if . . . ?*"

Cee-Saw paused. Then she got angry.

"Why you comin' 'round here, bein' all negative, trying to destroy the positive things I got goin' on in my life?"

"The positive things?" I asked.

"Oh, havin' a baby ain't a positive thing to you?"

"Yeah, yeah, no, I didn't mean it like that. Sure, no, I—that's positive, of course. I meant like plans and things like that," I said.

"You just a hater, Tee."

"Naw, Cee, it ain't like that."

"Yeah, it is. You a hater."

Cee-Saw pushed up from her chair in that fat way all preggo ladies do, then walked out of the room, leaving me all alone.

"I was just trying to help," I said, but she had closed her bedroom door.

After a moment alone I exited the apartment, turning the little lock on the handle and shutting the door behind me. Again I thought to myself about how I was only trying to help.

Suddenly, I saw a lime-green four-door Lincoln oozing white exhaust out of the tailpipe pulling into the parking lot. I dashed into the second-floor's garbage room.

Damn, it stinks in here!

I took out my cellie and checked the time. For

eleven full minutes I remained dead quiet while I breathed in the foul smell of two-week-old Chinese food and empty ashtrays. Then, feeling it was finally safe, I poked my head out the door. It looked to be all clear, so I snuck down the back stairs and walked quickly away from the building.

Thank goodness I hadn't run into Ms. Sawyer.

Classes started back again on January 7. By January 22 I had noticed a real change in Sonia. She was now a C student who always looked tired.

Then I didn't see her again at school until February 11.

"Dang, where you been, girl?" I said when we finally caught up again.

"I know, I've been missing a ton of school." She didn't really need to say it, though, the reason was crystal clear: *la familia.*

Instead of fighting with her about her duty to look out for number one, about how education was the only way she'd ever be able to break the cycle of poverty, and how it was unfair that she was the servant of her *familia* who always had to sacrifice her own needs for the sake of others, I simply asked one meaningful, deep, very important question: "Wanna share some fries?"

Our lunchtime ritual was almost a memory. Plus, I needed someone to chat with. After all, Valentine's Day was coming up the following week and once again, it was looking as if I was going to be without a man. As a freshman I could understand it. As a sophomore, I could understand it. But as a junior? This was becoming a *real* issue for me.

"I would love to share some fries," she said with her pretty smile.

"I'll get the chips and the soda," I answered, grinning.

"I'll get the fries," she said.

But our lunchtime ritual never got to happen.

Since it was February, Black History Month, our school had planned all sorts of "special events." Today the school schedule had been changed so that we had an extended double second period. This meant that for the first part of second period, half the school went to an MLK Day assembly in the auditorium while the other half of the school went to class.

Then everybody was supposed to switch. Half the school was supposed to go to the auditorium while the first group went to class. However, *supposed to* and *did* are two different things on our campus. About a hundred million kids ditched class and went to both assemblies. It was chaos. And then it was lunch. After lunch, we were all supposed to go to third period to finish out the rest of the day as usual. Once again, this is what we were "supposed to" do. It's not what happened.

Unfortunately, during the second MLK assembly, which was packed with about a thousand more students than there should have been, some Hispanic dudes were goofing off during the performance.

And some black dudes took it as a "disrespect" to our culture.

A fight broke out. It turned into a five-on-five brawl. Then lunchtime started.

The next thing anyone knew, a fuse had been lit and students were dividing up all over campus, throwing punches at one another for no reason other than the color of their skin. Hispanics and blacks fought while Samoans and Filipinos gathered their own and try to stay uninvolved. Kids were getting jumped left and right.

Of course, Sonia and I had had no idea any of this was happening when we planned to share french fries. Before I knew it, the whole campus was totally out of control, seized by a frenzy of violence.

Security had broken up the first few fights in the quad, but the action spread to pockets of other areas around the school—by the band room, behind the gym, in the science corridor. Roving gangs of students caused mayhem as they roamed the school. There just wasn't enough security to contain all the fighters. Troublemaking students cruised the campus like packs of jackals, attacking smaller groups of students who weren't with members of their own race to protect them.

Bam! Three black dudes stomped a Latino near a garbage can.

Pop! Four Latinos caught a baseball player and hit him in the kidneys with a bat.

Who-o-o-o-sh! Someone set a fire in the trash can.

Hmmvvvzzz! Hmmvvvzzz! Hmmvvvzzz!

The bell sounded. *As if a bell was going to make all the students stop rioting.*

It was teenage anarchy. I ran to go hide in my third-period class. This was totally insane.

Pow! A boy got clubbed with a backpack.

Whap! A dude got—

Oh my gracious . . . Sonia!

Blood poured from her nose like a faucet turned on full blast. *What had happened?* I rushed to her side.

"Come on, we gotta get you to the nurse."

"Tee-Ay, I think they broke my nose."

"I got you, Sonia. Come on, let's go!"

All of a sudden a group of five Latino boys turned

the corner. They were breathing hard, their cheeks were flushed and red. I could tell they'd been brawling.

And all they saw was me, a black girl, standing next to a bleeding Latina. Luckily, one of them was Rodrigo, a boy I had known for eight years.

"Step off, Tee-Ay!"

"Shut up, Rodrigo! I'm taking her to the nurse."

"Brown can take care of its own. Step off."

"This ain't a racial thing. My friend is hurt and I am—"

Next thing I know a group of four Latina girls turned the corner—and I didn't know a single one of them.

"Oh, you think you can whoop up on *mi gente* like that, huh, *chiquita?*"

"Naw," I said, backing up against a wall. "That ain't how it is."

"*Oye*, let's see how *her* pretty nose looks after a taste of spicy salsa gets applied."

The girls laughed and stepped closer to me. I backed up some more, but space was running out. I looked to my left. There was no place to run. I looked to my right. A railing cornered me in. Then I looked up and suddenly—

"Hey you!"

A teacher turned the corner. The Latinas scattered, scared off by the voice of an adult.

"Come back here!"

But they continued running. And they took Sonia with them.

"You okay?" the teacher asked me.

"Uh-huh," I answered as my heart pounded like a jackhammer inside my chest.

Hmmvvvzzz! Hmmvvvzzz! Hmmvvvzzz!

"Then get to class," he said as he took off to go help stop the madness somewhere else on campus.

I wandered, lost and confused, toward my third-period class. A group of black kids raced by me in the other direction, obviously up to no good.

Hmmvvvzzz! Hmmvvvzzz! Hmmvvvzzz!

The bell rang again and again. Police were called. Helicopters, better known as "ghetto birds" 'round these parts, flew over the school. TV news crews came to the scene so they could do an "Eyewitness News Special Report."

The school's loudspeaker went crazy.

"All students will return to class!"

"All students will return to class!"

Hmmvvvzzz! Hmmvvvzzz! Hmmvvvzzz!

"All students will return to class!"

I walked through our campus in a daze. The fire had been put out in the garbage cans, but the air around campus still smelled like smoke.

Things finally settled and order was restored. Flustered and dizzy, I walked into third period.

"Everyone take out a sheet of paper."

"What?" the class gasped.

"That's right, you heard me," Wardin ordered. "Take out a sheet of paper. It's essay time."

How in the world could he give us work and act as if there was nothing wrong?

"Earning acceptance into college is about triumphing over adversity," Wardin said as he wrote our task on the board. "So that makes this a perfect time for an assignment."

The class was stunned.

"Look, folks, life is not always going to be picture perfect, and if you want to reach your goals, you are going to have to learn to focus and move beyond temporary inconveniences toward realizing your ambitions."

Huh?

"Now, you'll have fifty-two minutes to complete this essay. Begin."

I read the board.

Compare and contrast two different countries from the Western Hemisphere in terms of their societal norms and cultural standards.

No freakin' way!

Wardin didn't care about the race riot. He didn't care about the MLK Day assembly, the fire in the garbage cans, or the ghetto birds either. He didn't care about anything. Honors classes had to "rise above," or so he said.

What a crock!

The only thing flowing through my mind was *Is Sonia okay?* It was hard to focus.

"Miss Theresa Anderson, will you be fulfilling this assignment?" Wardin asked, noticing my brain was a million miles away. I glared at him. "Is that a yes?"

"I'm thinking," I responded, with fire in my eyes.

"Thinking is good. But thoughts on paper are the only things that will receive points. Now write!"

I hated that man—hated him with all my heart. I bet things would be different if it were his daughter lying in the nurse's office with a smacked-up face, that was fo' sure! But his daughter didn't go to this kind of high school. His daughter probably went to one of them fancy high schools on the West Side. I once heard about the white girls over there and how they had reading parties with iced tea, classic literature, and sugar cookies baked by parents who took an active role in their kids' education.

Reading parties? What a joke! My school had helicopters, race riots, and wannabe gangstas. Why in the world did Wardin want me to write about two different countries in the Western Hemisphere when there were two different countries right here in our own city less than fifteen miles apart?

But the punk wanted an essay, so I gave him one. And I didn't hold back. Who cared if I got an F? It was over. It was all over.

I wrote about the unfairness and the injustice right under everyone's noses. I spoke about the rich and the poor, the haves and have-nots, and how it was just flat-out wrong the way some kids got the best schools, the best teachers, and the best resources, while other kids got nothing. I even used the word *bullshit* in my essay. Like I said, I didn't care if Wardin gave me an F. I didn't care about school anymore. This whole world was so smacked up, I didn't care about nothing. When the sweetest girl on the planet can have her nose smashed in because of the color of her skin on a high school campus, then hell, why should I care? Maybe Jax was the smart one. He had dropped out to quit playing society's game. People like us were set up to lose before we even started. Hip-hoppers understood this. Punks didn't. It was all a giant lie.

I turned my paper in, expecting never to see the inside of an Honors class again.

The next day, Wardin gave me my first A.

17

"I look like a Mexican raccoon."

"No you don't," I insisted. "Well, maybe . . . but the cute kind, like a stuffed animal."

We laughed. I was glad we could laugh. Truthfully, I was just glad that Sonia was okay.

It turned out that her nose was not broken—she had just gotten popped in the face in a way that caused both her eyes to turn purple, black, and blue. It had happened when some kid raced past her after a fire was set in one of the garbage cans and he nailed her with an accidental elbow. Noses always bleed a lot once they get going; and if you pop them in the right spot, your eyes look like a boxer's, too.

Her injury caused Sonia to miss three days of school. Then her drunken uncle got arrested for trying to steal a car stereo out of a BMW and faced prison time and deportation. That cost her six more days.

"Pero, yo no en-tee-endo 'familia,'" I said to her sarcastically.

I was now enrolled in Spanish III. We had just

started putting short sentences together. I wished I had worked harder in Spanish I and II.

"*Tu no entiendes mierda, Tee-Ay, y si quiero tirar mi vida al carajo, lo hago. Mételo en tu culo puto.*"

My Spanish wasn't that good, but I think she had just said something about how much she agreed with my wisdom.

On campus the bad blood had settled down, but there was still tension between the races. Latinos who walked the halls alone always feared for their safety. Blacks never went to the bathroom without two other peeps to watch their backs. For the girls it wasn't nearly as bad as it was for the guys, but all in all, no one really felt safe. Personally, I *never* went to the bathroom during passing periods—I always went to class and then got a pass from a teacher after the bell rang. There were just too many students with not enough security, so it was much safer to pee after the bell had rung. Besides, people smoked weed and stuff in the bathrooms in between classes and it was too easy to get caught in the wrong place at the wrong time, even if you hadn't done anything.

Principal Watkins thought a Thursday-Night Pep Rally for the basketball team might help the "morale" on campus, so he organized a school-wide party. Ninety-two percent of the people who showed up were black.

Latinos wondered how come the soccer team wasn't getting some kind of pep rally too. After all, the soccer team was better than the basketball team. They had advanced to the third round of the city playoffs, while the basketball team hadn't even finished up in the top five in our local bracket.

Principal Watkins, a black man, had never played soccer a day in his life. "Not enough scoring," he said.

So much for a pep rally to heal the school's spirit.

I never made it to the Thursday-Night Pep Rally, though. That's 'cause I was trying to make it to the hospital to be with Cee-Saw when she gave birth.

"Can I be with her?" I asked the nurse as I arrived at the third-floor maternity ward.

"No, sorry. Family only."

Thank goodness. I didn't really want to see a baby's head get squeezed through my best friend's vagina, anyway. I mean, how do you ever share a sandwich with a person after you've seen something like that happen to them?

"But there are some complications. She's going to have a C-section in thirty minutes."

A look of concern crossed my face.

"Don't worry," said the nurse. "We do this all the time."

"But won't that leave a scar?" I asked.

The nurse simply repeated what she had just told me. "Don't worry. We do this all the time."

Some preggo ladies had eight or nine people waiting in the maternity lobby for the slightest hint of news about their babies. I was the only one at the hospital for Cee-Saw other than her mother. Ms. Sawyer was in the delivery room with Cee, giving comfort and support, I suppose.

An hour and forty-five minutes passed. I felt alone and out of place. Occasionally some of the other people, people who were not all alone in the waiting room, would look at me. It felt like they were staring. Like they were feeling sorry for me or something. All I could do was lower my eyes and try not to pay attention.

Finally, the nurse returned.

"Is everything okay?"

"It's a girl," she said.

"A girl?" I repeated.

"And the mother's fine. The baby's name is," the nurse read from the piece of paper in her hand, "Ricita Dunstona Sawyer. She weighs seven pounds, two ounces and is as healthy as an oak tree."

The nurse then exited to go fill out some forms.

Wow, I thought. A baby girl.

I decided to go downstairs to the hospital gift shop

to get the baby a present. I bought a pink stuffed elephant. It cost eighteen dollars. Those places always rip you off when you have nowhere else to shop. I came back up and found the nurse.

"Can I go see her?" I asked, holding the pink elephant.

"Sorry, only family."

"But I'm like family."

"Her mother is the only family identified on the forms."

"Oh," I said, looking down.

"She'll be home in two days. You'll see them then." Then the nurse walked away.

What could I do other than wait the two days? I turned to leave and saw an older lady with curly hair staring at me. She smiled weakly.

"Congratulations," she said to me softly.

I weakly smiled back at her and went to go catch the bus home. Two days later, I showed up at Cee's apartment at ten o'clock in the morning.

As soon as I walked in I realized that one little pink stuffed elephant wasn't hardly enough. That's because other people had brought balloons, stuffed animals, cards, flowers—the whole living room was filled with all kinds of WELCOME HOME—CONGRATULATIONS—IT'S A GIRL! type of gifts.

All from Jaxson.

He had landed another gig as an album designer, this time for $2,500, and it looked as if he had spent his whole check on gifts for the baby. The apartment was filled top to bottom with awesome new stuff.

Cee-Saw looked tired but glowing in her own way.

"Hey-hey, Momma," I said with a smile.

"Hey-hey, Tee-Ay," Cee answered.

"Hi, Jax," I added.

"Hi, Tee-Ay," Jax answered as we hugged.

Ms. Sawyer took the stuffed elephant from me and closed the door. Though Cee's mother was definitely not happy about any of this, she was nevertheless overwhelmed with joy at the sight of her new grand-daughter's shiny cheeks.

"Ain't she cute?" Ms. Sawyer asked me.

I looked at little Ricita. I thought she looked like a chicken. New babies, in my opinion, aren't really that cute at all. But of course, I couldn't say that.

"Oh, she's adorable!" I responded, wanting to mean it. In a few months I am sure she would be adorable, too. But right now Ricita looked like a chicken.

Jax took the baby from Cee-Saw and cradled her tenderly. Was he now her man? I didn't know.

But, was he?

He wanted to be, that was for sure. And he'd

certainly make a good father. Better than Rickee, at least. That was for sure too.

I was freaking out. And I mean freaking out!

The SAT will do that to you. The very next day, Saturday at eight A.M., I was scheduled to take the hugest test of my life.

"Theresa, what's the matter with you? Why you so tense?" Pops asked after dinner.

"I'm not tense!" I snapped.

"Then why do you keep combing your hair so hard? You yankin' it so much, you're gonna make yourself bald."

"Bald would be an improvement over the nappy mess she usually got goin' on."

"Shut up, Teddy!"

"Theresa's taking the SAT tomorrow," my mother told Pops.

"What's the SQV?"

"The S-A-T!" my mother repeated loudly so that Pops could understand. His hearing problem sometimes drove us all crazy.

"Oh, tomorrow? Hey, I got a great idea," Pops said, rising from his chair. "How 'bout I take you for a scoop of ice cream to bring ya some good luck."

"She does not need ice cream for good luck."

"Now how you know that, woman? Some cookies 'n' cream might just be the thing she needs in order to kick some butt."

"There will be no ice cream," my mother said firmly.

"Dang, woman, why you always messing with superstitions?" Pops said as he sat back down.

"Why are you always messing with your high cholesterol?"

"She's gonna fail, anyway," Teddy said.

"For your information, Mr. Dinglehead, the SAT is not a test you 'pass' or 'fail,' " I said to Teddy. "It's a test you just try to earn a good score on."

And I would only get three tries to do so. Once now, toward the end of my junior year, then two more times during the first semester of my senior year.

Three times and *that's all!* Everything was riding on these scores.

No wonder I felt tense. Lying in bed that Friday night all I could feel was *pressure!*

I set my alarm for 6:01 and went to bed at 9:30 to get a good night's rest.

At 11:00 P.M. I got a drink of water.

At 12:30 A.M. I took a pee.

At 12:45 A.M. I took another pee.

At 2:15 A.M. I made a peanut-butter and jelly sandwich. I didn't eat it, though. All I really wanted to do was make it.

At 3:00 A.M. I started to really panic!

Calm down, Tee, I told myself. You've done a lot to get into college. Quit freaking out, girl.

And I had done a lot to get into college. I'd taken all the required high school classes, plus I'd raised my GPA. However, it was still nothing astounding.

Astounding is a good word to know for the SAT. It means, "amazing or astonishing." Maybe *astounding* would be on the test tomorrow.

Maybe it wouldn't.

I'm gonna get killed! I'm gonna die! Oh my gracious!

Calm down, Tee-Ay. Calm down.

I took a deep breath. Breathing is supposed to be a good thing to do when you're panicking.

I thought about the other things I'd done, too, like extracurricular stuff. Extracurricular stuff is big on college applications. That's why I had joined a few clubs, to fatten up my resumé.

I had joined the Spanish Club and sold raspberry cookies in the halls for 50 cents a bag to raise money for a trip to Spain. By my estimation, I needed each kid in the high school to buy three bags of cookies a day four times a week for 286 days in a row in order to pay for the cost of my plane ticket. Yeah, Madrid and me would be hooking up sometime soon, that was for sure.

I had joined the Math Club and Science Club, too, even though I hated math and science. But since it would look good on my resumé, I did it. The only thing I had to do for them, anyway, was sell Twix and Snickers bars. The profits went to help with the cost of lab experiments we never got to conduct because of school safety issues with conducting lab experiments.

Some things in the world are just so stupid they can only happen in school.

But still they told me I had to sell candy bars to be a part of the club, so I sold candy bars. Who was I to cause drama? Plus, I did get a field trip out of it to the Museum of Science, and a full day out of class on a field trip is *always* worth it, so I guess there was a bright side.

The other club I joined was the Economics Club. For them we had to sell "ornate desktop globes." *Ornate* is another good word to know for the SAT. It means, "really fancy."

No one bought the globes though. I guess they weren't ornate enough. The Economics Club was the only organization on campus that year in and year out consistently lost money.

I wondered why the school was so damn broke all the time that they had to turn me into a candy pimp in order to have all their clubs function. We got about ninety-seven gajillion dollars to spend on missiles and tanks to blow up other countries, but if I don't find a ninth grader with a sweet tooth, my chemistry class isn't gonna function? What kinda sense does that make?

Aw, what difference? I'd qualified for club membership and my resumé was better as a result. Who cared if I was a sugar dealer? The fat kids on campus loved me. I was their source for breakfast.

At 7:21 A.M. my mother started shaking me like there was a fire.

"Theresa, wake up. Wake up! You're gonna be late."

Shit! I had overslept. *Why didn't my alarm go off? Didn't I set it for 6:01?*

I looked at my clock. I had set it for 6:01—P.M., not A.M.

What an idiot!

I tossed on a hat, took two seconds to brush my teeth, and ran out of the house.

My mother got me to the test site, a high school sixteen minutes in the opposite direction from my own school, at 7:58 A.M.

"Good luck!" she said as I slammed the door and ran off toward a sign written in magic marker that said SAT >>>.

When I turned the corner I saw a line of about twelve students and joined in. My heart thumped, my eyeballs still had a speck of sleep in them, and my stomach felt twitchy from nerves and a lack of food.

But at least I had made it.

Within the next ten minutes another six kids arrived. All of them wore hats, all of them looked like they still had specks of sleep in their eyes and, if I had to guess, I would say their hearts were pounding and their stomachs were twitchy too.

The last boy to arrive was a fat dude wearing a rock 'n' roll T-shirt. He showed up breathing so hard, it sounded like an elephant had been chasing him. The whole line turned to stare.

"Whew, made it," he said with a small chuckle, embarrassed at all the noise he had made. A drop of sweat ran down his cheek and I noticed a layer of yellow scum across his braces. It looked like this dude was so late, he hadn't even had a chance to brush his teeth.

Gross!

I turned around, took out my student ID, and

faced the front of the line. The last thing I wanted to do was smell his breath.

Dear God, please don't let Mr. Yellow Scummy Braces sit next to me.

God, it turns out, had a different seating location for me in mind. Right next to Mrs. Bill Gates, the smartest, nerdiest, dorkiest-looking white girl I had ever seen.

Of course she wore glasses. Of course she had a sweater. Of course she had all her pencils and erasers and ID and admission ticket and calculator lined up neatly on her desk.

Calculator?

"We can use those?" I asked.

"Of course, on the math section," she answered. "Handheld minicomputers or laptops are not allowed, but basic calculators are permitted."

She double-checked to make sure her batteries were working. Yep, just fine.

Gulp. I didn't know you were allowed to use calculators.

"Good morning, ladies and gentleman," I heard the voice of an adult say from the front of the room. "Welcome to the SAT. Please have your picture ID and admission ticket placed on top of your desk."

I took a deep breath.

Here we go.

. . .

There were a lot of tough questions on the SAT. On some of the sections I ran out of time. A calculator would have helped for sure, but the math section was loaded with stuff that I had to solve in my cranium, anyway.

Unfortunately, about two-thirds of the way through the test, my cranium got fuzzy from too much thinking. Words were blurry. Numbers were confusing. And the whole test seemed designed as if it were one big trick trying to fool me at every corner. And that essay section . . . What the hell was that about?

Other than that, I thought I did a pretty okay job, though. Overall, that is.

Aw, who was I kidding? It was a monster and I had been fed to the dragons.

Well, I thought as I walked down the halls of my school on Monday, At least I'm a member of the Science, Math, Spanish, and Economics clubs.

"Yo, cookie girl, how much them raspberry things?"

"Fifty cents."

"Gimme two."

As the ninth-grader handed me a dollar I saw Devon Hampton.

"Hey-hey, Dev."

"What's up, Tee-Ay. You selling raspberries?"

"For the Spanish Club."

He laughed. "Got my Snickers right here," Dev said, pointing to his backpack. "AP Calculus Club."

We walked down the hall in the same direction.

"How'd you do on the SAT this weekend?" I asked.

"Didn't take it."

Huh?

"What you mean, you didn't take it? You don't want to go to college?"

"Of course, but the SAT is a test you gotta "crack." You can't just take it. There's all sorts of study secrets and tricks a person's gotta know to do well."

"Secrets and tricks?"

"Man, all those kids on the West Side, they take special classes, have private tutors, and spend months getting extra assistance to learn the ins and outs of the test. Unless you've done all this prep work—'cause the test ain't *all* about knowledge but a lot about strategy, too—it's like playing a game of cards against a loaded deck."

"A loaded deck?"

"A loaded deck. And if you haven't taken any special classes or anything, you're cooked before you even face question number one."

"Jeez," I said. "I had no idea."

"Most students like us don't. We just sign up and go take the thing 'cause we're told to do so and then we get killed. That's why folks who go to schools like this one usually do so bad. We're set up to fail and we're too stupid to even know it."

My stomach sank. Devon was talking about me.

"Up to now, I've only taken the PSAT. It's good practice and gave me a solid sense of where I'll be."

"I mean, I knew you had to study, but . . . How much do these private tutors and special classes cost?"

"Like, about a thousand dollars."

"A thousand dollars? My parents don't have a thousand dollars to spend on this."

"Mine neither," Dev answered. "But there are books for sale for, like, twenty-five dollars. Or you can go to the library. Libraries have all the stuff you need and they're free."

"Free is good."

"There's free stuff on the Internet, too. Check out www.FreeSATessayPrep.com—they have a ton of awesome stuff on just the essay-writing section alone and it's really good."

When I went home I checked the Web site Dev had told me about. It was true—there was a lot of really good stuff available on the Web at no charge. Dang, I wished I had known that earlier.

As I looked at my grades for the end of my junior year I realized that really, they weren't so bad. After all, it was the first time in forever that I hadn't gotten any C's.

A   Honors English
B   Honors Algebra II
A   Spanish III
A   Computers
B–   Honors American History
B–   Honors Chemistry

But still, I wasn't breaking any academic records either.

Some peeps go to Hawaii for their summer vacation. Other peeps go to Europe. 'Round my 'hood, some peeps go to jail. Me, I decided to go somewhere unusual for summer vacation as well.

To the local library.

No, I wouldn't be needin' suntan lotion, but at least I'd be joined by my two new best friends: the *SAT Prep Guide* and Devon Hampton.

18

At first it was weird having a boy as such a tight friend. But I discovered that there were all sorts of things I felt comfortable telling Devon that I had never felt good about discussing with any of my girlfriends, not even Sonia. It was as if I could show him a side of myself I had never shown to any one before and be *real* about it. And it wasn't about sex either, though I certainly thought Devon was cute.

I just didn't want to spoil our friendship with romance. And though we never talked about it, I had a feeling he felt the same way. We just became great friends. Nothing more.

Matter of fact, we even teased each other about trying to hook up one another with other people we came into contact with. We made up our own little game called Library Hookup.

Essentially, before we would start to study every day, each of us had to match the other with a mate. Sometimes we'd waste twenty-five minutes scanning the library for the nastiest, funkiest, most stank-breath—looking stranger we could find. Then we'd make up stories for each other about how happy their married life in the future would be, with their spouse scooping out their belly button cheese onto Q-Tips that they'd carelessly leave by the sink, and have kids who would turn out like wicked rodents with buck teeth and hooked noses, stuff like that. Libraries are supposed to be quiet places, and the ladies who worked there had to come and shush us from laughing all the time, but the smiles helped offset the hard prep work we were doing for the SAT. Sure, we joked around a lot. But for at least three hours every day, we studied, too.

After all, neither of us had $1,000 for SAT test prep and damn, did I need the work. I was almost too embarrassed to even show Devon my results from my first attempt on the test when I got them in the mail. I had scored a 460 on the Reading, a 530 on the Writing, and a 390 on the Math. My grand total for all three sections was a 1380. The average score for incoming freshman at USC was 1900. I felt like a loser/moron/idiot/worthless piece of crap. Dev tried to cheer me up.

"Don't sweat it, Tee. It was just your first time. We'll get your scores up."

I smiled through my tears and shame. Devon was the nicest person I had ever met.

"And then your life with Huang-lo, the dude in the

corner, will be happy and content and filled with lots of adorable, cuddly little babies."

I turned my head to see who Devon was referring to. It was the fattest man I'd ever seen. He was so round, he looked like a four-hundred-pound baked potato wearing dress shoes. His sweaty black hair and thick Coke-bottle glasses, the pimples on the back of his neck, and the combination of both belt and suspenders (a major no-no in the world of fashion) had me do not one, but two, double takes.

Oh my gracious!

"Dang, he's so fat," Devon added, "I bet if you kick him in the butt a bag of chocolate-chip cookies would fall out of his ass."

I laughed so hard, I snorted. Mr. Baked Potato wobbled over to the magazine rack.

"Oh, I'm sure you'll have many nights of marital bliss," Devon said, laughing, rubbing it in. "Much romance and passion." Suddenly, my 1390 didn't seem so bad and I felt like there was hope for the future.

"Sssshhh!" said a librarian. "We're happy to have you here, but please remember to be considerate of others."

"Sorry," I answered, trying to cover up my smile.

Those librarians must have *sssshhh*ed me another ten thousand times before the summer ended. But, I have to admit, they were always cool about it. Plus, every time I had a question, the librarians were really helpful. I guess I'd expected them all to be these really old ladies who farted dust and snapped at people from morning to night. Truth is, they were completely the opposite. Librarians were nice, smart, and friendly.

But still, I bet they weren't bummed when the "back to school" season came around and all us pain-in-the-butt kids cleared out. That was *fo' sure!*

19

On my first day of senior year I walked through the front gate and saw a new crew of hip-hoppers and beat-boxers flowing rhymes by the fence. I paused for a moment to hear 'em bust their best stuff.

MixMaster Mytch was no longer around. He had dropped out. Rumor 'round the 'hood said he was on the verge of signing a major record deal. It wasn't the same without him. I mean, some of these peeps by the fence were okay, but others sucked.

Hmmvvvzzz! Hmmvvvzzz! Hmmvvvzzz!

And of course, none of them moved an inch toward class at the sound of the first bell. But did they need to get to class? Oh, hell yeah.

I mean, some of those fools only had a fourth-grade reading level. That's fine if you're in fourth grade, but these peeps were fifteen and sixteen years old. I guess they thought since they could flow a few rhymes they were gonna be international hip-hop superstars one day, bringing home the big dollar bills.

Yeah, right.

There was no way that all nine of these dudes were each going to have a hit on the charts. The math just didn't add up. And I knew math. I'd just spent the whole freakin' summer studying it for the SAT.

However, the peeps who weren't going for the sweet record contract had a plan too—the NBA. Don't matter that not a damn one of them was taller than five-eleven, they still thought that the League would one day be theirs. Even the shortest boy believed it. He was five-foot-six, 211 pounds, and fat as a fried chicken. That's why they called him KFC.

"My name is KFC,
I love to par-tee!
One, two, three—
All the ladies love me!"

Rappers, hip-hoppers, and ballers, that was the plan for way too many folks at my school, particularly way too many of the black folks. Why didn't they wake up? Endorsement deals, shoes contracts, and bling-bling jewelry hadn't been locked down for their futures yet. Matter of fact, there was a better chance that one day in their futures they'd be locked up. What else happens to a peep who ain't got no education and doesn't make it in the League or the Biz?

Low-wage jobs, drugs, or jail—that's what happens. It happened all the time to peeps in my 'hood. I couldn't even stand to watch the folks by the fence anymore. By not going to class they were sacrificing their own futures and were too stupid to even realize it.

I grabbed my backpack, double-checked my class schedule, and made my way toward first period. I had somewhere to get to.

"Hey-hey, fine sista, don't you wanna stick around and listen to me bust some mo' of my flows?"

"Excuse me? Are you talking to me?" I asked.

"O' course I'm talkin' to you, bay-bee. This is KFC and I am all about da luv."

I could not believe this little freshman was trying to run some game on me.

"I'm going to class. And you should be, too."

"School's for fools, sweet sista, and I got me much planz that are bigger than dis 'round here."

I paused. "Plans like what?" I asked.

KFC took this as an invitation to come get a rap in with me. He winked at his friends, jogged over from the fence, and threw his arm around my shoulder.

"Why don'tcha gimme your digits and you and me can chat about my big planz some time," he said with a superwide smile.

KFC looked back again at his crew, thinking he was *all that*. I tossed his arm off my shoulder.

"With those weak rhymes, you need to get your little bowling-ball ass to class, maybe think about being an accountant or something someday."

I walked away. Behind me I heard his peeps bust out laughing.

"Aw, homie, she broke yo' ass ba-a-ad!"

KFC, needing to get the last word in, shouted at me after I was fifteen feet away.

"You ain't nothin' but a hater! Hatin' on a young black man's dreams! That's the problem with all ya'll sistas these days. You don't know how to support a man, bitch!"

Hoist is a good word to know for the SAT. It means, "to lift or raise."

And that's what I did. Without bothering to turn around, I hoisted my middle finger in the air and gave KFC a wave good-bye.

Like I said, I had to get to class, and the best part about it, which I knew for one-hundred-percent certain, is that it would *not* be a class taught by Wardin.

Because Wardin was no longer a teacher at our school.

He was a guidance counselor, the one in charge of College-bound Advisement.

Whatever.

I never interacted with the counselors 'round here anyway and I certainly didn't see a reason for me to start doing so now that the punk of all punks was running the show.

Yep, Wardin was out of my life—for good.

Thank the Lord in heaven.

As I cruised toward Calculus, taught this year by the Turkey Baster, I finally understood why seniors were the only students in the school who got color pictures in the yearbook. Every activity, every dance, practically every event would revolve around us, our memories and our graduation. Being in twelfth grade meant being the big fish in the campus pond in a way I had never understood until I became one. Us seniors owned the school.

Yet, I was already looking forward to leaving this place, even though it was only the first day of class. I mean, sure, I had some decent friends, but there's a lot of cliques of people I had never really cliqued with. Peeps always be in each other's business too. How many times can I look over at Angela and Stephanee and feel like they are superior to me just because they're prettier and their families have more money and all the guys in the school would do anything to sleep with them? I sure hope the rest of life after high school isn't so immature.

I passed by the candy machines, where three boys were buying their breakfast.

"Yo, lemme borrow a dolla' to get me a soda, homes."

"Fool, you still owe me three dollas from last week."

"I'm-a get you back, homes. Come on."

"Dis my lunch money, fool. You better hook me up wit' some chips or somethin' later."

"We'll handle it, homes. We'll handle it."

The dude gave the other guy a dollar and their lunch plans were set. I was jealous. I had no lunch plans. Sonia had transferred to Home Studies.

Home Studies was a program that allowed students to work on weekly assignments at home and then turn them in to the district office by the end of the week. Sure, Sonia'd be able to earn a degree, but most of the students who moved to Home Studies ended up not graduating. There's paperwork to be done, a few extra tests that have to be taken, and the Home Study office is only open from Monday through Thursday, nine A.M. until two P.M.—which is fine, 'cause a lot of Home Studies students go to Juvenile Court on Friday or meet with their P.O. in the afternoons. Plus, the people who work in the Home Studies office are weak. Most of them are former classroom teachers who are burned out, but since they're only a year or two away from retirement, they take a position in Home Studies because the hours are shorter and the workload is a lot less. What do they care if they lose an important file or some gangbanger doesn't learn how to reduce a fraction properly? In eighteen months, they'll be retired and on full pension.

Naw, Home Studies is *not* a place where students get maximum education, that's *fo' sure!* And why had Sonia transferred there? Because of the F word . . . *familia.*

Since I had no one to share french fries with by the flagpole I decided I'd spend most of my lunchtimes in the library. Sure, there'd be times when I'd hang with other seniors and dress up in the goofy outfits on Hippie Day and do stuff like that, but in the library I'd be able to access SAT Web sites or use the materials our school has to prep for all the college things a senior needs to do. That's another thing about being a senior: there's a lot less time to fool around. I could already tell that for each extra minute I seemed to have, I'd have two minutes worth of stuff to do.

Yep, I could see that senior year meant *pressure!* After all, the whole college application process was a Beast with a capital B. Unless, of course, you're on the cover of the most prestigious high school football recruiting magazine in the country. Then things probably weren't so tough.

When I walked into the library at lunch I didn't even want to read the article. I told myself I wouldn't read the article. Not even glance at it. But how couldn't I? Everyone else on the planet had. Basically, the cover story gave a full rundown on the "glorious Rickee Dunston." He'd grown to six foot three and 220 pounds, and although he was the size of a linebacker, he had the speed and cover skills of a cornerback. *Blah, blah, blah.* He hit so hard in the secondary, sportswriters had nicknamed him the Freight Train. *Blah, blah, blah.* He'd "grown up in tough circumstances but managed to survive the streets and make good choices in his life." *Yeah, real deep, investigative reporting going on there.* Ninety-six colleges were interested in offering him a full, one-hundred-percent paid scholarship to play football for their university. *Blah, blah, blah.*

But Rickee had narrowed his choices to three schools: Oklahoma University, Notre Dame, and USC.

USC? No, not USC! Oh my gracious!

I reread the magazine to make sure. Yep, it said USC.

Dev walked over just as this realization washed over me and could immediately tell I was despondent.

Despondent is a good word to know for the SAT. It means, "really bummed out." It is an antonym to the word *exhilarated*.

Being able to define words in terms of their

opposites is a helpful way to tackle tough vocabulary on the SAT. I had learned that over the summer while studying with Devon.

"Hey-hey, Tee-Ay. What's up?"

"I'm despondent."

Dev laughed. "Good word."

"Naw, I'm serious," I said, tossing the magazine on the table. "Some stuff just ain't fair."

Devon looked at me and saw I was serious. I was about to cry.

"Hey, I got a game," he said trying to make me feel better. "Tell me one thing about yourself that no one at our high school knows and I'll—"

"Dev, I don't feel like—"

"What's the matter, you don't trust me with a secret?"

"No, it ain't that, it's just—"

"What?"

I looked up. He had soft eyes. *Aw, what the heck.*

"Okay—but you gotta tell me something, too, right?"

"Deal," he said, and we *slap-slap-bump*ed on it.

"I want to go to the University of Southern California," I said.

"Who doesn't?" Dev responded.

"Naw, I'm serious, Devon. I desperately want to

go. Like, ever since sixth grade my only goal in life has been to get accepted to USC. It's the ultimate, deepest dream in my entire universe."

"Wow, you're more ambitious than I thought."

"I never told no one before 'cause our school is full of haters and they'd just try to bring me down. But this is something I have been dreaming about for years. No one else knows."

Devon spied the magazine with Rickee on the cover. "Isn't Rickee thinking about SC?"

"Don't remind me," I replied. "It's a lot easier for football players to get into college no matter where they go to school, especially if they are athletic studs. You better not mention nothing, Dev," I threatened. "I'm serious. Ain't nothing worse than when peeps be laughing at your dreams."

"I won't say a word, I promise," he said to me. "But *dang*, USC—that's the big time right there."

"What, you don't think I'm smart enough?"

Devon paused.

"Naw, girl, I think you got all kinds of skillz you don't even know about yourself."

I looked away, avoiding that type of soul-to-soul eye contact a person can make when they look too deeply into another person's eyes.

"Now you," I said.

"Naw, I don't wanna play anymore. See ya later, Tee. Gotta go."

He grabbed his stuff and walked out of the library.

Aw, hell no!

"Devon Hampton, come back here right now!" I said as I chased him down.

I caught up to him by the bench outside.

"Okay, okay," he answered with a grin when I grabbed him. He checked to make sure no one was anywhere near us and pulled me around the corner by the stairs. He leaned forward, practically whispering in my ear. My blood got hot.

Oh my gracious, what was he about to say?

I paused—tense, excited and hopeful.

"I don't know karate."

"What?"

"I don't know karate."

"You don't know karate? But—"

"Sssshhh!" he said, looking around to make sure no one could hear.

"You're lying. Tell me something real."

"Naw, it's the truth. I don't know a damn kick or a punch or a chop or nothing. Not a bit."

"But the whole school thinks you know kung fu."

"I know," he said with a sneaky smile.

I shook my head and stared at him. I could see he

was telling me the truth. A giant grin broke out across my face.

"But why? I don't get it."

"See, a long time ago I got my momma to buy me this T-shirt that said 'Shaolin kung fu' on it. I didn't know anything about Shaolin kung fu, I just liked the cool dragon on the back. When I wore the shirt to school on the first day of fourth grade—I mean, you just had to wear fresh clothes on the first day of school in fourth grade—people automatically assumed I knew karate."

"So you never told anyone?"

"Better than that, I've bought a new Shaolin kung fu T-shirt every year since then and made sure to wear it on the first week of classes ever since. Ain't nobody ever messed with me my whole life. Like you said, we got a bunch of haters at this school. You do good in class and they'll want to take you down."

"You mean if someone messed with you right now, they wouldn't get blasted into a million little pieces."

"Naw," he grinned. "I hate violence."

I laughed and let one of those embarrassing snorts escape from my nose.

"Then where do you be going every Tuesday and Thursday afternoon?"

"Dance class."

"Dance class?"

"Yeah, rhythm tap. Old school. Been studyin' it for years. What can I say, I like to bust moves." Devon did a little wiggle and ripped off a fresh *ta-bamm!* with his heels.

Dang, he was good. But dance class? *Oh my gracious!*

"You know you can't tell anyone, right?" he said to me.

"Yeah, I know," I said and we *slap-slap-bump*ed a high five on the down low. Now each of us knew the other's secrets. I would do anything to go to USC, and Devon was a kung fu–less tap dancer who had the whole school fooled into believing he was Bruce Lee.

20

I didn't miss one day of school—not one period of class, not one homework assignment, not nothing for the first two months of senior year.

Even when Pops had a heart attack.

I got the news on a Friday after school that my father had suffered "a mild cardiac arrest" and within forty-five minutes I was at the hospital.

Pops was sitting up in bed with a tube in his nose. Machines bleeped with his vital signs. He looked tired but okay other than that.

"It's not that uncommon for black males over the age of fifty to suffer such incidents," his doctor informed us. "Too much salt, too much sugar, too much fried food."

My mother glared at Pops as the doctor described exactly the things she always nagged him about.

"Heart disease happens to be the number-one killer of African American males over the age of twenty-five," he added.

"What's the number one killer of African American males *under* the age of twenty-five?" I asked innocently enough.

"Murder," the doctor replied. "Black-on-black violence."

"Oh," I answered.

The room got silent.

"Hey, this is the same hospital I was in."

Everyone turned—it was Andre. He had jumped a flight from Stanford, which was only about an hour north. He rushed to the bed to give Pops a hug. Andre and my mother had already spoken about a hundred times by cellie, so he knew that there was no need to be panicked, but still, I could see, he was glad to be able to hug Pops and make sure for himself.

"And I've got good news, Pops. The Salisbury steak here is terrible."

"How's that good news?" Pops asked. The tube in his nose looked uncomfortable.

"'Cause you're not gonna be allowed to eat it anyway."

"That's right," my mother added. "No more red meat. No more salt. And definitely, no more ice cream."

"Is that true, doc? No more ice cream?" Pops asked.

"No, you can have ice cream, Mr. Anderson," the

doctor replied. My mother looked at him with a face full of shock.

"Unless, of course, you want to live," he added.

Mom smiled. Pops frowned. Teddy stared at the bleeps on the EKG machine.

"The pattern shifts every four cycles."

"Very perceptive, young man. That's correct." The doctor smiled and patted Teddy on the shoulder. "Maybe you'll become a doctor one day."

"Naw, I got bigger plans than that," Teddy replied.

"*Teddy*," my mother said. "I'm sorry, doctor, he didn't mean to be rude."

Teddy sat back down, bored with looking at the machines now that he had cracked their mystery. The doctor faked a smile.

"I'm going to keep him overnight for observation, but if everything maintains the way I think it will, he can go home in the morning."

"Thank you, doctor."

"Yeah, thanks, doc."

The doctor left the room and Andre bonked Teddy on the top of his head.

"What? It's true," Teddy said.

"You need to learn some manners," Andre replied.

And just as the doctor had said, Pops came home the next day.

• • •

It's amazing how much more I knew about the SAT the second time I took it. First of all, I slept with two alarm clocks next to my bed. Plus I had my mother set hers so that she'd be up by 5:45 A.M., too.

Showing up sleepy was no way to start off the day.

Okay, okay, having Devon call the house at 5:48 A.M. just to be on the safe side might have been a bit excessive—and I apologized to Pops about a thousand times for the phone ringing so early—but hey, I couldn't risk oversleeping again. Or running out of mental energy. That's why I had eggs, toast, and fresh raspberries before I stepped out of my front door. Devon had told me a hundred times that having mental fuel in the tank—a.k.a. breakfast—was a big part of proper strategy.

Proper strategy also meant wearing a watch to stay aware of the time, skipping superhard questions to concentrate on the ones I had a better chance of answering, using the process of elimination to get rid of wrong answers, knowing the directions beforehand so I didn't waste time reading them, understanding when to guess, knowing that questions in most sections went from easy to hard, making sure my essay had a thesis, topic sentences for each paragraph, vivid details, a point of view, solid structure, minimal grammatical mistakes, and—*whew!*

Strategy really could make a huge difference on this test and most of this strategy stuff had very little to do with measuring my intelligence. However, without knowing these things, there was just no way to do well.

And *dang*, I sure knew a lot. I mean I hadn't even looked at a single question yet, but already I knew I was going to get a higher score. All because I had a strategy. And a calculator. Of course, I couldn't forget that.

When I found out that Dev and I had been assigned to the same testing location, my confidence grew even more. Sure, it meant we had to travel to a high school on the West Side, but since Dev had his own car, getting there would be no problem.

Dev's mother had scraped together enough money a few months before to get him an old Toyota Corolla, and even though it had no horsepower and a dented roof, Dev loved it like a Rolls-Royce.

My own mother wouldn't so much as let me roll down the windows in her car, much less drive it, even though I already had my license and had passed the test the first time with a great score.

I didn't understand why my mother couldn't hook me up. She had just gotten yet another promotion at the bank—*dang*, they must really love her—but none of those dollar bills she was bringing in ever seemed to roll my way.

Dev pulled up to the front of my house just as the sun was rising. The peacefulness of the early morning can be kinda cool sometimes. Even though it wasn't the greatest car in the world he was driving, I was grateful for the ride—but a bit jealous, too.

"You fill up with mental fuel?" he asked as I climbed into the front seat. By "mental fuel" he didn't mean candy bars and junk food either.

"All good," I answered.

"Then let's do this," he said, as if we were both soldiers and it was time to go to war.

We *slap-slap-bump*ed a high five on the down low and Dev put a hard-bumpin' beat on the boom box in the backseat. His car didn't have a stereo. Some fools at school had stolen it while his wheels were parked in the student parking lot.

But now wasn't a time to think about the haters. It was a time to rise above, and a boom box spittin' hard beats was plenty good enough for both me and him.

After all, it was wartime.

• • •

"*Dang*, look at this place," I said as we walked onto the West Side's campus. "Look at all this grass."

"Place is pretty sweet, huh?"

Dev told me about how this school had a swimming pool, offered cinema classes, and had won the state's Mock Trial competition three out of the past five years. Impressive. But I still couldn't get over all the grass. I just loved the fact that there was so much space for students to kick back all over campus and chill. The whole place felt relaxed. Heck, there wasn't even a front gate for security. Or tagging.

"Goodness, Jax would have a field day bombing over here," I said to Dev as we followed the signs pointing us to where we needed to go. "What's the matter, white people don't know about graffiti?" I said with a laugh. Devon didn't answer. "Or maybe their janitors are just about a hundred times better than ours, huh?"

"Maybe the students just take pride in their school," Dev said.

"Oh," I responded.

We walked the rest of the way in silence. In a thousand different ways, the West Side was a different world.

As we walked along I thought about how lucky I was to have a friend like Devon in my life. Without knowing all the stuff about strategy he had taught me, there was no way I could have done well. That's what he meant when he had said the deck was loaded against students like us. In high schools like this one on the West Side, everyone knew this stuff. In high schools like the one we attended, you had to figure it out for yourself.

And just as I thought I would, when I finished the test after almost four hours of hard work, I *knew* my scores had risen. By a lot.

"How'd you do?" I asked Devon as we walked back to the parking lot.

"I think I did all right," he responded.

Turns out Devon scored a 2170. Only brainiacs get over the 2100 level. Only geniuses break into the 2200s. A perfect score is 2400, and almost no one gets a *perfect* score. Devon's digits were off the hook— and on his first try. I was so proud of him.

And so bummed with myself. I had only scored a 1710.

A 1710 was more than a 300-point jump in my scores—a *huge* leap—but still, they weren't good enough to get me into USC. Not even close. USC's average SAT score was 1900. I needed almost 200 more points.

The old me would have felt like crying. The new

me looked up at my posters, one of Tupac, one [
Malcolm X, and knew I just had to work harder. I sti
had one more chance to take the test again, and feeling
sorry for myself wasn't gonna do anyone any good.

Students who get into top colleges rise up to chal-
lenges, I told myself. They don't get down on themselves—they work harder.

Yep, I would take the test again.

So would Devon, he told me one afternoon

"Why?" I asked. "With your GPA and these SATs,
you can pretty much go to any school in the country."

"I can do better," he answered.

"What, you trying to get into Harvard?" I joked.

"Uh-huh," he answered.

"You wanna go to Harvard?" I said in shock.

"Yeah, or maybe Princeton. I don't know. But the
East Coast is sweet and would be a tight place to go to
college. I'm pretty sure Harvard is my number one."

"So you're only applying to two schools, Harvard
and Princeton?"

"Naw, you gotta apply to more than that—who
knows what can happen? I'm applying to Georgetown,
NYU, Yale, and . . ." He paused.

"Where?" I asked.

"USC," he answered. "It's my one West Coast
school. I hope that's okay, Tee. That college is tight."

"Of course it is," I responded. I wanted to be happy for him—I really did. But a part of me hurt bad on the inside. With the kind of student he was, I knew Devon would get into USC no problem. I also knew that it was looking like I wouldn't.

"Hey, it ain't over, Tee. You still got another chance."

"Yeah," I said. But I knew he was just trying to make me feel better.

When I got home I sank into my bed and stared at the posters of Malcolm and Tupac. Sometimes it was tough to stay positive.

The other major part of applying to a college is the application essay. Basically, the point is to tell the school everything there is to know about you and your entire life in a page and a half. *Yeah, right.*

It's like a homework assignment with the consequences of a nuclear bomb. Some peeps spent two months writing it. All schools pretty much asked the same questions though, so my plan was to write one really smoking essay for my top school—USC—and then adapt the essay so that it would fit in as an answer for all the other schools' essay questions I was going to have to write. Essentially, that's what most kids do anyway.

I'd heard that kids on the West Side had private

tutors who helped them with this, too. Rumor even had it that some kids simply paid cash for someone else to write their essay for them.

Of course, that could never be proven.

Heck, in my neighborhood, we were lucky to find someone to coach a Little League team much less write a college application essay.

Two different worlds. Two totally different worlds.

The essay question for the USC application was simple, yet kinda complicated.

Our lives are shaped by many factors, some of them small, some of them significant and unforgettable. Please write a brief essay about how an event, an encounter, or a specific life experience has helped shape your character and influence your perspective on life. This essay should be a maximum of 700 words. You may use the back of this page or attach additional sheets if necessary.

Basically a lot of good bullshit came to mind, but I had no idea what to write about.

I spent three weeks trying really hard to think about something. Finally—and I don't know why—I decided to ask for help.

"Mom, what life experience do I have?"

"Why do you ask?"

"'Cause I don't think I have any."

"You've got plenty, Theresa."

"I mean, good life experience. The kind that has helped shape my character and influence my perspective on life."

"Did you put the dishes away as I asked?"

"Yes, I put the dishes away. How about an encounter that has helped mold my viewpoint?"

"Viewpoint on what?"

"On life."

"You know, I think we're missing a fork. Did you take a fork with you to school and forget to bring it home?"

"No, I didn't take a fork."

"Are you sure?"

"Yes, I'm sure."

"Well, I still think we're missing one. What was it you asked about my viewpoint again?"

"Forget it, Mom."

I knew it was a dumb idea to ask for help. Especially hers.

"Wait, I want you to go to the store and get some broccoli. We need some green vegetables to go with dinner."

"I hate broccoli. Can't you make mashed potatoes?"

"Mashed potatoes are not green and they have too many carbohydrates for your father. Now go get some broccoli—take the car."

Did she just say "Take the car"?

"And come right home."

It was the first time ever I got to drive my mother's new car—which was not really that new anymore, but still, I didn't care. I was taking it.

I put the key in the ignition. The engine came to life with a quiet *hummm*.

Nice, I thought. Some old-person music played softly on the radio. I quickly turned the dial to the number-one hip-hop station in the nation.

And turned it up loud!

Moms wouldn't mind a few tunes, I thought as a fresh beat started to thump. I put the car in reverse and started to back out of the driveway.

Ho-o-o-onk!

"Whadya—crazy? Watch where you're goin'!"

"Ooops, my bad, sir."

I had better pay better attention.

After making a right at the light one of my favorite songs ever came on the radio and I turned up the volume even louder. Moms needed a subwoofer in the worst way.

But still, it was cool that she let me drive.

21

The pressure of being a senior was killing me. Every day, every moment, every everything just felt like this overwhelming responsibility, which was just *too* much. Goodness knows I needed the four-day Thanksgiving weekend, but still, I couldn't relax. The only thing on my mind was *pressure! I was freaking out!*

It got so bad, I caught a case of the "butterfingers." I mean, I dropped everything—pencils, notebooks, milk. Ain't nothing worse than dropping milk, because if you don't clean it up real good, it stinks up the place something fierce for days.

I don't even like milk. It grosses me out. The only time I ever use it is in my coffee. I must have been drinking four or five cups a day. That's too many. I know because my eyelids would occasionally twitch. *Twitching eyelids? Girl, you need a break.*

When I got to math class I dropped my calculator. The batteries rolled thirty feet across the floor. When I got to English class I dropped the dictionary. Then the thesaurus. Then *The Anthology of Great English Poets.*

Good thing I wasn't studying the art of making stained glass.

When I got to Honors Econ I dropped a chart about the risks of inflation. Then, when I went to pick it up, I knocked over the stapler on Debbie Mullen's desk and it landed on my pinkie finger.

Freakin' ouch!

While a stapler is not that heavy, when it falls from three feet above your hand and smashes you on the tip of the finger when you're not ready for the impact, the damn thing can hurt.

I looked down at my pinkie. It throbbed. And *jeez*, my nails looked like crap.

Dev approached from the other side of the room. "We gonna study this Saturday?" he asked.

"What the hell do I want to study this Saturday for? It's Thanksgiving weekend, can't we take a break? I mean I ain't even gonna get into the college I want and you probably already got into yours, so quit taking pity on me, huh, Dev?"

"Whoa."

I looked at my finger again. It continued to throb. I could tell an ugly bruise was going to form.

"No, Devon, I do not want to go study this Saturday."

Hmmvvvzzz! Hmmvvvzzz! Hmmvvvzzz!

The bell rang. I grabbed up my stuff, and walked out of class.

Thanksgiving weekend at our house always meant two things: a big turkey dinner and a family fight.

"*Mmm*, this is delicious, baby."

"And don't you dare put salt on it."

"*Aw, woman*," Pops responded. My father was feeling better, but he still added butter to his biscuits when Mom wasn't looking.

"Teddy, can you please stop tapping on the table?"

"I'm not tapping, Theresa. I'm doing Morse code."

He tapped some more.

"Can you please stop?" I repeated. "You're giving me a headache."

"Wanna know what I just spelled out?" he asked Tina.

"What?" she answered.

Teddy started tapping again,

"The . . . boo-gie . . . man . . . will . . . vi-sit . . . Ti-na . . . to-night."

It took Tina a moment to follow along, but when she did her eyes got huge and she got scared—real scared. Tina had been having nightmares lately and for the past week and a half she had gone to sleep in my parents' room because of the "noises."

Some of us thought the "noises" might be coming from her older brother, Teddy, but we couldn't prove it.

"Mo-o-om!" She started to cry.

"Teddy, why'd you do that to her?" I snapped.

"Can't we just have a nice Thanksgiving dinner?" my mother asked. "I know it's not the same without Andre here but . . ."

"Pass the gravy, please."

"No, you cannot have any more gravy!"

"Aw, woman."

"May I be excused?" I said, my head pounding. But it wasn't really a question. I was old enough now to leave the table whenever I wanted, so I got up and headed into the other room.

"I know you'll be back to help with the dishes."

"Of course," I answered as I walked away. "Of course."

"Come on, baby. Just a touch more gravy."

"No!"

I flopped on the couch and grabbed the remote control. The stupid Dallas Cowboys football game was on. I changed the station to the History Channel. It was a commercial.

I watched a dumb ad for a phone company about the spirit of Thanksgiving and reaching out to old friends. Then the craziest thing happened. A tear came to my eye. A real tear! I hadn't reached out to my old friends in over two months.

Dang, I miss my homegirls. I miss 'em bad.

"You cryin' from a commercial?" Teddy asked as he snatched the remote control from me. "What a wuss!"

Without asking, he flipped the station back to the football game. I decided not to pound his face into the floor over it. Let him watch his stupid game. I went to my room.

After closing the door behind me I looked in my secret savings drawer. It had been a really long time since I had worked at the movie theater and put any money in. All I had done lately was take money out. But I still had four twenty-dollar bills, a ten, a five, and three ones left.

I grabbed the twenties and started dialing my cellie.

The next morning at ten A.M. Cee-Saw, Sonia, and I were sitting side by side by side in Nancy's Nail Salon, having manicures, pedicures, and iced café mochas. My treat.

No, we were never Mousketeers or nothing like that, but as the three of us sat there soaking our feet and having our nails done, a huge layer of stress melted off each of us. It was just a different stress for each of us, that's all.

And the truth was, after I heard Cee talk about the three A.M. feedings and Sonia gripe about how sometimes it felt like other people in her house purposely avoided doing things because they knew she would eventually do them anyway, I realized my stress was much better than their stress. That was *fo' sure!*

Actually, I kinda felt sorry for them . . . and lucky for me. They had burdens. I had opportunities.

When I got home after having my toenails painted cotton-candy pink, I picked up my cellie and called Devon.

"Library tomorrow?"

"You know it," he answered.

I had never apologized for biting his head off, but he didn't hold it against me. He probably just thought it was PMS. That's the only good part about getting your period—you always have an excuse to be a real bitch. Well, that and the fact that it means you're not pregnant.

Devon and I worked hard in the library for the next three weeks. *Very hard.* Harder than I had ever worked in my entire life. We always stayed until closing time, when one of the librarians would announce over the PA: *"The library will be closing in fifteen minutes. Please proceed to the checkout counter. Thank you for visiting."*

"How many times have we heard that?" I asked as we packed up our stuff.

"Lots," he replied, folding over his notebook. "Hey, you fill out your FAFSA yet?"

"What's a FAFSA?"

"What's a FAFSA? It's only the most important form you have to fill out for college. Without it, you're not eligible for scholarships and financial aid. You haven't filled it out yet, have you?"

"Uh . . ."

"You'd better get on that, Tee."

"Where do I get it?"

"From the College Admissions Counselor, where else?"

Oh, great.

"Well, if it isn't Miss Theresa Anderson."

"Hi, Mr. Wardin."

I sat down and he pulled my file. I didn't ask him to pull my file, he just did it.

"A three-point-three-eight GPA—I see you have raised your grades since you were in my class," he commented. "Involved in a few campus clubs, too, I see. That was a pretty intelligent decision."

I didn't reply.

"Hmm, SATs, let's see. . . . Ooh, haven't really worked too hard there, have you?"

"I still have the December test."

"In eight days? Well, yes, but, how much can a student really improve in eight days? I imagine you're thinking of community college?"

Why did everything out that man's mouth sound like a put-down? I mean, talk about a hater—all this dude ever did was make me feel bad. All he ever did to any of the students was make them feel bad.

I *detested* him. I *loathed* him. I *abhorred* him. He was *despicable, abominable, insufferable, intolerable,* and *repulsive.* I went SAT crazy on his ass!

But just in my brain, of course. However, I did look him firmly in the eye.

"My plan is to go to USC."

I don't know what happened. I don't know why I said it. Really, it just came out. And how did he respond? With a chuckle, of course.

"The University of Southern California? Miss Theresa Anderson, maybe you are not familiar with the type of student top-tier universities are seeking. Maybe if you would have started focusing a bit earlier on school instead of your social life, you'd be in a better position right now. Unfortunately, however, *reality* is a word you need to understand when it comes to your future. At this juncture, my guess is the only way you'll be getting into USC is by transferring in after two years of community college. Two stellar years of community college, might I add, and you'll be lucky at that."

Mock is a good word to know for the SAT. It means "to ridicule and make fun of." I knew he'd just mock me. Wardin's whole career was all about mocking students.

"I just need a FAFSA," I said.

He gave it to me and I left.

What a punk.

Dev and I studied like mad for the next eight days. After all, that's what Malcolm and Tupac would have done.

On the morning of the SAT, Devon couldn't pick me up. Not because he didn't want to but because this time we'd been assigned to different testing locations.

Me, I was heading back to the West Side. Devon was assigned to a place closer around our 'hood. Who knew why certain people got placed where for the test? It was all random.

Luckily, my mother allowed me to take her car,

mostly because she didn't want to get up ridiculously early on a Saturday morning to drive me and then pick me up again.

"But come right home!" she said.

"Yes, Mom."

Devon and I made a plan to meet for "mental fuel" at 5:45 A.M. at Denny's. Denny's is always open.

I had scrambled egg whites, whole-wheat toast, and a sliced banana. Devon had a spinach omelet with an English muffin and hash browns. Both of us drank two cups of coffee. Dev treated.

"Now, remember," he said to me in the parking lot as we were getting ready to part ways. "No one question is worth any more than any other question, so don't get tripped up trying to crack something too difficult. Stick with your strategy."

"I will."

"And stay positive."

"I will."

"Remember, attack the test."

"I will," I said again.

He looked at his watch.

"Okay, time to do this. Got all your stuff?"

I pointed to my backpack. "All good. You?"

He pointed to his car. "All good."

"Well, here we go. Best of luck, Tee."

"You too, Dev." And we gave each other a hug.

A big hug. But there was more to it than that. I felt an energy between us, like some kind of sizzle of electricity that came from his body into mine. *Could it be . . . ?* No.

As I drove to the West Side I had one of those out-loud conversations with myself, the kind that crazy people have when they are talking to themselves and no one else is around to hear.

Oh, come on, girl. You got to focus! This is the SAT. Chance number three! Put that romance out of your head. Strategy, Tee-Ay. Think about strategy!

But it was no use. My whole drive to the West Side was filled with only one thought: *doin' da freak between da sheets* with Devon Hampton.

Focus, Tee-Ay, focus!

Fuzziness clouded my mind. Thoughts about holding hands and Valentine's Day and what kind of nose our baby would have should we ever get married floated through my brain. I don't even remember driving the car to the test site. It's like the vehicle was on automatic pilot while I daydreamed about romance.

However, once I parked and saw the sign that read SAT >>> I got it back together. Love would have to wait. Love always had to wait when it came to war. I learned that on the History Channel.

"Good morning, ladies and gentleman," I heard the voice of an adult say from the front of the room. "Welcome to the SAT. Please have your picture ID and admission ticket placed on top of your desk."

As I calmly placed all of my materials on my desk, I noticed a plump Hispanic boy sitting next to me, looking like he had just woken up six minutes before. He stared at my desk with his forehead crinkled.

"I didn't know we was allowed to use calculators."

I nodded my head. "As long as they don't have minicomputers in them."

"Oh," he replied.

I turned back around to face the front, calmly closed my eyes, and took three deep breaths. *Strategy, Tee-Ay. Stay calm. Stick to your strategy. Focus.*

I opened my eyes, feeling strong, refreshed, and confident. Then the idea of Devon popped into my head again.

And I felt even better. It would be a good day.

"How'd ya do?" Devon asked when we met up that afternoon.

"My best yet."

"Yeah?"

"Fo' sure!" I responded. "What's the word *reconcile* mean?"

"It means 'to fix up,' like 'to heal,'" Dev replied.

"Awesome! Got that one right. How'd you do?"

"I think I did okay," he replied. I didn't even know what that meant. A 2200? A 2350? A perfect score? Dev was not only shooting for Harvard, he was shooting for the big scholarship money that came with having elite SAT scores. "The essay writing is always a little challenging, though."

"Sure it is, Dev. Sure it is."

"You hungry?" he asked.

"Starved," I answered, looking down at my menu. "May I please have a cheeseburger with a side of avocado, no onions, extra tomato, and a side order of chili fries?"

"You got it, darling. And you?"

I looked at Dev. "You are not allowed to order 'mental fuel,'" I said. He grinned.

"Give me the same thing as my friend here, except no avocado, and double the cheese," Devon said. "And a strawberry milk shake, please," he added.

"Strawberry? Make mine chocolate," I said to the waitress as she scribbled down our orders and went to turn them in to the cook. "Don't you know anything about milk shakes? What's this strawberry nonsense?" I bounced up and down in my chair. "I've always wanted to bake a strawberry pie. Baking pies is something

my mom does to relax, but she's never made strawberry before. Maybe when I go home, I'll make a strawberry pie to relax."

I peeled the paper off my straw and blew real
hard, shooting the end of the tip toward Devon's
head, but my aim was off and it sailed crookedly
through the air, hit the window, and fell to the floor.

"Maybe you need to make a truckful of strawberry
pies," Devon said.

Truthfully, I was drained and exhausted, but it was
like I had this buzz of good vibes running through me
and couldn't sit still. I was tired but juiced up. There
was no way I could sleep but, *wow*, I really needed to
hit the pillow for about three days.

"Now comes the hard part," Devon said with a
sigh. "The wait."

"Yeah, I *ha-a-a-ate* the wait," I replied. "I mean, the
math is whack, the reading passages are *so-o-o-o* boring, and the twelve-letter vocabulary words that no
one uses in real life anyway are completely insane. But
the wait . . ."

"It's torture," Devon said, speaking my thoughts
exactly. "Four to six weeks to get your scores is
forever."

"I mean, a person works their butt off for months

and months preparing for the most important exam of their life and then they say, 'Chill, dude, give us four to six weeks and after that we'll let you know if you're going to have a future or not.'"

"It's just wrong," Dev replied. "You'd think with all these computers on the planet, they'd be able to do something about it."

"Arrrgghh! I am such a mess!" I said, shaking my head and neck and fingers to get some of the pent-up energy out of me. "Thank goodness winter break starts next week."

"Yeah, I'm going to Oakland for three weeks. What are you doing?"

Huh?

"Oakland?" I repeated. I had to play it chill. "What's in Oakland?" I asked softly as the waitress brought over our milk shakes. I wanted to dump mine on Devon's head.

"My cousin, Trey," he answered. "He's a bit on the wild side, but we've been tight since we were five. You know, Christmas, family, that kinda thing. Made the plans months ago."

Suddenly, all of the energy was sucked from my body and I stopped bouncing in my chair. Dev wasn't just informing me about a trip to Oakland, what Dev was really saying was that our "dee-veloping sit-u-ation" wasn't going to have a chance to "dee-velop" for at least three weeks.

"Yeah, I get it. That's cool. The family thing and all," I responded.

The SAT needed six weeks. Dev needed three weeks. This whole "needing weeks" thing was totally weak.

Our food came. I nibbled at a chili fry. "Want some ketchup?" he asked.

"Sure," I answered. But I wanted to pour that on his head, too.

We ate our food, the check came, and we split it.

"Good work today, Tee," Dev said as we walked to our cars.

"Thanks, Dev. Thanks for all your help." We hugged again, but this time without electricity. I headed home totally exhausted.

On the drive back to my house I thought about how at least I'd be able to focus on finishing all my college applications without distraction over the winter break. There was still a lot of work to be done, like calculating my unweighted GPA in core classes, getting copies of my parents' tax return, rounding up three letters of recommendation, that sort of thing. After all, everything was due in full by February 15 and college application deadlines are absolutely set in stone. You either make them or you don't—there are never any exceptions. Plus, I still had the application essays to write.

I had decided my basic topic would be how this whole process of studying for the SAT was a momentous moment in my life, and had taught me the valuable value of pursuing my dreams. Or something like that. I didn't have it all figured out yet. But I would be writing something about how triumphing on the SAT had taught me the true meaning of life. When I got my scores, I'd figure out the details.

I had no idea what Dev was going to write about. It didn't seem like he wanted to share it with me, so I didn't ask. Probably some super genius thing on how he would one day save the world from famine, poverty, disease, war, bad television shows, and people with body odor. I didn't even care what his stupid essay was going to be about. I mean, why should I care about *Mr. Oakland?*

I walked in the door of my house, tossed my stuff on the table, and took a four-hour nap. Then I woke up, drank a glass of orange juice, and went back to bed for another eleven hours.

The next thing I knew, Dev was gone to northern California. I decided to visit Ricita.

Thank goodness that girl no longer looked like a chicken. Matter of fact, she was cute, dressed in pink pajamas and fluffy socks. When I walked into the room she even smiled at me. Ain't nothing like a baby's smile to make your heart feel warm. And Ricita's glow seemed to be contagious.

Maybe it was all the bright colors in the apartment from all the kiddie stuff lying around, but Cee's house didn't feel as depressing as it had the last time I was there. Cee-Saw even seemed to be trying to roll forward with good vibes herself. She had even gotten a job.

Yeah, it was only part-time, but at least it was employment. She worked at Starbucks.

"Come by tomorrow and I'll hook you up with a latte," she said to me while Ricita sucked on her titty.

It was weird to watch a baby suck on my friend's titty, especially since Cee-Saw didn't think twice about whipping it out right in front of me to nurse her baby. I guess she saw me staring at her nipple. It was big and dark and round.

"Don't worry, I won't use this stuff," she said, looking at her boobie. "Breast-milk lattes are only on the kiddie menu."

We both laughed. Ricita continued to suck.

"Good deal, I'll be there."

"Come by around two."

"Perfect," I answered.

That morning, before I met Cee-Saw at Starbucks I went to score little Ricita a tiny present, maybe a rattle or something. I took the bus to the mini-mall.

"Mytch, is that you?"

It was the MixMaster.

"Yo-yo, how's it goin', homegirl?" he said, approaching. Was he collecting shopping carts in the parking lot?

"Hey, it's me, Tee-Ay," I said. I knew he didn't remember my name, but he tried to play it off like he did.

"Yeah, yeah, Tee-Ay, o' course. What's up?" He tugged at the yellow shirt of his supermarket uniform, trying to wear it like it was some kind of fresh and stylin' jersey he would have chosen to wear that morning even if he weren't headed to a minimum-wage job.

He gave me a hug, a bigger hug than our relationship really would have called for. I was the first to pull away.

"Things are good. Things are good. You still in school?"

"Yeah, senior year," I said.

"Sweet," he answered.

"How's the music biz?" I asked. After all, MixMaster Mytch was the most talented dude I had ever known. He had a tongue like a serpent.

Maybe I didn't really need to ask. After all, he was wearing a yellow supermarket T-shirt, collecting shopping carts in a parking lot.

"Things are workin', you know. They're workin'. I mean that record deal I was hoping for, well, it kinda didn't come like some peeps promised it would—there some real punks in the music biz—but things are good. I mean, I got some new stuff happenin' and I'm gonna make a demo pretty soon."

"Sounds cool," I said.

"Just a matter of time. A matter of time. Don't miss school at all, though, dat's fo' sure!"

"Not at all, huh?"

"Well, the peeps maybe. But not the teachers and all the hatin' they did on me."

"Mytchell!" a bossy-looking, dorky dude shouted from across the parking lot. "We need those carts. Chat time is over."

Mytch glared at his boss with a look of hate. "This just temporary, you know, till I get my demo done. Just a matter of time. Matter of time."

But what if it isn't temporary, Mytch? I mean, what if the music thing don't come through? Then what are you going to do, collect shopping carts in a parking lot for the rest of your life? I mean, that's what school and education is all about. People with degrees don't do this kind of stuff. People with degrees end up with real jobs and high-paying careers. I mean, what is your Plan with a capital P, dude? 'Cause I can't see it.

Well, that's what I wanted to ask him. Instead all I said was, "Cool." After all, he had to go. Customers needed carts.

"You take care o' yourself," I said.

"So," he asked before I walked off. "Can I get those digits or what?"

Asking me for my phone number caught me by surprise. A while back, I woulda given anything for this boy to ask me for my digits. But now, well, what about all those other girls he used to go with? Did he have any babies of his own floating around? Maybe a long time ago, I woulda melted at the thought of a date with MixMaster Mytch. But those days ain't these days.

"Naw, I kinda got a man, already," I said as I started toward the toy store. "But you take care and good luck with your music."

"Just a matter of time," he answered. "Just a matter of time."

"Yo, Mytchell. I am warning you!"

"I'm coming. *Shee-it!*"

303

I heard the clank of a couple of shopping carts behind me as I walked into the toy store. I hoped I hadn't come off like a hater to Mytch—'cause nothing is worse than when someone is hating on your dreams—but who doesn't want to be rich and famous and an international celebrity and *all dat*? The question is, what happens if you don't get there? Does it have to be a minimum-wage job at the supermarket collecting shopping carts?

I cruised up to a sista who was wearing a blue apron, standing behind the cash register and filing her nails. "Yes, can I help you?" she asked without looking up.

"Yeah, I need a rattle."

"Aisle eight," she answered.

"I'm looking for the kind that'll give a fatherless black baby a future," I added. "You got any of those?"

She put down her nail file.

"Girl, if we sold those, do you think I'd be workin' here?"

22

Every Valentine's Day throughout high school I'd been dateless. But this year, senior year, my unlucky streak was going to end.

I knew because I had just gotten a flower-gram from a secret admirer. But the identity of the secret admirer wasn't much of a secret. After all, who else would send a single rose with a sealed note asking, *Would you acquiesce to a resplendent rendezvous on the 14th evening of February?*

I had never had more fun looking up words in the dictionary. *Acquiesce* means "agree to." *Resplendent* means "dazzling." *Rendezvous* means "a meeting or date."

Devon's plan was to "rendezvous" at a superfancy restaurant where the food would be expensive, the portions would be small, and the table would be set with at least three forks. I eagerly "acquiesced" to this "resplendent" invitation.

"So you'll be my valentine?" he asked when I saw him on his way to the Big Brother Meeting for Special

Education Students. Devon was president of that club. Heck, he could have been president of the whole student body if he'd wanted, but he preferred to lay low and avoid the spotlight. But helping out the kids with disabilities was something he cared deeply about.

"I would love to be your valentine," I answered. "Blithesomely so."

"Blithesomely so?"

"Blithesomely so," I repeated.

"I'm gonna have to look that one up."

"Be my guest," I said. After all, it had taken me twenty minutes to come up with the damn word myself.

Hmmvvvzzz! Hmmvvvzzz! Hmmvvvzzz!

Ah, love was in the air.

"This FAFSA needs to be redone, it's all wrong."

Anything you wish, my dearest Mr. Wardin.

"I need you to go to the dry cleaners and the supermarket and then come home and chop two cups of onions before five o'clock."

Anything you wish, my dearest, beloved mother.

"Put it on channel eight—I wanna watch ESPN!"

Shove it up your ass with a flaming hot jalapeño pepper, Teddy!

After all, love only goes so far.

· · ·

For the next few days, I didn't see much of Devon around school, but I thought about him all the time. And I hoped he was thinking about me.

Then I got the envelope. My SAT scores had arrived.

It was Thursday, February 7. I marked it down on my planner before I opened my test results 'cause I wanted to remember this day always. The day my future arrived.

Hey, that's a good line to include somewhere in my application essay, I thought.

I trembled and my stomach churned. I wanted to pretend that the contents of this envelope weren't really that important to me, but they were. I knew it. Devon knew it. The University of Southern California knew it.

I used a letter opener to make a clean cut. It was the first time I had ever used a letter opener in my life. They actually work pretty well.

I scanned down . . . 1790.

A 1790? Oh my gracious, I had stunk it up! Was that right?

Fear raced through my veins. Maybe I was reading it wrong. No, it said 1790. There it was, all official. I would never get into USC, not with an SAT score that was more than a hundred points lower than the average accepted applicant's.

It's over. It's all over.

A tear came to my eye and my head sank. It really was all over.

I ditched school the next day. It was a Friday anyway and zillions of kids ditched on Fridays. So what if it was the first day of class I had missed all year? I mean, did anyone really care, anyway?

I stayed in bed, turned off my cellie, and tried to sleep away the pain. It didn't work, so I went to plan B and started eating buckets of ice cream.

"Theresa, are you all right?" my mother asked when she saw me working over my second pint of Häagen-Dazs that afternoon.

"I'm sick," I answered. "Please leave me alone." I stomped up to my bedroom and closed the door.

I was ashamed of myself, ashamed to tell my family. Most of all, I was ashamed to tell Devon. But I had to.

Finally, on Sunday night around ten o'clock I got up the courage to call him. I picked up my house phone and dialed, tears getting ready to fall from my eyes.

There was no answer on his cellie. My tears ended up not having a chance to rain. I didn't leave a message.

Since I had used the house phone to call Devon, I figured I'd go check my own cellie for messages. After all, I hadn't turned it on in three days. I'd missed a few calls.

Cee-Saw. Devon. Another one from Devon. Something about how he was taking his cousin from Oakland out on the town Saturday night. Cee-Saw. Cee-Saw again. Sonia hardly never called me anymore, I thought.

I tried Devon's cellie one more time at eleven-thirty. Still no answer. I went to bed, figuring I'd just rap with him at school the next day.

I ate some more ice cream before I went to sleep. So much cream and sugar in my stomach made me want to throw up. Or maybe I wanted to yak because I now had nothing to write my application essay about.

Shit! It was really over.

On Monday when I walked through the front gate of school I felt an air of weirdness on campus. None of the hip-hoppers and beat-boxers were spitting rhymes by the fence. I saw two of the vice principals whispering and walking with very purposeful strides.

Definitely, something was going on.

"Yo, what's the four-one-one 'round here?" I asked a little freshman.

"Some dude got capped on Saturday night."

"Who?" I asked

"Don't know. The valedictorian or some shit like that."

Oh my gracious! Devon Hampton had been shot.

23

At the hospital on Monday night I felt lost in a dream of tubes, medical machines, and eerie silence in the halls. Devon had caught a stray bullet in his neck thirty-seven hours before. He had yet to regain consciousness.

"It's touch and go whether or not he'll live," his mother informed me. Over the past day and a half she had cried enough tears to fill a lake.

The story was pretty simple, almost a cliché. Devon had gone out for the night with his cousin Trey from Oakland. Thinking he was tough, Trey had started "representin' Oak-town." Some boys from the East Side decided to shut him up. Gunshots were fired in a drive-by next to a burger joint and Devon caught a stray bullet in the neck. Trey escaped without a scratch. The shooters were still at large. The story didn't make the papers.

I thought about what Jax had said that one time about needing to die to make the local news. I thought about what the doctor had told me about black-on-black violence being the number-one cause of death for African American males under the age of twenty-five. I thought about how when my brother Andre was attacked by a gang of racists I was really too young to understand what it meant to be waiting forever for some kind of information in a hospital about someone you loved.

For two days I experienced fear, frustration, hurt, rage, and emptiness, over and over again, all in different, weird combinations. And while these emotions kept racing through me, switching and shifting and changing on a moment's notice without any warning, we waited for news from the doctors.

None came. There was no improvement, no deterioration, no nothing. Like waiting for my SAT results, it was torture.

Naw, this was nothing like the SAT. This was Real with a capital R.

There was nothing to do except stare at Devon as he lay there with tubes in him teetering on the brink of death. Watching the pain on the face of Devon's mom hurt my soul too.

It all became too much for me. Just *too* much.

On day three I decided to go get some air and wander around the hospital halls. Maybe seeing other sick people would make me feel better.

I know, it was a twisted idea, but my brain was fuzzy and clouded.

Most of the patients' doors on Devon's floor were closed. As I walked the hospital halls I tried to peek into some of the rooms that were open, but all I saw were blue shower-type curtains. I didn't have the guts to just walk into anybody's room, so I just kind of wandered.

I heard a voice say behind me, "Pardon me, comin' through." I stepped to the side to let a smiling older man who was carrying a giant heart-shaped balloon and a monster bouquet of flowers enter one of the rooms with a closed door. It looked like this guy had bought the whole damn flower shop.

At the nurses' station three ladies dressed in light yellow hospital uniforms stared at the door he had just entered with grins on their face.

"What's going on?" I asked.

"That lady he's going to see lost one of her breasts to cancer and still her husband shows up with all that stuff for Valentine's day. Just makes my heart melt."

"You know, no matter how much medicine we apply, there's nothing like love to cure the sick."

"That is so true," the other nurse answered. "That is so true."

I paused and looked back at the closed door.

Then I started to cry. Uncontrollably.

One of the ladies in yellow came around from behind the desk and hugged me. "There's gotta be something I can do," I said. "There's just gotta." Tears streamed down my face.

"The doctors are doing the best they can, honey. The best they can," she reassured me. "But if you really want to do something, think about helping his mom. That woman hasn't eaten a bite of food in three days."

"Good idea," I said as I wiped the tears from my face. I headed down to the hospital cafeteria to buy Ms. Hampton something to eat.

Unfortunately, the hospital food looked like, well—hospital food—and I didn't think she'd eat anything I'd buy her.

But I did come up with another idea. I raced back to Devon's room to get the keys.

"Back in an hour," I told Ms. Hampton. "Maybe less."

My plan was to get Devon's mom some fresh clothes, maybe grab Devon's favorite MJ 23 hat, bring the mail in, that type of thing. Personally, I'd gone home every night around nine o'clock, but Devon's mom had stayed 'round the clock in the room by Dev's bedside, ever since the moment she got there.

Some fresh stuff to wear would probably make her feel better.

I turned the key and opened the door. Their apartment was small but tidy. While I had never been here before, I could tell, though there was only the two of them living here, they shared a lot of love. The pictures all around said it all.

I brought in the mail, opened the fridge, and poured out a half-full container of milk. The expiration date had passed two days before and it was starting to stink.

Some Valentine's day, I thought as I turned my nose to avoid breathing in the nasty scent of the liquid, white goop. I was supposed to be chowing down on a fancy dinner in a ritzy restaurant with three forks and now I'm about to go through Ms. Hampton's dresser drawers and pick her out a clean pair of undies.

I tossed the empty milk carton into the garbage, tied up the bag, and put it by the door to throw it away in the Dumpster on the way out, then headed to Ms. Hampton's bedroom.

I opened a door, but it wasn't Ms. Hampton's

bedroom, it was Devon's. College application materials were everywhere. Harvard, Yale, Princeton, everything was filled out. But why weren't they mailed off?

Oh my gracious, I realized Devon hasn't finished his application essays yet.

I mean, I knew I'd been struggling with them, but Devon? I guess he meant to finish it this past week. I started looking through all the papers on his desk. *What a mess!*

I counted eleven different versions of Devon's essay, all of them half and three-quarters of the way finished, with another thirty-eight pages of notes, thoughts, ideas, scribbles, and jottings all over the place. It was a tornado of disorganized paperwork, virtually unusable the way it was. Pieces of this, parts of that—nothing fully assembled and yet a whole lot of potentially great material.

What's today? I thought. Oh yeah, Valentine's day. Duh. The application deadline was the next day. *Tomorrow!*

I threw some stuff in a bag, raced back to the hospital—still no news—and then dashed back to Devon's apartment.

I knew what I had to do. Luckily, Ms. Hampton had a pound of coffee in the freezer.

Screw my own application, I would write Devon's essay.

After all, Wardin was probably right. I needed to wake up to "reality." Since it looked like I would have to take the community college path to USC anyway, the reality was that the best way I could help Devon right now was to get him accepted into a university for the fall. If he lived.

Come on, Tee. Focus, girl. You can't think like that.

I set to work.

Tenacious is a good word to know for the SAT. It means, "persistent." A tenacious person never gives up, no matter what. As I read through all the work, sorted through all of Devon's ideas, organized all his notes, considered all of his achievements, and reflected upon the essay questions being asked I realized one very important thing.

This was impossible.

I only had nineteen hours to finish the entire thing and get a postmark. Plus, Devon was a more brilliant writer than I could ever hope to be. What I was about to do might not even be allowable—or legal. I didn't have any of Devon's passwords, so I couldn't apply online, and I had to go the old-school, snail-mail route, which many of the universities had tried to move away from in the past few years. In addition, my head was still conflicted about whether or not I should really be giving up on applying to USC myself. On top of that, every ten minutes I was staring and praying for my cellie to ring with good news about Devon's recovery. And I hadn't really had any sleep in four days. By the way, there was no milk for my coffee.

Then three images popped into my head: Malcolm, Tupac, and Devon. I would be Tenacious with a capital T. At least I could make coffee. Screw the milk!

Eight hours later at three o'clock in the morning I finally figured out what I would write about. At 5:25 A.M. I finished the first three sentences. (But in all fairness, the first three sentences on any essay are *huge!*) At 6:15 A.M. I ordered a pizza.

"What do you mean you don't deliver pizzas at six-fifteen in the morning?" I said. "Haven't you people ever heard of breakfast?"

"We're just the cleaning crew, ma'am. I shouldn't have even answered the phone."

"Okay, then how about just a salad?"

"Ma'am, I don't know how to make a salad."

"You don't know how to make a salad?"

"No, I mean, I know how to make a salad, but . . . Ma'am, the kitchen is closed."

"Whatever."

I slammed down the phone and found some cereal. I ate it dry. No milk.

By 3:15 P.M. on February 15, I had finished typing up Devon's essay and written the following letter. Since all application essays basically ask for the same thing, an account of some "life-influencing experience," I simply answered the prompt for Devon's USC application, added a small letter of introduction about the "unique circumstances," and sent the same essay on to all the other six colleges on Devon's wish list.

Dear USC,

Enclosed is the application essay for my best friend in the whole world, Devon Hampton. I hope you will accept him into your college. But if you do, please be aware that he may not come.

That's because he may not live. Devon Hampton was shot in the neck in a drive-by three nights ago.

Every bit of this application had been completed by Devon himself before this happened, except for finishing his essay, which I did for him, using his own notes. He really wanted to apply to your school. Since today is the deadline, I decided to finish this part for him. While I know that this is "out of the ordinary," please take a look.

Sincerely,

Theresa Anderson

P.S. I did the best I could. Please don't disqualify him for my attempt to help. I am sure he would have done a better job than this.

Our lives are shaped by many factors, some of them small, some of them significant and unforgettable. Please write a brief essay about how an event, an encounter, or a specific life experience has helped shape your character and influence your perspective on life. This essay should be a maximum of 700 words. You may use the back of this page or attach additional sheets if necessary.

Pitch-black with sterling silver speckles, charcoal-black rims, drag-racing stickers, and fat cylinder pegs in the front and back. It even had hand and back brakes!

That was Devon's bike. He always wanted a

"racer" and repeatedly begged his mom for one. However, his family's economic situation left him walking. Then his twelfth birthday came. Just as he had hoped, he finally received a bike. As soon as he saw the speeder, his eyes lit up. It was any twelve-year-old's dream.

Unfortunately, this dream would be short- lived. Three days after receiving the bike, Devon decided to go out for a spin. Suddenly, he noticed two guys eyeing him. One of them was riding his own bike, the other was on the handlebars. Devon turned his head for a second and when he turned back around they were right in front of him.

"Get off!"

Devon's first thought was that this guy had to be kidding, so he responded, "No way!"

All of a sudden, the guy pulled out a knife and jammed the tip next to Devon's belly. "Get off!"

Terrified for his life, Devon got off. After they rode away, Devon ran home with tears in his eyes.

His initial reaction was fright and confusion. How could someone steal a little kid's prized possession? Devon promised himself he would never ride a bike again and he didn't go outside for a week—didn't even look out the window. He hadn't owned the bike for more than two days! How could something he had wanted to own for so long be stripped from him so quickly? The injustice made Devon want to go out and violate someone else. He wanted to deprive someone else of their dream, to leave them heartbroken, just as he was.

With time, Devon's feelings changed. He began to sympathize with the thieves. Maybe they came from a broken home? Maybe they were on drugs? Maybe no one loved them? Instead of being sad, Devon started to feel grateful. Thank goodness they did not hurt him physically, he thought. He started to take some positives from the negative experience. He began to use this misfortune as a motivational tool to work even harder so that he could become a success in life. He decided not to become a thief but instead to become a scholar. Devon Hampton has a 4.93 GPA and is the valedictorian of our high school. He has won the top prize for Calculus AP, earned the California Educational Achievement Citation for Scholastic Accomplishment, and has a room filled with more academic trophies than I can even count. (I know, I am sitting in his room right now.) Devon is active in numerous outreach programs that help those less fortunate than he is. Devon Hampton could have become a victim. Instead he became a role model.

Ironically, the saddest moment in Devon's life (up until now) turned out to be his most inspirational. He has forgiven the guys who took his bike at knifepoint. I read about how he doesn't hate them. Instead, Devon is sort of thankful to them. They taught him a lesson about life that he feels will stay with him for the rest of his days. They showed Devon what he did not want to become. In fact, Devon even took notes about how they showed him the type of people that he one day hopes to help if he ever gets the chance. Years from now, after Devon graduates from college (your college, I hope) Devon says that he plans to look back upon the day when two hoodlums stripped him of the best gift he ever got and realize that they replaced it with something even better. They gave Devon "purpose." (That's a direct quote.)

Ultimately, as crazy as this sounds, Devon says that he is forever grateful that he encountered these thieves.

EXTRA NOTE: I personally have two prayers: 1. That Devon survives, and 2. you admit him into your university.

Thanks!

J.A.

I completed the applications for Harvard, Georgetown, Princeton, Yale, NYU, and USC. I guess I started with USC 'cause I wanted it to be me applying there.

But it wasn't.

However, when I got to the post office and watched the lady behind the counter stamp a postmark dated February 15 on each of the applications, I felt better, as if I had just delivered balloons and flowers and smiles and love to the room of Devon Hampton.

Now, if he would only regain consciousness.

24

On February 17 Devon opened his eyes. On February 19 he chewed some food. On March 4 he complained about the food. On March 14 the doctors told everyone that, although Devon was still not able to walk, they felt he would have . . .

"A full recovery."

"Full?" asked Ms. Hampton.

"Yes, full. But for now, he's still going to need a lot of rest."

Ms. Hampton raised her eyes to heaven and looked at God with gratitude as I had never seen before. I smiled so big I must have been flashing every tooth in my mouth—even the back ones with cavities. She and I hugged. We'd become family.

I visited Devon every day. My ritual was to come home from school, make Teddy and Tina an after-school snack, do some homework, tidy up the house before my mother got home, then take the bus to the hospital and chill with Dev until visiting hours were over, usually around nine o'clock.

But the nurses were cool and they basically let me stay until whenever I wanted.

Then one day I came home and found a letter addressed to me, from Princeton University.

Screw using a letter opener, those things are bad luck.

I tore open the envelope with my bare hands and a prayer in my heart.

Dear Ms. Anderson,

Thank you for your recent application to Princeton University. As you know, admissions are extremely competitive and we receive many more requests for enrollment than we can accommodate. Regrettably, this letter is to inform you that your application for admission has not been accepted.

We thank you for considering Princeton University and hope that you will . . .

Blah, blah, blah . . . I stopped reading.

It was a form letter. Not a personal note. Not a reason explaining their decision. Just a cookie-cutter, regular old letter of rejection.

My heart sank. Devon had just been rejected by Princeton.

I spent the next two and a half hours debating how to break the news to him. After all, I had to tell him. It was his news. I was just like a messenger or something. *Yeah, the messenger who wrote the crappy essay that caused him to get denied.*

I felt guilty, as if it were somehow my fault. Devon's mother and I had agreed that we wouldn't tell Devon about what I had done with his applications until after he had gotten some acceptance letters. We figured they could be used as a tool to cheer him up. Sometimes his spirits weren't that good. I guess getting shot in the neck will do that to you.

Now, however, we had bad news. I hadn't thought about that. Was it up to me to judge whether or not he got the bad news or only to deliver it? I didn't know what to do. After all, he'd have to find out at some point.

I walked through the hospital halls with the letter in my purse, trying to decide the right course of action to take. Devon would find out at some point, eventually—that was *fo sure!* And he would probably get mad at me for holding back on him if he knew I knew way before he did.

This whole situation reminded me of something I had once heard this person on the History Channel explain. He said that some things in life were black, some things in life were white, and other things in life were like the gray in between. I had never known what he meant. Until now. This was definitely the gray in between.

I finally decided Devon deserved to know. After all, there were still five other applications out that he'd be hearing back from any day now, so all hope was not lost. Besides, Princeton wasn't even his number-one choice. I mean, jeez, they were insane for not accepting him. I wish they'd given a reason. But they didn't. Colleges never do. They just said yes or no and they never explained why.

I entered the hospital room, hugged Devon hello, and reached into my purse.

"Hey-hey, Dev. Got some news."

"Hey-hey, Tee-Ay. What's up?"

I paused and reached my hand into my bag. feeling for the letter with my fingertips.

"The situation is this . . ." I pulled out my cellie. "I am 'bout to lose it *big-time*! Can you please figure out how to change this dang ringer on my phone? The sound is so annoying, I know there's got to be another choice."

He smiled. I passed him my phone.

"I don't know why you don't get this yet, Tee. What's this, the third time I've changed it this week?"

"Yeah, something like that."

The doctor said Dev needed his strength. I didn't want to do anything that might get him down or break his spirits. Positivity is what this room needed, not rejection.

I'd wait until the next day's mail when one of the letters of acceptance came and then show him that first. Then I'd let him know about the rejection.

Yeah, good plan, Tee. Positivity, that's good.

Dev still wasn't walking yet, and even though the doctor had said "full recovery," Dev was not making as much progress as everyone had hoped. Devon's "lack of progress" wasn't something any of us really talked about though. We just kept focusing on the encouragement and the optimism and the hopefulness. No room for haters here.

Screw Princeton!

"Here, I got it. You like this one better? Listen . . ."

The phone played a new ring. I didn't really pay attention.

"Much better," I said as I pushed the Princeton letter deep into my purse. "Much."

The next day I raced home from school to check the mail. Nothing. The day after that I raced home from school again. Still nothing. The day after that was a

Saturday and I bum-rushed the mailman as soon as I saw his little truck parked on my street. Still nothing!

Sunday came. There's no mail on Sundays. The post office is closed. *Slackers!*

On Monday I got a letter from Harvard.

My stomach fluttered and I got tense.

Harvard's envelope was really nice. It felt like a letter from the Queen or something.

Damn, Dev's number one. Here we go . . .

Dear Ms. Anderson,

We greatly appreciate your interest in Harvard University. Each fall many prospective students apply and yet we are only able to offer a limited number of Freshman admissions. Though it is no reflection of your worthiness as an applicant, Harvard regrets to inform you that your request for fall admission has not been granted.

Please know that Harvard is an extremely competitive school and that this is by no means an indication of your ability to succeed at the collegiate level. We receive . . .

Blah, blah, blah . . . I stopped reading. Harvard had said no. *What was wrong with these people?*

I collapsed in a chair. For twenty minutes I sat there confused and sad. Finally, I knew what I had to do. I picked up my cellie and dialed.

"Room 3106, please . . . Hey Dev, it's me. I don't think I am gonna make it today."

This would be the first time in seven weeks that I would not visit the hospital.

"That's cool, Tee. No big thing."

"But you know I want to be there. I just—got some stuff to do. You know, like for Honors Econ, there's that paper."

"Don't sweat it, girl. You've been great."

"And I have an upset stomach," I added.

"Tee, don't worry about it."

"Plus, I think I broke my boom box, I shrunk my mom's favorite blouse, I gave Tina a French-tip manicure but cut off half her fingernail, and I promised Pops I'd shine the leather of his calf-skin boots to get the scuffmarks out before going to wash out the garbage bins in the back of the house . . ."

There was a pause.

"Hey, Tee . . ."

"Yeah, Dev?"

"Everything okay?"

I knew he'd know I was lying. That is why I

couldn't go to the hospital in the first place—I'd give everything away. I had to get off the phone, quick.

"Yeah, everything's good. I just don't think I am gonna be able to make it today."

"It's cool, Tee. It's totally chill."

"You sure?"

"I'm sure."

"Much love to ya, Tee. Much love."

"Bye." I clicked off the phone, looked at the Harvard letter, and felt a sense of stabbing heat in my rib cage.

Please God. Please let a letter come tomorrow with some good news!

I guess God had his headphones on that evening, 'cause the next day I got an envelope from USC.

A thick envelope. Right away, I knew what it was.

I guess I shoulda known right away that Devon had been rejected by Princeton and Harvard because everyone knows the colleges have that thick-or-thin envelope thing going on. Thin envelopes contain one-page rejection letters that are written in a nice tone of voice not to make you feel bad. On the other hand, thick envelopes contain not only letters of acceptance, but applications for student housing, information on freshman orientation meetings, schedules of events that you are going to need to plan for, response cards that serve sort of like contracts that inform the university whether or not you are choosing to accept their acceptance, and stuff like that.

Rejections are thin 'cause they really have nothing to say other than, *Sorry, dude, you're screwed.* Acceptances are thick cause they have lots of stuff to say like, *Welcome, dude, you're not screwed, we want you.*

The envelope I was holding from the University of Southern California was thick. I carefully peeled it open.

Dang, USC had nice stationery.

Dear Ms. Anderson,

Congratulations on your acceptance to the University of Southern California. Enclosed is a variety of materials you will need in order to . . .

Oh—my—God!

I screamed so loud I almost burst my own eardrums and my heart started beating so fast in my chest I thought I was going to have to run to the medicine cabinet and take some of Pops's cardiac pills.

Devon had gotten into USC! Oh my god!

I raced to the hospital. Screw Harvard. Screw Princeton. It was all about the Trojans of USC!

• • •

"Look Devon, you're in! You're in! You've been accepted to USC!" I screamed, out of breath, as I dashed into his room. "You're in!"

"I know, I know!" He was smiling from ear to ear.

"Amazing, huh? I mean, I know it's not the East Coast but . . . Whadya mean, you know?"

"I mean, I know. My mom just brought me the mail fifteen minutes ago. I got into USC, Georgetown, and—are you ready for this—Harvard!"

"Harvard?"

"Yes, Harvard, my number one!"

Huh?

"What's up, Tee?"

"I . . . I don't get it," I stuttered.

"What do you mean, you don't get it? Look, I'm holding the letters right here. All four came today. Thick envelopes."

"But . . ."

"And my mom said it's 'cause of you." A tear rolled down Devon's cheek. "I can't believe you did that for me. I mean, I'm blown away that. . . . Hey . . . What's wrong with you, Tee?"

I slowly dug into my purse and pulled out the letters from Princeton and Harvard. Yep, they were rejection letters. Then I looked again at the letter from USC and read it.

Dear Ms. Anderson,

Congratulations on your acceptance to the University of Southern California. Enclosed is a variety of materials you will need in order to . . .

"What's that?" Dev asked.

I felt dazed. "I . . . I'm not sure," I said.

I handed Dev my letter with a shaky hand.

Dev took a moment to read it thoroughly. "Hey, Tee," he said. He held his USC letter up to mine. They looked exactly the same. "Congratulations, looks like you just became a Trojan."

25

*C*onfounded is a good word to know for the SAT. It means "extremely confused." When I rose from the chair into which I had collapsed, I was monumentally confounded.

Filling in the missing pieces for Dev about how I had finished his essays for him on Valentine's eve seven weeks before and sent them off to all his colleges on his behalf was easy. Filling in the missing pieces for me about how I had been rejected from Princeton, rejected from Harvard, and accepted to USC when I hadn't even applied to any of them was another matter entirely.

"There's only one possible explanation," Dev said.

I paused to think about it.

"No way. There's no way."

"It's gotta be," he said.

I repeated it again. "No way. No freakin' way!"

"Yes, way, Tee-Ay. It must have been Wardin."

• • •

I showed up at the door to Wardin's office just as he was finishing up chewing out a tenth grader about how she'd never get into college unless she shaped up.

"And I mean, you need to start *yesterday*. Education is your life raft and the seas are filled with drowning teenagers. Young lady, I advise to you to clutch it and never let go."

The tenth grader looked at her shoes in shame.

"Well, that's all. Leave. Go to class. Just don't say the world never told you so because guess what—the world just told you so."

The tenth grader left with her tail between her legs.

"Miss Theresa Anderson. Come in, close the door, have a seat."

I did.

"You know, you put me in a very awkward situation with some very important people. Do you know how unprofessional I sounded when the chair of Harvard's admissions committee called me to ask about the unconventional nature of Devon Hampton's college application and I had no idea what he was talking about?"

Wardin reached into a filing cabinet.

"After Harvard faxed this to me"—he tossed the essay I had written on his desk—"I was very soon thereafter contacted by NYU, Georgetown, Princeton,

USC, and Yale, all of them inquiring about a Mr. Devon Hampton. What could I say, other than in my nineteen years as a professional educator, Mr. Devon Hampton might be the finest, most well-prepared high-school student I have ever encountered."

Wow, I thought.

"And then I insisted that each of the universities consider the candidacy of another one of our students and that I'd be overnighting all of her records immediately. It cost this school thirty-four dollars to FedEx your files to Harvard alone."

"You think I'm good enough to go to Harvard, Mr. Wardin?"

"Miss Theresa Anderson, let me be bluntly honest with you for a moment." He leaned forward in his chair and looked deeply into my eyes. "I believe you're worthy of admission to any university in the United States of America." *Wow.* Blood rushed to my cheeks. "But I don't get paid to make those decisions, other people do. Unfortunately, Harvard, Princeton, and Yale didn't agree with me. But USC, Georgetown, and NYU did. And let me tell you, when you're applying to some of the best schools in the nation, three out of six ain't bad. It ain't bad at all," he said, reclining in his chair.

"You mean I got into NYU and Georgetown, too?"

"You haven't received their letters yet? Oops. Ruined that one."

Oh my gracious.

"Devon, as you probably know, went six for six. He was accepted everywhere he applied."

"Uhm. I didn't know that. And I don't think he knows either. He's still waiting to hear from Yale and NYU."

"Well, screw it, the secret is out. Notifications can be weird. Some colleges send out their rejections first and then their acceptance letters. Some wait and do it all at the same time. Some do it alphabetically. Some students find out on a Tuesday while their neighbors don't get their letters until the following Monday. Between the mail crossing the country and all the paperwork for these tens of thousands of applicants, it's amazing anyone gets notified at all. But off the record, I'm told your decision at those other Ivy League schools was razor close. Razor close."

"But, my SATs . . ."

"SAT scores aren't everything, Miss Theresa Anderson. And God help us when they are."

I looked up at the wall. There it was again, that ugly, scrawny, nondecorated, raggedy little sign.

GOOD THINGS HAPPEN TO PEOPLE WHO TRY.

A lump formed in my throat. It was the prettiest poster on anybody's wall I'd ever seen in my entire life.

"This is a damn fine essay. Damn fine," Wardin said, picking up the paper on the desk and thumbing through it, even though he'd probably already read it a few times. "I would have liked to see a bit more vivid vocabulary myself, but overall, mighty solid. You Andersons are pretty good writers, huh? How's your brother Andre, anyway?"

My brother? He wanted to know about Andre just as I was experiencing the best news of my life?

"Just fine," I replied, without a drop of envy or hate or disgust in my heart. "Andre is doing just fine, sir."

"Well, he won't be when USC kicks the crap out of Stanford this year in football, that's for sure. I've a feeling he's got a sister who might give him a bit of grief about that one, huh?"

We both laughed. After three years of being tortured by this man, I could not believe I was actually sharing a smile, much less genuine human-to-human interaction, with him.

"That is, if SC is still your number-one choice? I mean, goodness, NYU and Georgetown, those are tremendous schools. Plus, the East Coast can be a great place to live. Maybe you still need time to decide. That's okay, you have a few weeks."

"I don't need another damn second, Mr. Wardin. I'm going to USC." A huge smile came to my face. "I'm gonna be a Trojan."

Wardin grinned. "An excellent choice, Miss Theresa Anderson. An excellent choice. It's an outstanding school." He turned to refile Devon's essay in the cabinet. "And if you should run into Mr. Rickee Dunston over the course of the next four years, be sure to say hello for me."

"Rickee chose SC?" I asked as my stomach dropped to the floor.

"Yep," Wardin answered. "But USC didn't choose him. Grades weren't good enough. Plus, there were some 'ethical questions' as to his overall character, too."

I breathed a sigh of relief.

"So, where's he going?" I asked.

"Notre Dame," Wardin responded. "Notre Dame."

The USC Trojans had hated the Notre Dame Fighting Irish with a bitter passion ever since the early 1900s. Now Rickee was headed for ice-cold South Bend, Indiana, while I was staying in sunny southern California and we'd be sworn enemies forevermore.

Perfect!

Wardin stood from his chair and grabbed a file off his desk.

"Well, time for a meeting with the parents of some knucklehead who got caught ditching class by the locker rooms. Kid has a one-point-two-eight GPA, hasn't been to his third-period class in three weeks, and his mom wants to know why we're 'hating on' her son. Do people even know that one cannot 'hate on' another person without being in violation of about thirty-six rules of grammar?"

I smiled.

"You need a hall pass?" he asked.

"No, I'm okay," I answered. "But . . ."

Wardin paused. "Yes, Miss Theresa Anderson?"

"Well, why'd you do it, Mr. Wardin? I mean, well—yeah. Why'd you do it for me?"

Wardin stopped and a warm grin came across his face. "It's simple, Miss Theresa Anderson. Like all teachers, I care. After all, this is what I've dedicated my life to doing. Being able to help someone like yourself was both an honor and a pleasure."

Paradox is a good word to know for the SAT. It means, "when things don't add up with one another when you add them all up."

No, I didn't need to know any more words for the

SAT, I did, however, still need to know more words and ideas to be successful in college—and in life. Attending a university would help me with that. And Mr. Wardin was the reason I was getting the opportunity to go to a university. And Mr. Wardin was a paradox.

"Good-bye, Mr. Wardin. And if I haven't said it yet already, thank you."

I wanted to hug him, but for some reason it seemed like it wouldn't be very professional, so I reached out my hand to give him a firm shake.

I had expected his thick fingers to crush my hand. Instead, his palm turned out to be soft and smooth.

"You're welcome, Miss Theresa Anderson. You're very welcome."

We shook, he opened the door, and we exited the office together. Once in the hall, Wardin spotted a student he had obviously known from before.

"Well, if it isn't Mr. Freddy Johnson sitting outside the dean's office, probably waiting to get more demerits placed on his academic record. Young man, do you even realize the stupidity you demonstrate by consistently showing your face in here? Class is where you belong, son. I mean, where are you gonna be at the age of twenty-five with no education?"

This Freddy Johnson kid stared defiantly back at Wardin without saying a word.

"What, am I *'hatin'* on' you? You know what your problem is, son? I think you listen to too much hip-hop."

All I could do was shake my head and laugh.

26

The human body is a weird thing. Although Devon had taken a bullet in the neck—it missed his spine and cleanly exited, leaving an in-and-out wound that pretty much only tore through flesh and muscle—Devon still suffered from a random inability to balance. As a result, almost three months after the injury, he was still in the hospital, and could not consistently walk.

The doctors were at a loss for answers.

"The human body is a delicate mechanism," one of them explained to me. "And bullets are violent pieces of metal built to cause damage. Unfortunately, sometimes they work too well."

"But what about 'full recovery'? I mean, those were your words. 'Full recovery.'"

"We're still hopeful."

News about Devon's recovery (and setbacks) were practically broadcast over the loudspeaker every day because all the seniors wanted to know how he was coming along. Not just cause they wanted to know, but because Amanda Hardison, the second-smartest student in twelfth grade and our student body president, had turned into some kind of psychotic trial lawyer, arguing with the school's administration, the event planners at the local hotels, and the rest of the students' council over how all the senior events were going to be arranged and carried out.

Everything had become a huge confrontation with her, as if she were on some kind of insane mission from God or something. At any other high school, Amanda would have probably been the number-one student in the senior class. Here, she was number two to Devon. Always had been.

For twelve years she had been bitter about it, too. But now was her chance to seize the rank of number one. And she didn't want it. Devon's tragedy had brought out a totally different side of her. The only thing she now cared about was "honoring our valedictorian" and she was on a warpath.

She closed the "top ten list" so no one could move ahead or fall back in the academic rankings, forced a huge production delay in the annual yearbook until a two-page spread about Devon's tragedy could be printed, and led a ferocious charge on the mayor's office for the street in front of the school to be renamed Devon Hampton Drive within the next fifteen days. It got to the point that when she walked down the halls even Principal Watkins avoided her, fearing that she was going to chew him out for something.

Then one day she tracked me down. "Hey, Tee," she said.

Amanda and I had never been tight like a kite, but I wasn't scared of no one.

"Wuzzup, Amanda?"

"Mind being the one to tell Dev that we will not be having a prom on May fourteenth?"

"You canceled the senior prom?"

"It's within my authority," she replied. "But we're not canceling it, we're simply changing the date. The student council voted eighteen to zero this morning to move it to the night of graduation because there's a better chance that Devon will be out of the hospital by then."

"Isn't the prom usually about three weeks before graduation?" I asked, concerned about all the haters on campus who'd have a problem with such special arrangements being made for one student, even if he was our school's best.

"If they don't like it, they don't have to come. It's to honor our valedictorian." *Damn, she was firm.* "And I feel it's my duty as salutatorian and senior class president to do so. Would you mind being the one to tell Dev?"

349

"Naw, I'll be happy to."

"Thank you." Amanda walked off, all business. She'd be going to Duke University in the fall and I felt sorry for the folks who were going to have to deal with her in the student government over there, that was *fo' sure!*

Much to my surprise, however, everyone—black, brown, Asian, and Pacific Islander—all of them thought that this nontraditional prom/graduation night was a dope idea and no one complained a bit.

It wasn't because they feared Amanda Hardison, either. It was because everyone knew it was the right thing to do.

That's what I love about my high school, the sense that, just like hip-hop, in the end, we were all about Unity with a capital U.

Ever since my mother had got that big job promotion a few months before, I had been making two grilled cheeses—one with tomato for Teddy, and one without for Tina—at three-fifteen every day when my brother and sister came home from school. Mom working a bit later at the office meant dinner was being served a bit later than it used to be, so they needed a snack to get them through to the evening.

No one complained about my mother's job, though, because it meant more prestige and bigger paychecks for her.

And she deserved it. She worked her tail off for those peeps at the bank, and in my eyes, her promotion to manager of corporate trusts was long overdue.

But today I had really exciting news for Dev, so I figured I'd put my homework off until later, let Teddy and Tina make their own snack—I prayed that they wouldn't wreck the entire kitchen—and rush straight to the hospital.

However, when I walked in my house, my mother was already home.

"Hi, Mom, something wrong? Why are you home early?" I put down my backpack, thinking, Great, now I can get to the hospital even earlier.

"Theresa, I need you to go to the market to get a few things. Here's a list." She stopped chopping the red peppers she was going to use for dinner and handed me a sheet of paper with about twenty items on it.

Avocado, eggs, whipping cream . . . It was about forty-five minutes' worth of shopping.

"But, Mom, I want to get over to the hospital. I've got some news that I—"

"You're going to the market," she said, cutting me off. "Then you can go do whatever you want. My car keys are on the table along with some cash."

I had learned long ago that when my Mom took that tone with me, I had two choices. I could either fight and scream and yell and do what she told me, or I could forget the fighting and screaming and yelling . . . and just do what she told me.

Either way, I was gonna end up doing what she told me.

Since I wanted to catch the bus to make it to the hospital—I'd probably be there earlier than usual any-way because I was putting my homework on the back burner until later—I decided to just do it.

"You just want the stuff on the list?"

"That'll be fine, Theresa. Drive safely, please."

Four bags of groceries and an hour and ten minutes later I returned to the house, but some jerk was parked in our driveway. His car didn't even have license plates on it yet. It was too new.

I double-parked behind it and grabbed all the bags. Charcoal gray, tan leather interior, a sunroof . . .

Pretty phat ride, I thought. For a jerk, that is.

I opened the door.

"Mom, some jackass is blocking our driveway so I had to . . .

"Surprise!"

The first thing I saw staring at me when I opened the door was a cake decorated in the colors of USC. On a platform in the middle of the cake were a set of car keys for the new Honda Accord parked in the driveway.

Pops, Tina, Teddy, my mom, and Andre all stared at me, waiting for a response.

"You bought me a car?"

"Not me," said Pops. "Your mother."

Now it was my turn to have a heart attack. I set all the groceries down on the floor and turned to my mom.

"So you didn't really need all this stuff from the supermarket."

"Not really," she said with a smile.

"And you bought me a car so I could get to school?"

"No baby, I didn't buy you a car so you could get to school. I bought you a car so you could come home from school to visit."

There was a pause. I didn't know what to say.

"I am so proud of you, Theresa, my heart feels like it's gonna burst. You have become an amazing young woman. I'm just so proud."

I hugged my mom like I hadn't hugged her since I was eleven years old.

"Good job, Theresa," Andre said, giving me a squeeze. "But you know we're gonna spank you on the hoops floor."

"I'm sorry, what was last year's football score?"

"See the problem is, you don't have anybody who can rebound."

"First of all," I said. "We're looking sweet this year on the basketball front. Got some solid recruits. Second of all, need I remind you about the football term *National Championship*? How many of those do you guys have?"

"Come on, come on, let's eat some cake already and quit this foolish rivalry stuff," Pops interrupted, licking his lips. "I can't wait to get me a bite of that homemade good stuff."

"Oh no, you are *not* getting any cake, not with your cholesterol the way it is. I made you a nice bowl of fruit salad."

"Fruit salad? Lord, woman! If God didn't intend man to eat cake, why in the world did he invent frosting?"

My mother handed me the keys to my new car. The first place I drove to was the hospital.

27

I rolled Devon in his wheelchair down to the parking lot to show him my new ride. The hospital always insisted on us using the wheelchair and was very strict about Devon getting up out of it when he was not in his room or in physical therapy.

"Your moms got you this? Oh my goodness, it's beautiful. How's the sound system?"

"Totally bumpin'."

I turned the key and cranked a beat that rocked the whole parking lot. Devon started to groove, nodding his head in time.

"This machine is off the hook."

I lowered the stereo.

"Amanda Hardison told me today that the student council voted unanimously to cancel senior prom."

"What? That girl abuses her power."

"And then the plan is to combine graduation and prom into one event. They're hoping it will give you some extra time to be there."

Devon paused.

"The school's gonna do that for me?"

"That's the plan."

Devon paused.

"What about the haters?"

"Ain't a one. All is chill with every peep in the senior class."

Devon paused.

"*Dang*, I don't know what to say. What about all the deposits at the hotels and with the photographers and stuff? All those things are nonrefundable."

"Amanda took care of it all."

"Jeez, that Amanda Hardison's a tiger."

I could see Dev was humbled that so many people were so supportive of him.

"So, what do you think?" I asked after another quiet moment.

"I think I might have to ask Amanda Hardison to the prom."

Dev saw my eyes shoot out of my head and he smiled from ear to ear.

"Naw, just playing. What do I think of what?"

"Well, do you think, you know . . ." I got all tense and serious. Dev and I never rapped about his recovery. "Do you think you'll be able to . . . walk by then?"

"Walk?" Devon said as he struggled to lift himself out of his wheelchair. "I'll do better than that."

"Devon, don't. The hospital doesn't want you to . . ."

"My plan is to dance!"

Devon wouldn't listen. He climbed out of his wheelchair, took a step back, and did a little head-shake *ta-bam!* groove move with a 360-degree twist.

Whoa, where'd that come from?

"I been stayin' up till one o'clock in the morning doing leg lifts and knee bends and stuff. Now I'm gonna stay up till three."

A tear came to my eye.

"You just tell everyone I'll be there. Be there to dance and party and do it to it all night long."

It felt like my grin was plastered to my face and I couldn't get it off, his determination was just so inspiring.

"Be there with you, that is," Dev continued as he walked toward me. "I mean, if you'll be my prom date, Miss Theresa Anderson?"

I looked him in the eye—in that deep, soul-to-soul eye-contact way that let me see his inner glow.

"I would love to be your prom date, Mr. Devon Hampton."

And we kissed for the very first time.

• • •

Shopping for my prom dress wasn't really that big a deal to me, though I know for most girls it's a huge event. I was just happy I'd be going to the prom— going with Devon, of course.

The truth was that the best part of the whole experience was that my mother and I got to take a Saturday afternoon to ourselves to go buy the dress. We shopped at three different stores even though I found exactly what I was looking for at the first place we went. Then we shared a casual lunch at an outdoor café where we each ordered raspberry iced tea and a Cobb salad, mine without bacon.

Afterward we went to a shoe store. My mother was having such a good time, she went a bit crazy. Each of us left with our hands full of shopping bags. I scored fancy prom shoes and a pair of loafers. For some reason, my mother decided she needed two pairs of flats, two pairs of supercute open-toe strapless heels, and flip-flops.

She never even wore flip-flops.

"But we won't tell your father," she giggled. "Men don't understand when it comes to shoes."

"My lips are sealed," I answered. "My lips are sealed."

Our day was nice. So was our graduation ceremony.

The whole experience was almost like a movie,

filled with little scenes and encounters and images that flowed one into another. It was a bit hard to concentrate, because the whole thing was almost a blur. There was just so much emotion. I couldn't believe this was it. I was graduating from high school.

As I looked for my assigned seat in row E, wearing my robe, fixing my hat, and playing with my tassel—boy, I really liked my tassel—a zillion ideas swam through my mind. First, I had not become just another "minority dropout statistic" from the 'hood. That was *huge*. I had earned a degree and no one could ever take that away from me. Plus, I was off to earn another one. USC was just two months away. I still couldn't believe that either.

This led me to think about Cee-Saw. She'd be spending the night at home with her baby tonight. If she was lucky, Jax might rent a movie from Blockbuster and come over to watch it with her, but Jax had been starting to show a little less interest in Cee and Ricita lately. After all, what man really wants to be father to another man's baby—especially at the age of eighteen?

But since it was graduation/prom night, Jax would probably show up, maybe with some Chinese food takeout, too. He was just that kind of person.

Walking through the crowd, I bumped into peeps and shared smiles, hugs, and "*Wuzzup?*"s with all the folks I had been seeing virtually every day of my life for each of the past twelve years. Hard to believe I might never really see most of these folks again.

Then, when I saw Stephanee and Angela, the dynamic duo of cheerleading, bouncing around, shouting fake hellos to people, and pretending everyone in the entire world was their best friends and that they would always and forever remember each and every one of them and that they'd always keep in touch and were just so proud of all of everyone's accomplishments, it dawned on me that not seeing some of these peeps ever again might not really be such a bad thing.

Then I turned to go to my seat and bumped into someone. Wow, it was crowded.

"Oops, excuse me," I said.

"Hello, Tee-Ay."

I stopped. A smile came to my face.

"Sonia . . ." I said and we shared a warm hug.

I don't know what had really happened to me and Sonia. I guess peeps just drift apart in high school at different times and for different reasons. But, despite the overwhelming odds, Sonia had apparently done what she needed to do in Home Studies, because here she was, wearing a silk graduation robe, a tassel dangling from her square hat just like mine.

She looked terrific, her perfect white teeth sparkling like diamonds.

"So good to see ya, girl," I said squeezing her a second time after we got done with our first hug. "What is up?"

"Well, I'm starting community college in the fall."

"Amazing," I said.

"I mean, I know it's not USC but . . ."

"Don't even think like that, Sonia. Really, that is awesome."

"But, I won't be able to take a full load of classes 'cause I need to work at my cousin's auto shop as a bookkeeper for some money, but . . . well, you know how it is."

"Sonia, *un* picture, *un sólo,* come on." I turned around. The person speaking to Sonia was the most drop-dead handsome Latino dude I'd ever seen before in my life. He stood six feet tall, must have weighed 190 pounds, and had a smile like an Aztec god.

"Geraldo, *venga,* I want you to meet one of my best friends in the whole world. This is Tee-Ay, the girl I told you about," Sonia said, introducing us. "Tee-Ay, this is my boyfriend, Geraldo."

Her boyfriend? Damn, he was hot!

"Very nice to meet you," Geraldo said, extending his hand to shake mine. His palm was as soft as cotton, his fingernails were clean, and his light accent made words drip from his tongue, as if everything he said was a romantic love song.

"Hi," I replied, trying not to act like he was the most gorgeous dude I had ever met. I mean, Devon had it going on, but . . . well, this dude was H-O-T!

A Latin lover like no other—dang, Sonia!

"Congratulations on your good news," he said to me. "Sonia has told me many nice things about you. I hope that maybe one day we can all go out for a lunch. It will be my treat."

And polite, too. Yo, Sonia, marry this boy!

Then it dawned on me . . . *Oh my gracious, she just might.*

"I would love to have lunch sometime," I responded. "But it'll have to be french fries—"

"And a Diet Pepsi," Sonia said, finishing my sentence. We both laughed. Geraldo looked confused.

"Well, it is a strange lunch, this one you talk about, but if that is what you wish . . . okay," he said. "Now, how about a picture?"

Sonia and I pressed our cheeks together and Geraldo snapped a photograph that I knew would one day sit in a frame on my dresser for the rest of my life.

Some pictures are just like that. You know when you take them that they're going to last forever.

Graduating from a CC and transferring to a four-year university afterward while working to support an extended family was asking a lot of a person. But for a Latina—a *girl*—to be the first one ever in her family to graduate from high school in America, this was truly amazing. A part of me understood that Sonia had already won. She'd not only moved herself into a better position for the future, but she had managed to move all future generations of her *familia* into a better position for the future.

Maybe she'd only go this far and drop out of school after a year or two to start a family of her own. Like I said, things were going to be tough. But one day, someone in her family would go farther because Sonia had broken through this barrier first. I respected her tremendously for that and the idea of sacrifice for *familia* suddenly took on a whole new meaning for me. All those years Sonia wasn't just slaving for the needs of the older generation, she was hooking up the needs of the future ones, as well. One day, there might even be a Dr. Rodriguez in her *familia*. Better yet, a woman doctor. And it would only have happened because of Sonia.

However, I had a feeling that even if it took her fifteen years, Sonia was going to earn a college degree. Maybe even a master's. Becoming a family therapist had always been a huge interest of hers. After all, what could stop her?

We hugged and cried. "I'm so proud of you," I told her.

"And what do you expect me to say about you?" she answered. "Lunch for sure?"

"Fo' sure!" I responded. We hugged one last time as Principal Watkins approached the microphone. The ceremony was starting and everyone began scrambling to their seats.

Principal Watkins began saying all the things that all principals say at every high school graduation. He was proud of us. We should be proud of ourselves. The future was ours.

Blah, blah, blah . . . boring.

Finally he got to the part that everyone had been waiting for.

"And now I introduce to you our school's valedictorian, Devon Hampton."

As the salutatorian, Amanda Hardison wore a yellow robe. Devon's robe was pure white. The crowd rose to their feet and gave Devon a standing ovation. For three minutes it was so loud he couldn't begin.

Over the past month I had been asking Devon to give me a hint of what his speech would be about, but he wouldn't let me know a clue. Not even a speck of an idea. All I knew was that he had worked on it really hard for the last eighteen nights in a row to get it absolutely perfect. And he hadn't shown it to anyone. I guess he had too much to say. I sat in the audience, like everyone else, and waited. And like everyone else, just the sight of him up there delivering the speech, standing on both of his feet without a wheel-chair or a wobble or a trace of anything wrong with him whatsoever brought tears to my eyes. Tears were in everyone's eyes and he hadn't even said a word yet.

Oh my gracious, I need a tissue.

Devon waited at the microphone until the huge crowd of people in the audience were completely silent.

"We made it," he began.

The crowd went crazy with cheers, especially the seniors. Smiles, roars, applause was everywhere. Finally, we settled back down.

"I made it," Devon said next.

The crowd cheered even more. It was like the chairs were electrified. The room was just crazy! We settled down again.

"And now it is time for us to make it more. Make—it—more!"

Devon turned and went back to his seat. There was a pause. That was it. It might have been the shortest valedictorian speech in history. It also might have been the best, too. One person clapped and then all of the sudden the crowd exploded and went nuts!

Every soul in the building rose to their feet and roared. Security guards, janitors, even the lighting technicians were on their feet hugging and clapping and they didn't even have any relatives in the audience.

My face was so wet with tears it was hard for me to see. I turned around. I needed a freakin' tissue.

And so did Rickee Dunston. He was crying like a little girl.

After that, there was more blur.

I kinda remember walking across the stage to get my diploma, but I kinda don't. They don't give you the real thing anyway, just a token piece of paper. The real diploma gets picked up at the secretary's window the next day after you pay all your library fines and do stuff like that.

My family greeted me in the hall. While I hugged all of them—Andre, Pops, Tina, even Teddy, who looked like he was scoping out the butts of all the various high school girls in the room—I squeezed my mother especially tight with everything I had in me. I'd been so wrong about her. She wasn't *the man* who had been holding me back my whole teenage life. How could I ever have thought that? Would my little sister Tina one day think that as well on her own way to graduation?

"I'm sorry, Mom," I said.

"Sorry, Theresa? Why would you ever say you are sorry to me right now?"

"Because there's no way I will ever be able to thank you," I said.

"Girl," my mother answered, "one day you'll do this for your own daughter and that's when you'll have paid me back. Paid me back and then some."

I smiled and we hugged again. Was there a stronger being on this planet than a determined African American woman? I doubted it, and having one in your corner was like having lion by your side, ready to attack, defend, and die for you at the drop of a dime.

"For your granddaughter, huh?" I teased her.

She smiled.

"Grandaughter? What the hell is all this talk about a granddaughter? Theresa, am I gonna have to whip some little boy's ass?"

"Sssh, be quiet, Pops. Tee and I are having a private conversation," my mother said.

"Mom . . ." I said.

"Yes, dear?"

"Please call me Theresa."

She smiled softly. "Yes, dear."

And we hugged again.

I didn't think I had any tears left in me to cry any more. And then I cried when I saw Mr. Wardin, I cried when I saw Ms. Hampton, and I cried—wow, did I cry—when I finally saw Devon.

"I think my eyes are broken," I told him. "I can't turn off the water spout."

Yep, it was a day that would live forever.

And a night, too.

Because, as I climbed inside my car, bumped some hip-hop on the stereo system, and headed home to change into my prom dress, I knew one sweet thing was certain.

I had a future.

COMING APRIL 2007

HOMEBOYZ

by Alan Lawrence Sitomer

A sneak peek at Alan Lawrence Sitomer's
darkest, most dramatic, and most hopeful work yet.

1

Everybody who's anybody in the 'hood has got a street name. Some of the a.k.a.'s threaten danger, like Monster or Li'l Killa. Others are kind of playful, like Loopy or Mouse. A few make no sense at all but sound cool, like Z-Pop and Quysm. Meeksha Livingston became known as Li'l Gal Blinkie—Blink for short.

And Blink was out of control.

At the age of nine, Meeksha shouted, "Eat my ass!" to a teacher. At the age of eleven, she got busted for trying to shoplift a pair of brass knuckles at the Swap Meet. At the age of thirteen, she got caught in the act of stealing a car stereo out of a Toyota Camry. When the sixty-three-year-old woman who owned the car said, "Give it back," Blink responded, "Okay," and slammed the three-pound metal box directly into the white lady's face. The radio's jagged steel edge ripped the soft flesh from the lady's lower lip, broke three of her teeth, and caused a gush of blue-and-black blood to pour from the her gums, like a faucet turned on all the way. Despite multiple plastic surgeries, this nice old grandmother, who had only stopped in at the local Target to get some laundry detergent for her housekeeper, was permanently stuck with a smile that made her look like a demented clown.

Meeksha got away. The police description of a five-foot-four black girl with black hair and a light-colored short-sleeved T-shirt only matched about 300,000 other young women in the area.

Not only didn't Meeksha get popped by the po-po for her crime, she bragged about it. The attempted theft had been her first real mission, her first chance to prove that she was down for the 'hood. Obviously, she was.

Someone passed Meeksha a hit of weed.

"So what's it gonna be?" a raspy voice asked in a tone of approval. It was late at night on the back stoop of an abandoned house.

The question was simple. For a girl, there were two ways to join a gang. The first was to get jumped in. That meant getting into the center of a circle and fighting your way through an attack by four to six other gang members as they stomped and beat and kicked and punched until you proved your worth by proving your heart. Would you fight for your homies? Would you represent for your homies? Would you die for your homies? The circle was where you proved that you would.

But girls had another way in, too. They could be sexed in. That meant giving up a piece of lovin' to every member of the crew.

"So, like, what's it gonna be?" the voice asked again.

Meeksha looked up. "Both."

"Both?" the gang's leader said with a smile.

"You heard me," Meeksha said. "Both."

Four gangsta girls started taking off their earrings so their lobes wouldn't get torn off during the fight. Then they circled Meeksha. Six homeboyz drank forty-ouncers of malt and got ready to watch the action.

"Yo, let me tag some of that boo-tay before ya'll whoop up on her," one of the guys shouted with a smile.

"Too late," replied a hardcore chola with a nasty look in her eye. If Meeksha was gonna be sexin' her man, she wanted to make sure that it would be a one-time event, associated with a lot of pain.

An overhand left flew and the beat-down was on.

Meeksha fought like a wolf. Black and brown fists and feet flew everywhere. The 22nd Street Merks (short for Mercenaries) were a clique made up of both blacks and Hispanics. Their crew wasn't about color, it was about territory. Meeksha wanted in. Ever since the age of six, all she had ever wanted was in. The Merks were her idols, her role models, her ultimate fantasy. Tonight was the night Meeksha had dreamed about. She sucked in school. Her mother was a drug addict. She had never met her father. Causing trouble was the only thing Meeksha was any good at. Finally, it was paying off. Meeksha wasn't just getting pounded, she was getting a family. Gangsta love, is what it's called.

Over the course of the next year, Meeksha got even crazier. She started sniffing glue, putting in work for her crew, and getting tatts. MERKS 4 LIFE was scripted across the top of her left breast, with the 22nd Street logo, just over her heart:

$$\text{MerKs 4 Life} \atop \text{22nd Street}$$

Smoking. Drinking. Flunking. Fighting. Dropping out. Building a rep. Running up a criminal record. In juvee hall. Out of juvee hall. Doing drugs. Selling drugs. Beefing with the 0-1-0's. Oh yeah, beefing big-time with the 0-1-0's.

The 0-1-0's were the archenemy of the 22nd Street Merks. They had taken their gang name from the middle three numbers of their neighborhood ZIP code. Nobody could count how many teenagers had died in the years that they'd been feuding, but the bitterness ran long and deep. Even if there was only one Merk and six 0-1-0's, a Merk was expected to claim their 'hood and fight—pain and death be damned. The brawling had been going on for so long that adults in the community didn't even try to interfere. Random violence had become a part of everyday life, like stop signs and supermarkets.

One Tuesday afternoon, Meeksha heard the jingly bells of an ice-cream truck pulling up to the curb by the park where she was hanging out and decided she wanted something sweet.

"Gimme a chocolate Bomb Pop."

"That'll be two dollars."

"Here." Meeksha pulled out a ten-dollar bill and slapped it on the counter.

"Sorry, I'm out of singles," the ice-cream man said. "You have nothing smaller?"

"Naw, this all I got. Hey girl, you got change fo' a ten-dolla' bill?" Meeksha asked a kid nearby.

"Maybe . . ."

As Meeksha waited to see if her ten could be

broken, a crew of gangbangers rolled up, creepin' style, in a green Ford Escort. They had caught Meeksha slippin'.

"No, it looks like I only have eight . . ."

"Oh, shit!" Meeksha screamed.

"That's right, bitch . . . O-One-O!"

A semiautomatic handgun sprayed Meeksha with bullets. She tried to run, but only made it five feet before her chest was pumped with hollow points.

The ice-cream man dove to the floor of his truck. Little kids screamed and took off for the playground. The girl who had tried to make change for Meeksha's ten-dollar bill didn't even try to run. She didn't know Meeksha. All she had wanted was a Rainbow Éclair.

"That's right, bitch . . . O-One-O!"

And that's how Tina Maryssa Anderson died. With eight dollars in her wallet at the age of fourteen.

2

R P, RT. That's how Tina's death was known around the 'hood. It was nothing more than a simple RP, RT—"wrong place, wrong time."

Each member of the Anderson family took the news of Tina's murder in a different way. Mrs. Anderson was devastated. Losing her baby girl to gang violence left an empty, hollow stare in her eyes. Pops, Tina's father, was equally wounded, but concealed his suffering more than his wife could. Guilt as much as grief filled his heart. As a father, Pops viewed his role in the family to be both provider and protector. Now his baby girl was dead. He had failed.

Andre, Tina's oldest brother, known affectionately as "the Hoopster" for his skills on the local pickup basketball court, struggled with his feelings. Andre knew violence: as a teenager, he had been assaulted by racists—but he had lived, and come back even stronger in the end. Reflective by nature, Andre retreated into his thoughts, few of which found their way to his lips. His silence spoke for him.

Theresa—"Tee-Ay" as she was called by her friends—rushed back from college as soon as she heard the news. *How could something like this happen again?* was the question that rolled over and over through her mind. Her best friend had been randomly shot in a drive-by in her senior year of high school, and now bullets were flying through her life yet again. *I just don't understand,* she said to herself, like a broken stereo playing the same song over and over. *I just don't understand.*

Teddy, however, the youngest brother in the Anderson family, shared none of his parents' or siblings' emotions. At seventeen years old, he had grown to be six-foot-one, weighing 195 pounds—all of it rock-hard rippled muscle. Sadness wasn't his style. Nor were hugging, consoling, grieving, weeping, or moaning. T-Bear—that was Teddy's a.k.a. on the streets—only cared about one thing . . . revenge.

Late at night in the inner city, the streets are dangerous. Drunks beg. Drug addicts fiend. Prostitutes carry blades the way lawyers carry briefcases—simply as tools of their trade. Legal businesses operate as well. Bright lights in the windows of bail bondsmen flash like Vegas casinos to attract customers. Tattoo parlors ink up most of their clients after one a.m. Run-down liquor/convenience marts that sell overproof booze, the kinds of wine and beer hardly ever seen on the shelves of stores in the white parts of town, stay open all night. Smokes, condoms, potato chips, and a bottle of forty—it's like a kiddie meal at a fast-food restaurant, except that it's made for grown-ups and there's no fun prize at the bottom, other than the huge buzz of debauchery.

Tonight, however, Teddy cruised the streets hunting for something else: 0-1-0's. This was their territory and he knew they'd be out.

He turned right at the corner of Martin Luther King Jr. Boulevard, driving his older brother Andre's hand-me-down Honda Accord. The blue paint no longer shone, rust speckled the back bumper, and the exhaust pipe occasionally spit out a cloud of black dust. But the beat-up old car blended in perfectly with its surroundings. The digital clock on the dashboard struck midnight.

Though Teddy was alone in the car, he wasn't alone in his quest. The night air was thick with the unseen presence of the 22nd Street Merks. It wasn't a question of *if* the rival gangstas would strike to avenge Blink, their fallen homegirl, but *when*. The cops were out everywhere, trying to prevent "retaliatory action." Among gangstas there was always retaliation. It's the law of the streets: *You take out one of our homeboyz, we gotta take out one of yours.*

The local media had been obsessed with coverage of Tina's death, which only aggravated the tension in the streets.

Innocent honors student gunned down by ruthless gang members: Where does the madness stop?

If Blink had been the only one to get blasted, the entire episode in the park would have flown under the radar. Gang members killing other gang members happened all the time—it wasn't even page-eight newspaper material any longer. But gang members killing innocent honor students in an RP, RT situation—now that made for attention-grabbing headlines. The pressure was on the police to find Tina's killer as the media screamed for justice.

Teddy turned left on Elm Avenue, cruising along with one eye peeled for cops, the other for gangstas. The 0-1-0's, as Teddy knew, would be easy to find. On a night like this they could be counted on to show their faces, throw their gang signs, and stand their ground. The law of the streets said they had to. If the 22nd Street Merks had the guts to come into enemy territory seeking payback, the 0-1-0's attitude had to be, *Bring it on!* If the 0-1-0's didn't maintain a presence on the streets and defend their territory against enemy invaders, their gang would gain a rep as punks—and then gangstas in all the other surrounding neighborhoods would think the 0-1-0's could be punked, and so, stupid as it may have been to stay out on the streets while they were being hunted, the 0-1-0's did exactly that. They had a point to prove. It is known as *gangsta logic.*

Gangsta logic affected every aspect of life in the 'hood, and no one was immune to its reasoning. The routes kindergarten kids walked home from school were dictated by it. The times when the phone company scheduled repair visits were ruled by it. The number of people who had to sleep on the floor in their living rooms to avoid stray bullets zipping through their bedroom windows was governed by it. Gangsta logic didn't just change small behaviors, it altered the entire lifestyle of every inner-city resident.

Behind gangsta logic lay the conviction shared by most gangbangers that they had little chance of living to see the age of twenty-one. If they were gonna die young, they meant to die with their T-shirts pressed, their tattoos bold, and their guns blazing. No tears, no fears, no regrets. Any conversation among teens ensnarled in the web of *la vida loca* always came back around to the same idea: *If it's my time, it's my time, homie. Ain't nothin' I can do.* Cavemen had a longer life expectancy.

Death or jail was just part of the Game in the world of homeboyz. The Game was full of pain, but if a homeboy simply followed the three commandments of gangsterism all would be cool:

NEVER SNITCH.

ALWAYS REPRESENT FOR YOUR HOMEBOYZ.

PLAY FOR KEEPS—THERE IS NO TOMORROW.

Danger sizzled through the night air, but Teddy remained cool and calm. There was ice in his veins as he circled onto Greenhill Drive, scanning the streets for prey. Suddenly, Teddy spied what he was looking for and slowed the car.

A crew of six homeboyz were kickin' it by the side of a ghetto convenience mart whose large, faded signs in the windows advertised cheap cigarettes and cold beer. Just as dogs marked their territory with piss, graffiti clearly marked this territory as 0-1-0's.

Teddy made a slow, sly righthand turn, then circled a couple of blocks so he could approach from the other direction, on the opposite side of the street. The homies hadn't seen him. Teddy killed the lights, cut the ignition, and let his car roll softly into a parking spot diagonally across the way, with the front of his car facing the front of the ragged-looking store.

Once parked, Teddy covered the front windshield with a visor, a silver sunshade that prevented anyone's seeing into his car, then sat in the dark and waited. From outside, the car appeared to be empty. But a rectangular hole Teddy had cut in the fabric of the sunshade a few hours earlier created a small window through which he could see out without anyone being able to see in. It was ideal for spying on the enemy.

And the cops. The police concerned Teddy much more than the homeboyz did. Teddy had already crafted a plan for how to deal with the 0-1-0's. But he still had to work out how to execute his scheme without getting pinched by the po-po.

Teddy reached into the glove compartment, feeling for a notepad, a pencil, and a digital watch with a timer. What he needed was to discover a pattern in the night's activity. Teddy knew if he waited patiently and observed the environment long enough, the magic answer would present itself.

To some people, the world appeared as chaos, a jumble of events crashing into one another haphazardly. But to Teddy, the world had always unveiled itself in patterns. It was a gift he had. Teddy didn't know why he understood things the way he did, he didn't know why complicated chains of deductive reasoning and analysis made sense to him—they just did, the way music made sense to Mozart or paint made sense to Picasso. The challenge that lay before him now was to simply discover the patterns so he could interfere with them to his own advantage. Soon enough, he observed one of the patterns he was looking for.

Typically, the police would patrol an area such as this about once every hour. But on this night, because of the heightened gang activity, Teddy knew that the black-and-whites would be rolling through much more frequently. After an hour and a half of patient observation, Teddy figured out that two patrol cars were crisscrossing this part of the 'hood—one, then the other, passing by every twenty minutes. Teddy scribbled a few numbers on his pad of paper. Plenty of time, he thought.

While Teddy observed the street traffic, he noticed a few other details beyond the police officers' pattern of surveillance. He saw bums buy bottles of cheap wine with handfuls of change. He saw homeboyz in white T-shirts and baggy pants come and go so that the number of 0-1-0's hanging out in front of the convenience store was always in flux: sometimes it swelled to nine, other times it shrank to four. Teddy also saw the owner of the liquor mart come out a few times and try to shoo the homeboyz away.

Teddy felt an itch to get out of his car and go deal with the situation he had come to deal with right at that very moment, but he held back. He knew that emotion was not the right thing to guide him. Emotion led to erratic behavior. Emotion led to weakness. Emotion led to failure. Logic, reason, and ice-cold, dispassionate judgment were Teddy's tools for success. Teddy took three slow, deep breaths through his nostrils and relaxed the grip on his pencil. Be patient, he thought. Then strike without mercy when the moment is right.

The right moment arrived twenty-seven minutes later.